1347:

Faith in the Face of Death

1347:

Faith in the Face of Death

Ken A. Gauthier

Legend ☐ Press

Independent Book Publisher

Legend Press Ltd, 2 London Wall Buildings,
London EC2M 5UU
info@legend-paperbooks.co.uk
www.legendpress.co.uk

Contents © Ken A. Gauthier 2011

British Library Cataloguing in Publication Data available.

ISBN 978-1-9077560-2-3

Set in Times
Printed by CPI Books, UK

Cover designed by Gudrun Jobst
www.yotedesign.com

Legend Press

Independent Book Publisher

Acknowledgements

The tireless editing of writer and friend Lorraine Lordi went above my highest expectations. Her patience with this fledgling author seemed to know no limit, so neither will my gratitude. This kind woman has touched many lives, and so now touches you by unearthing this novel from me.

My early critics and typo police include my mother Barbara Ashley, son Cuyler, and mother-in-law Shirley Montanaro. It took my devoted wife (and heavyweight reader) Sue some time to read this work for fear of how she might have to let me down gently. I am so glad you like it, because nobody else is more honest to me. Thank you also to Marsha Libby for a fine red pen, and for pushing me toward publication with an ever so gentle slap on the back of the head.

Thank you to Lauren and Tom, and the folks at Legend Press for, well, everything. Thank you Darin Jewell at The Inspira Group for taking a chance. Thanks go to several websites for providing some necessary historical information: Eyewitnesstohistory.com, Insecta-inspecta.com, themiddleages.net, and Aboutmilan.com.

This book is dedicated to Princess Taylor.

Chapter 1

Frederico Gallinelli marvels at the grape's simplicity. Its vine climbs toward the sky however it can, and then meanders off with soft green tentacles in any direction to bring forth its bunches in a display no other plant can match.

Red, purple and blue berries huddle together in various sizes, owing to their order of ripeness. Green and yellow leaves hang over their heads as a roof protecting its occupants, while curling tendrils willfully accept Frederico's direction over trellis and twine. His awe of the contrast between his work and the labour of the plant itself continues. The more he learns about how a vine produces fruit, the more he realises he knows little about it at all.

"Papa!" cries a voice from the distance.

Pulled away from his work, Frederico knows this call from all of his children. It is Ambrogino, his youngest boy of eight years. His two other sons and three daughters have shown less enthusiasm for working the vineyards than Ambrogino. Of course, they have always done as their father has commanded, but the joy of Ambrogino's delight to be working in the vineyard continues to draw Frederico's favour.

"Gino!" he calls back.

It is all that is needed for Ambrogino to find his way to his father. Amidst long rows of mature plantings, he will find his father as though it is a game. Frederico plays this game every day, for he knows his boy will be grown soon, and little time will remain for such frivolity.

"Papa! I've found you!"

"I cannot hide from you, Gino. You find me so quickly."

"I always know where you will be, Father. By now, you are nearing the end of the last row, because Isabetta and Alessandra have finished with the horses."

"This happens every day like this?"

"Yes, Father."

"Well then, you are the clever one, aren't you? Perhaps tomorrow, I will work in the opposite direction to fool you."

"That's okay," Ambrogino glows.

"Since you know so much, Gino, has Maria left her bed today?"

"No, Father," he replies. "Mother has been tending to her, but she hasn't gotten up yet."

"Well, I'm sure she will soon, son. God knows of your sister's pain, and will ease it soon. Don't you agree?"

"Oh yes, Father. Yes I do!"

"Good, then let us finish this work. You can carry these clippings back for the hogs, and I will meet you in the barn for cleaning."

"Yes, Father. It's a beautiful day, isn't it?"

"It is, Gino. God has given this splendid day to us, and He has also blessed this vineyard with a bountiful crop this season."

"I love the smell of the grapes," Ambrogino inhales with joy. "Our wine will be better than ever this year, Father."

Frederico knows, too, that it will be a top wine season for the Gallinelli farm this year, and it will please Lord Visconti. The Lord's fondness for Frederico's wine has made the Gallinelli vineyard renowned in all of Milan, and has allowed for good fortune for the Gallinellis.

Upon arriving at the barn, he sees Ambrogino already cleaning the sheep pens.

"You are a hard worker," Frederico declares.

"I can do as much work as Antonio can do, Father."

"I see that you can. I don't know if it's because you work so hard, or your brother works so little," Frederico amuses.

"He can't even carry this bucket!" yells the now visible Antonio from the doorway. "He fills it and then cries for me to carry it!"

"You are both good workers, but you could do a little bit more, Antonio."

Antonio waddles over to the placid sheep with the full bucket of fresh water. He places it carefully down without any spillage while his father watches.

"I do twice as much as Gino, Father. I can carry three buckets to his one."

"You should, Antonio, as you have four years on him. When Gino is your age, he too will carry three buckets, maybe four."

"Maybe five!" fires Ambrogino.

"Maybe zero!" argues Antonio. "Maybe you will be ill like Maria when you are my age, and you don't have to do anything but lie in bed!"

"Antonio! Are you angry with Maria? Would you rather be in her place instead?"

"She is not so ill, Father," Antonio replies as he walks toward the doorway. "She could get out of bed if she wished."

"Continue with the sheep, Gino. I will be right back," directs Frederico as he walks after Antonio.

The father and middle son clear the doorway and grab two more empty buckets on their way toward the stream together.

"Say whatever you will, Antonio. I will not admonish you for your words if they are true."

"When you are in the vineyard Father, Maria is being nursed by all of us. She speaks to us in a different way than she speaks to you. She is always so tired and uncomfortable when you are around. But when you leave, she yells at us with the energy of a healthy person."

"So you feel she is taking advantage of her condition to free herself from her chores?"

"Yes I do, Father."

"I believe that you too, Antonio, are always looking for ways to share your chores, but I can see in your eyes that there is some truth to what you are saying. I will speak with her, and you will stop teasing. Is that a fair deal?"

"Yes, Father."

Over in the main house, Maria and her mother are knitting a new jumper for Frederico. The house is the colour of sandstone, and has several arched windows adorned with dark green shutters. Maria is always aware of who is approaching by their particular noises. Her father often spits on the ground before entering the house, relieving himself of the dirt of the day before coming inside.

"Father's coming," whispers Maria to her mother.

She gathers the secret jumper and hides it beneath Maria's pillow – a routine they have perfected for a few days now. Reaching for the half-made robes that they are otherwise working on, mother prepares the knitting scene to be viewed by Frederico.

"Where is my lovely bride?" Frederico asks as he enters the main house right on cue.

"Performing God's work as always," replies Margherita, a slender woman of strength and confidence.

"When is it you are not performing God's work, my dear?" asks Frederico upon entering the room.

"Only when He allows me to stop to catch my breath," she replies in a clever fashion that Frederico adores so much. "Your daughter has almost all of my knitting skills, as this fine robe shows."

"Yes, I see that, I think our mild summer will give way to a cold winter this year, Maria. Your excellent skills will be necessary to lessen the burden on your mother."

"I have no such burdens, Rico."

"None you will admit to."

"I will knit all of our garments this year, Father, in all the colours of the rainbow," Maria boasts. "And you will both be proud of my work."

"Indeed," agrees Frederico. "And I will use your eye for detail to help me in the vineyards at harvest soon."

"The vineyards?"

"Yes, of course. Only the grapes of the proper colour are selected for the Lord of Milan's wines, and your brothers' poor choices cause me great work to oversee. I would trust you to harvest on your own without my oversight."

Unsure of how to take her father's compliments, Maria replies, "I don't know if I can, Father."

"She's not able to work the vineyards, Rico. She has all the work she can do right here," asserts Margherita.

"I am certain Maria will be pleased when she is on her feet again, and enjoying the delightful sun that shines so warmly. Will you not, my sweet cherub?"

"Of course, Father. I do wish for that day."

"Then that day shall be tomorrow! We will walk hand in hand through the vineyard as we have done a hundred times. And if I must carry you on my back, then so be it."

Silence consumes the room for a moment. While there should be great joy in the recovering of Maria, both she and her mother feel a sense of loss at the ending of their special time together.

"Yes! Yes it shall be tomorrow then," Margherita proclaims, seeming to abandon Maria. "You shall go with Father tomorrow as your assistance in the vineyard is needed."

"But Mother, I have only been out of bed to use the bucket. I haven't worked for such a long time... I don't think I can do it."

"Your condition will be weak, but your strength must be used for more than knitting before it abandons you forever, don't you agree?"

There is silence from Maria again as she is unsure of the answer, and now looks to her father.

"That is true, Maria," Frederico replies. "You will be fine in my care, and your strength will be tested. Continue your knitting, and do a good job."

Gently stroking Maria's rich black hair, Margherita nods to her daughter and places a firm kiss of reassurance on her forehead. Standing up to leave, Frederico takes her hand and guides her away from the bed and out the door.

"You have taught this one well, my love. If she shows the same skills at knitting that her sisters show with the horses, then we will be rich with the sales of robes!"

"We're already rich," Margherita replies.

"Perhaps, but we can't work this farm forever, and these children are of the age that requires them to have skills."

"Oh, must you make them grow up so fast, Rico? Will you have Ambrogino managing the vineyards next week?"

"You know, I am beginning to think he could do it!" Frederico laughs. "I do understand your point, my dear. It just troubles me that we have such a successful farm and vineyard only at my daily scrutiny. Our children rely on me for every direction, and assume little of their own. I fear they will never understand the proper ways that my father taught me."

"Bartolomeo certainly has this knowledge."

"Yes, but it does not come with a desire to put his hands into the soil. That yearning must come from inside. A good farmer has to feel the earth, and the rain, and then react to those feelings in order to get the best crops. Without it, we would struggle like everyone else, always complaining about this and that, instead of applying knowledge and feelings to produce a fine crop."

"Give them time, my love, and you will see that they will exceed your expectations."

"Time? Bartolomeo has all the time in the world, and he chooses the University in Bologna – all because Guisseppe's father insists he goes. He is so bright and all he wants to do is read books about nothing."

"You regard his studying as a bad thing? You have given Bartolomeo your blessing, and you have assured him he will be going with your favour."

"Of course, of course that's true. I know he will become a fine and most learned man and I have a great amount of pride for him in my heart. But my heart also tells me that he will forge his own way, and never want to come back to his family's farm."

"You don't know that, Rico. I don't have any idea what he will wish for himself one day. The mere fact that he is free to choose is a tribute to the wealth you have provided for all of us. And I know he appreciates that."

"Well, suppose he chooses his own life in another town. Then we will have three daughters who are excellent animal keepers, and a son who never wants to work at anything. I get more cooperation from the mules than I do from Antonio."

"Yes, but look at Ambrogino. We've been blessed with a son who wants to perform every chore that you do. And when you are alone in the vineyard, he helps me prepare the meals. He's showing to be exceptionally bright for his age, too. The farm is in good hands with this one."

"Everything you say is true." Frederico smiles and cups his hand against his wife's soft cheek. "He is all that you say he is. But he needs another ten years, and I will be an old man when his time comes."

"No older than your father was when you came of age. Ambrogino is so much like you, in more ways than you can see."

Frederico settles down and places his rugged hands on her sturdy shoulders. "How is it you seem to know all there is to know?"

"Simple," she replies. "I tend to the family just as you tend to the vines… and I have the greatest crop in all of Milan."

Frederico laughs, "You certainly do!"

He squeezes her shoulders and kisses her squarely on the lips with a delightful humming sound as though eating her up. Margherita returns the energy, and they break apart smiling, hand in hand, walking toward the stalls to check the progress of the girls.

Chapter 2

As this year's berry harvest is now upon the farm, Frederico needs to gather his hired hands to discuss the activities. He is always certain to get complete agreement from Bernardo, his crew leader. If Bernardo comes to agreement with Frederico on any subject matter, then there will be no mistakes with the other men. Bernardo's size and strength contrast with his soft-spoken politeness and genuine affection for the Gallinelli family.

One of the many things that Frederico's father had taught him, was to hire the very best man in the land and his salary shall return tenfold.

"First thing as always," Frederico begins. "We shall cut ten of the best bunches for delivery to Lord Visconti."

Bernardo knows exactly why this is being done. After sixteen years, his enthusiasm remains high, and he accepts Frederico's orders with the delight of hearing them for the first time.

"Yes sir, the finest ten bunches for delivery to his Lordship Visconti. If I may say, this will be an easy choice this year, as you have cultivated a most fantastic crop."

"I merely set the direction, Bernardo, but it is you and your team who perform such fine work," Frederico heaps the respectful praise that maintains a happy and motivated crew.

"When the Lord Visconti smells and tastes these bunches, he will set my prices higher than ever. Our farm, and our tradesmen, and all of you will see great profits this year. All of Lombardia will remember the great wine of Gallinelli di Como, 1347.

"Cheers to Frederico!" one of the young hands cries out.

"Thank you my young friend, but we haven't produced a single keg yet! You go with Bernardo to make the cuttings, and he will show you how to choose. The rest of you will gather the harvesting supplies."

Bernardo, armed with sharp shears and a single crate, sets out with his helper to peruse the vineyard. From in between the rows, Bernardo hears a playful call of his name.

"Bernardo!"

"What are you doing here little Ambrogino?"

"I am tending to the grapes, can't you see?

"Yes, I see, I see. You are a careful steward of this vineyard. Perhaps you can lead us to the best bunches for Lord Visconti's inspection," Bernardo offers with warm intent.

For the next hour or so, Ambrogino guides the two men all around the vineyard, pointing out bunches for collection. Bernardo has no fear of the boy's choices, as the crop is so strong this year. On the occasion that Ambrogino's judgment was in error, Bernardo explains how he thought they could find a better one. The boy happily complies, as it means even more time to show off his skills in the vineyard.

Before long, the work is finished and Bernardo is hoisting the choice bunches into the family farm's best wagon. This wagon is colourfully painted with grape vines, summer flowers, and a white background as though it belonged to royalty. Frederico always uses it for his trips to Milan as it shows off the best qualities of the farm.

"Maria, do you have the horses ready for me?" he asks.

"They are ready and anxious Father. Mother has your provisions packed, and the weather looks good."

"You have done well, my dear. You have most of your strength back, and it pleases me to see you in this condition." Frederico gently pulls his daughter into his arms.

"Thank you, Father. When will you be leaving?"

"As soon as I find your little brother."

"Oh, how wonderful, Father! Gino is so anxious to go with you today. He was afraid you were going to take Bartolomeo again."

"He is old enough to not be a burden. He can help do what needs to be done."

"Shall I get him now?"

With her father's nod, Maria dashes off to the house with the energy of a colt, yelling Ambrogino's name the whole time. It is more common for the siblings to be fighting, but Maria has always cared deeply for Ambrogino, as he never complains, and always tended to her needs when she was ill.

As swiftly as Maria rushed to get Ambrogino, the boy now slowly walks from the main house with his mother. Ambrogino does all he can to hide his emotions, and act more like his older brother Bartolomeo did, all those years of going to town with father.

"Mother, have you prepared this one for a two-day journey?" Frederico asks, hiding his own enthusiasm.

"Yes, Husband. He is all yours and is ready for inspection now."

Frederico adopts a serious look, and slowly circles Ambrogino, inspecting him like a calf being sold at auction.

"Are you sure he's capable?" asks Frederico again, scratching his head and feigning uncertainty.

Margherita straightens Ambrogino's clothes and gives him a little shake, testing his sturdiness. "He's ready."

"Hmm," Frederico continues, now stroking his beard. "Let's go!" he yells with a big smile, shattering the manufactured tension.

Ambrogino leaps into his father's open arms. "Thank you, Father. I've wanted to go on the trips to Milan for so long now. I can't wait to go!"

Hoisting him onto the cart, Frederico hands over the reins to temporarily give him the feel of control.

"We shall return tomorrow by supper, everyone!"

Then one by one, Frederico kisses each daughter who has been dutifully standing by.

"Antonio, you are the man of the family until Bartolomeo returns this evening. You must take care of your mother and sisters," Frederico states with a hand upon Antonio's shoulders. "I trust you to do a good job."

The sternness in Frederico's voice has a more man-to-man tone then other previous conversations between the two.

With all other matters cared for, Frederico and Ambrogino depart. Side by side they sit, with two seasoned stallions pulling the well-equipped wagon. The road to Milan is well travelled, and Frederico expects many travellers over the next two days. He has brought along the regular necessities, and also sundry items that may never come in handy. But in any event, Frederico will be prepared, as always.

Again this day, the sun shines down big and round, as it has for the past several days. Good weather not only brings out more travellers, but also thieves. Even though Frederico is well known to the Viscontis, and to the surrounding farmers, it will be of little use should a thief attack. He keeps these thoughts only to himself, and maintains a happy smile.

"Wave to Mother, Gino."

"Goodbye, Mother!" Ambrogino shouts as he twists his body back to see her.

Margherita exaggerates her wave so he is sure to see her. Her feelings of uneasiness in seeing her youngest boy ride away without her are quickly replaced with the thought that Frederico would never let anything happen to Gino under any circumstances. Around the bend of the brown gravel road the bright white wagon rolls on, and away from her.

Feeling a hundred miles away from home, Ambrogino asks, "Will we see an army today Father?"

"I don't expect so, son. That was several years ago when Bartolomeo and I crossed paths with those soldiers."

"Yes, but you fed them all, and you saved their lives!"

"No, not at all," laughs Frederico. "We simply offered the food we had, since they appeared so tired and hungry."

"We have so much food with us today that it seems like we are going to feed another army, Father."

"I would rather have more than we will need, that's all. You never know how God will test us, so we should always be ready. That year when we met the soldiers, it had been a terrible year for crops, and you were only a year old. We were blessed with enough fortune to manage the most sizeable harvest in the area, so I decided to bring extra with me. There is no need to keep a surplus in your barn when others are going hungry."

"Because God will think we are selfish?"

"That's right. And do you see how we were rewarded for that day? We were given great fortune with the Viscontis and our wine business. That is why you, and your brothers and sisters, have everything you could ever want."

Ambrogino remains silent for a while, not ashamed or confused, but instead just contemplating his father's wisdom. He has always known how great his father was, but now he is starting to understand why, and he is pleased. "So God likes it when you make people happy."

"Son, I surmise that God is most pleased not by the happiness one creates, but by the despair one eliminates."

For several hours, they travel through the countryside, stopping here and there, visiting folks and resting the horses. At one point, Frederico shows Ambrogino a tree with carvings in its bark from dozens of passers-by. Ambrogino is enjoying himself thoroughly as he delights in the wonderment of the world, all while in the comfort of father's presence.

Not too far down the road, the Gallinellis come upon a fork in the road, where Frederico takes the left and begins toward a large hill.

"Wait until you see what I've got for you up here, Gino."

Bouncing in his seat, Ambrogino's eyes light up towards his father. They continue up a small pathway through some trees and up toward the top. Frederico stops the wagon, and the two of them walk hand in hand for about two hundred yards. The trees finally part, and Frederico hoists his son to the top of a large boulder. The view now unfolds for the young boy, and Ambrogino gasps at the sight. It is Milan. The city is larger and more spectacular than he had imagined. It's a magnificent sight – a gigantic city that has high walls, castle spires, and dozens of smoke plumes. It is alive with activity, and Ambrogino is speechless.

"It's quite a sight, isn't it, son?"

"It's amazing, Father, just amazing. Let's go!"

"Okay, okay," Frederico concedes, as the two retreat down the path and back to their cart.

"When will we get there, Father?"

"It will be about three more hours, so you can breathe easy for that time."

"But it seems so close, Father. I can't wait that long!"

"You'll have to find a way, little man."

Back on the main road, they notice that the number of travellers coming and going is increasing now, as other roads begin to converge. Ambrogino hears languages not known to him, but keeps his curiosity quiet, so as not to be a bother.

As they approach the outer wall of the city, merchant carts and small markets crop up on both sides of the road. To Ambrogino, nearly everything that could ever be sold in the whole world is right here. The noise continues to rise, and the variety of activities from so many people now start to blend into one as Frederico drives the cart into the city.

Unable to fully comprehend the magnitude of what he is seeing, Ambrogino remains silent. His father does, too, as he calculates the imagery he allows his son to absorb without inter-ruption.

"Frederico!"

Both father and son turn in the direction of the voice. There, at the blacksmith's station, Ambrogino sees a huge man with muscles on top of muscles. He is covered in soot, but his smile cuts through his appearance like the fires burning nearby.

"Beppe!" Frederico returns as he stops the cart and hops down to greet his friend. "How have you been, you big ox?"

"I am only a simple man trying to make a living," replies the gentle giant. "I see you have a new apprentice."

"Indeed I have," Frederico replies, reaching up to the cart to help his son down. "This is Ambrogino. He is on his first journey to the city today."

"A welcome sight you are, my friend."

"Hello," Ambrogino peeps.

Beppe walks right over and dwarfs the boy by his presence. Bending down into a crouch, he asks, "So how is your crop this year, Ambrogino?"

"It is excellent, as we can show you!"

"Alright, son," Frederico intervenes. "God has been most kind to us this year, Beppe, as I trust He has been to you as well."

"I have no complaints," softens Beppe as he lowers his head, "… no complaints."

"Your heart is heavy," Frederico observes.

"It is my Violeta, Frederico, she is with the Lord now."

"Oh, my dear Beppe. What happened?"

"She was thrown from a horse while learning to ride, and she struck her head on a rock," Beppe mumbles through a quivering lip.

"I can't even imagine such a tragedy, my friend. It must have been a terrible accident and not your fault."

"The rock was so small," Beppe recalls, staring at his hammer. "It took my wife some time to point it out to me. It was only out of the ground about the size of an apple. I don't understand how such damage was done to her. Most children would laugh after tumbling down to the ground. It is just so impossible that a fall like that could take a life."

"You are a strong and wise man, Beppe. There is no way you could have foreseen such a circumstance. I know you cared for her and protected her in the best way any father could have. You are not to blame. Do you understand?"

"Yes, I know, but our suffering is no less. She had a beauty greater than that of her mother. She was so... proud of herself. She would do anything at all that you would ask of her, with no hesitation. She had no equal in this world – no equal. Why would God take such a healthy child at only six years?"

"Only He knows, Beppe. You and I will never know until our own day comes."

"But until that wonderful moment, I can't find a way to clear my head of the memories of that horrible day."

"But why would you want to, my friend? You will want to hold onto every memory of her life as long as you can. All of those times that you can close your eyes and see her face, and hear her laugh, keeps her alive in your heart."

"You are right as always, but I would do anything to see her one more time, Frederico."

"But you have work to do here," Frederico pulls Beppe back into the moment. "Who will do your work? Look at this shop, there is so much to do; our farms and cities are growing, your goods are sought after by many, and your family thrives because of your skill."

"Of course, Frederico. There is much to do, of course."

"And besides, I have wine to trade with you."

"Yes, of course you do my friend. Has there ever been a Gallinelli wagon that did not carry wine to trade?" Beppe asks with a bit more cheer. "What do I have that you might call for?"

"I need a plow blade of your most rugged quality."

"But Father... " Ambrogino interjects. "We have two in the barn."

"Hush, Gino! Those are worn to half their size. Allow me to make my decisions, son."

"Yes, Father."

"What do you have, Beppe?"

"Have a look at this," Beppe says as he walks back into his shop.

Hoisting down a monstrous plow blade, Beppe handles it with one hand in a way that most men would need two.

"That's fine, indeed," Frederico says as he inspects the piece. "Excellent work." Frederico feels its weight and moves it around to inspect it from every angle, while Ambrogino inspects his father's conduct. "I don't suspect I have enough wine with me to trade for a piece so fine as this."

"It is expensive," positions Beppe. "I will have to ask for three kegs of the finest wine for it... or two kegs of yours, Frederico."

"Your flattery is kind, Beppe, but I will not cheapen the quality of your work. Three kegs is a fair price. Gino, roll them to the back of the wagon for me please."

Ambrogino obliges and pulls open the heavy covers from their load. Frederico walks around to where his son is working, and hefts out one keg at a time with the perfect balance of having done so a hundred times.

"Here you are, Beppe," Frederico lays the kegs down away from the action of the anvil. "And I've got one more for you." Frederico reaches into a small unmarked box and produces a misshapen old-looking bottle. "This is a special old friend of mine, from '29, a great year for me, my friend. May you celebrate with all of your family the precious gift of Violeta that was yours to cherish for six years."

Without saying a word, the stoic Beppe takes his gift and embraces Frederico. After hiding the rare bottle in a safe place, Beppe shouts to Ambrogino, "Your father is a great man, Ambrogino! A great man."

"I know," the boy beams.

"You embarrass me, Beppe. I will see you on our way back from our visit with Lord Visconti."

"I will look forward to it, although I do not know if you will find him today. There has been much secrecy in the palace these past few days. If you can find some news, I will be glad to hear it."

"I will have my ears open for you, Beppe. Goodbye, my friend."

"Goodbye."

"Goodbye!" shouts Ambrogino.

"Enjoy your visit, little one," Beppe waves.

As the two now continue toward Visconti's palace, Ambrogino asks his father, "Is Beppe a friend of yours?"

"Yes, Gino. He and I met on this road soon after Bartolomeo and I met those soldiers. We helped him fix his cart, and have been friends ever since."

"He is a nice man."

"Yes, he is. Now, son… you will need to stay in this cart at all times, and not stray until we reach the palace. It is easy for a person to get lost in this city."

Chapter 3

New sights grow and embrace Ambrogino. He is caught staring again and again at the strangeness of this city as Frederico keeps their horses moving at a steady pace. Vendors and pedestrians begin to close in on them while the road narrows into a cobblestone street. The clacking of horseshoes on stone startles Ambrogino as he looks down to make sense of the surface beneath them.

Frederico doesn't say a word, as he prefers only to answer questions from his boy. This way Ambrogino can try to understand things for himself and ask when he chooses.

It is a bit odd for so many folks to be gathered in groups, and Frederico is becoming concerned. Usually, folks are always on the go, with business to conduct and work to do. Perhaps they are speaking of the news that Beppe asked about. Not far ahead, the great palace is becoming visible to them.

"I saw this from the hill, Father. It is fantastic."

"This is our destination, son – Lord Visconti's palace."

"Are we going inside?"

"Of course we are. We are going to see Lord Visconti himself."

Feeling important, Ambrogino sits back and now enjoys the last few yards of his trip. He wants to seem relaxed and confident to anyone looking on.

As they approach the main gate, Frederico slows his pace so as not to disturb the guards. He has learned over the years that courtesy and respect for the guards will be rewarded with favour.

"Greetings," Frederico salutes.

"State your business," replies one of the guards.

"We are the Gallinellis, here to present Lord Visconti with a cutting from my finest berry crop as a gift, for him to judge and choose for his own personal wine."

"Lord Visconti is not seeing anyone today. You can leave your gifts with us."

Realising that Visconti is indeed present, Frederico states in a comforting tone, "Surely, you do not wish to be the one who denies his Lordship the specially selected gifts which he has been so eagerly waiting... every year at this time."

After conversing with the other guard for a moment, he speaks, "Your gifts are always welcome, Gallinelli. You may proceed."

Now unlocked, the large iron gate squeaks in announcement as it eases open, and the vintner and son are allowed inside.

"You are wise men," Frederico offers to the guards as he passes. "The Lord looks favourably upon both of you."

The two horses ease the cart through the gate and into the open air of the palace courtyard. There is a much cleaner and polished atmosphere inside as the inhabitants move about their paces with a more dignified presence than the rest of the city.

"It's a city inside a city, Father," Ambrogino attempts.

"Yes, it is."

He guides the horses over to the right near a large stable area where he hopes to keep them overnight. Hopping down from the cart, Frederico holds up his arms to help his boy down.

"I can do it," Ambrogino announces, and leaps down to the ground, barely keeping his balance.

"Soon you won't let me carry you anywhere!"

The attention comforts Ambrogino. Here they are in this strange place, yet Frederico is at ease, as confident as a member of Visconti's family.

"You there," Frederico calls out to the stable hand. "Would you be so kind as to tell one of the Lord's servants to call for me. I have gifts for him from the Gallinelli di Como vineyard."

"Certainly, sir," replies the boy as he heads into the main building.

"This is a grand place, Father. This is where you go every year?"

"Yes, it is, son. Your brother and I have delivered these bunches to this very spot for many years now."

"Do you get to see Lord Visconti?"

"Yes, of course. He needs to give me his opinion so that my prices can be set. By giving him these fresh bunches, he can tell by their flavour if this year's crop will be average, good, or great. I owe him a great deal for this effort."

"But you are always testing the flavour yourself, Father. Can't you tell if the crop is good?"

"Indeed, I have my own opinion, son. But consider having the most powerful man in Milan choosing your wine above everyone else's. Don't you think your price would then be the highest?"

"Then everyone else would want your wine, too?"

"That is right. That is why it is so important to make this visit today. And if everyone else... " Frederico is interrupted by the reappearance of the stable boy with one of the Lord's servants.

"Who requires business with the Lord?" the servant asks.

"I am Frederico Gallinelli, his Lord's most favoured wine-maker, bearing gifts for his Lord's pleasure."

"Yes, I remember you, Gallinelli. You must be patient. Lord Visconti is conducting many discussions today and is very busy."

"Lord Visconti's time is most valuable, of course. We shall tend to our horses and await your call."

Turning back to the main house, the servant disappears.

"Well, son, it appears we will have a bit of time. Let's get the brushes so we can groom the horses."

"Father, can't we just pay the stable boy to do it, so we can walk around?"

"We could, Gino, but that would be a waste of money when we are able to do it ourselves."

Just then, the doors of the main house fly open, and the servant calls out, "Gallinelli! You are wanted right away!"

Frederico, surprised by the timing, quickly stuffs two coins into the stable boy's hand. "Brush these horses, boy, and watch after my cart."

"Yes, sir!"

Frederico hurries to the back of the cart to pull out the crate of berries.

"Let's go, son!" he shouts to Ambrogino, and the two of them follow the servant into the house.

Instantly, Lord Visconti appears, his eyes fixated on Frederico.

"My Lord!" Frederico exclaims, and drops to one knee. Ambrogino does the same as he was instructed.

"Frederico, please rise. It is good to see you. Your timing is exquisite as usual," Lord Visconti exclaims with no fanfare. "Please come in. Your boy has shrunk! Ha, ha, please, please come with me."

Puzzled, Frederico bends to lift the crate of grapes.

"Leave them as they are," Lord Visconti directs. "Right there, that is good."

Frederico walks away from his crate and holds out his hand to Ambrogino, who quickly connects to his father. The two follow Lord Visconti down a large hallway and up a flight of brilliant marble stairs.

On the second floor, they are urged into a room where six other men are milling around. These men are all well dressed and strike Ambrogino as being important.

"Gentlemen, this is Frederico Gallinelli, and his son... "

"... Ambrogino," Frederico finishes.

"Ambro-gino, ooh, funny name," states Lord Visconti with feigned delight. "Ambrogino, we men are going to talk for a while. Wouldn't you rather see the city from the tower? It is a spectacular sight."

Although perplexed by his handling today, Frederico feels no real danger and reassures his son. "Go ahead, Gino. It is as he says it is. Go and have fun."

Ambrogino lets go of his father's hand and is lead down the hall by a servant.

"We'll call for you soon," Lord Visconti waves goodbye to the boy and closes the door.

"If I may, your Lordship, the crate downstairs has... "

"I know, Frederico. I know," Lord Visconti dismisses. "You have the most spectacular crop in the land this year."

All of the other men chuckle at his humour.

Visconti continues, "The weather has been most favourable, the pests have been few, the soil has been warm and moist, and God has been most kind to you. I hear it every year."

The men laugh even louder at Visconti's over-the-top sincerity.

"Frederico, your vineyard could be frozen with ice in June, and you would somehow manage a worthy crop. The men here in this room know of your great skill. They have been drinking your wine for years."

"Indeed!" one of the men proclaims.

"Frederico, if God were truly so generous to you and you alone, as you proclaim, then you would be Pope by now!"

Now the men howl in laughter.

Not appreciating the humour, Frederico defends, "I am but a simple farmer doing my best for my family."

"Rubbish!" another of the men responds. "Would such a simple farmer separate himself from all others year after year?"

Frederico stares at the man, but does not respond.

Lord Visconti now sees Frederico's discomfort and moves closer to him. "Frederico, let me ask you a question, have you ever lost a horse due to sickness?"

"Sickness?"

"Yes, sickness. Not from a broken leg, or old age, or even falling over a cliff, but from sickness."

Frederico contemplates for a moment. "I do not suppose so."

"Come sit down, Frederico. I have made jokes at your expense today, but it is only a reprieve from what we have been debating these past few days. Regrettably, it is becoming the worst time in our lives, and I require your opinion on the matter. Angelo has a story that is of great disturbance to me and everyone else, and I ask that he share it again for you."

The mood changes to reverence as each man gathers a seat in various places.

"One week ago, I was travelling on his Lord's behalf to Genoa. Upon arrival, I was witness to a great and fretful crowd, so I joined in and listened to what I could. They were speaking about a horrible sickness, plaguing the Eastern Mediterranean that was described to them in graphic detail by three fishermen from Cagliari. These fishermen had run up against a rogue galley that had arrived in deplorable condition, sailing non-stop all the way from Caffa. The crew of only five men had sailed out ahead of their caravan of fourteen other galleys, which were bound for Messina. Their ship was badly burned from the effects of infighting, and further was stripped bare for maximum speed. The men were starving, but refused to sail on with the rest of their party whom they believe were carrying the very sickness they were fleeing.

"Their warning to the Cagliari fishermen was simple. Run. Run as fast as they could, and as far away as they could, for death was growing like an uncontrollable fire fanned by the Devil himself. At the time, the Caffa sailors were convinced that the pestilence had already been delivered to Messina by their brethren, and had likely consumed all of Sicily. Many Sicilians will have escaped just as they had, and will have undoubtedly raced for the mainland, carrying the death with them. This particular pestilence, gentlemen, is no ordinary sickness that picks on the weak and the aged. They were speaking about deaths of the strongest and most able citizens on an unimaginable scale."

Even though the men have heard this story several times, they listen intently in case they had missed something before. Frederico, stunned and confused, listens with a discerning ear.

Angelo continues, "The scene from Caffa was straight from the depths of Hell itself. There were men, women, and children wailing in the streets, with no consolation to be found. The accounts of appalling human suffering is beyond my words, dear friends, but I can tell you this... when death comes to those who have been stricken, it is most welcomed for them. This sickness begins with walnut-sized buboes on the skin that soon turn black in colour. There are horrific pains in the arms and legs, which is soon followed with the vomiting of blood. So riddled with pain and suffering they become, that no doctor can find any type of comfort, let alone a cure. The worst part of all, is that this pestilence runs its course so rapidly it can take a full-grown man in three days time, while the young and the weak go even sooner. One thing is known to be certain: this wretched sickness passes from one person to the next simply by looking into the eyes of the stricken."

"These must be exaggerated stories. Perhaps they are trying to scare folks away from the great riches they might be hiding."

"But I have seen it with my own eyes, Frederico. Not only do these stories of horror come from Cagliari, but there was much talk about ships of death coming into their ports from Caffa. Five ships came in with only a few surviving men on board; all others having perished on the journey. The doomed survivors spoke vividly of the pestilence they were fleeing. Then the poor Corsicans who helped these men became afflicted too, and soon their whole families were sick, and then their entire neighbourhood and city."

Angelo now becomes more loud and animated, "This pestilence will not spare Milan, gentlemen. If this is not the work of Almighty God, punishing all of us for our sins, then please tell me now!"

"Did you journey to Corsica?" Frederico asks. "Is that where you saw it?"

"No, I would never go there with what I know now," replies Angelo. "It was in Genoa, here on the mainland, that I saw it. There was a woman carrying her daughter from church to church, and doctor to doctor. This poor child had the same afflictions that were being spoken about. I can only assume that the mother was soon afflicted as were the rest of her family and all who came to her aid. It was this sight that caused me to leave and return here."

"Then you might be afflicted as well."

"Precisely, Frederico. I thought I would be, so that is why I left when I did. But since it has been more than one week now, and I feel no pains, I have to say that I have been spared."

"And here we are," interjects Lord Visconti. "I know of no reason for this man to lie to me, Frederico. He is most trusted, and I believe his every word. I fear for all of us, and our families, yet I cannot show my fear to my people. I need to know what you make of this."

"I am no doctor, nor have I ever seen such a sickness that strikes so rapidly and with such force. I believe Angelo when he says it is God that chooses who will be afflicted. For that, we must all atone... or be afraid."

Angelo furthers, "It is a pestilence not only of the masses, but of doctors and priests as well. Nobody is spared, no matter how obedient! How can it be that the most pious man suffers the same fate as the most sinful man? When the priests refuse to give last rights to the dying, then you know that no blessing can save you."

The room falls quiet, and all eyes are fixed on Frederico, awaiting his comments.

Frederico breaks the silence, and measures his response, "I am not sure what to say. The stories being told here are upsetting me greatly as they have you. My immediate thoughts are of my own family."

The men nod in agreement.

"I have spent my life in the service of God, and will only pray more deeply now than ever before. I do not know what to do otherwise."

Lord Visconti adds, "We understand your thoughts, Frederico. We have all had the same thoughts ourselves, but you will soon find, as we have, a burning desire to stop this pestilence that is so taxing us. Just as Noah was tested to build the ark, we ask ourselves if there is an ark for us to build. We have wondered if there exists a sacrifice we can make whereby we can be spared. I am sorry, Frederico, if this is too much to ask of a humble farmer such as yourself so soon after hearing this news."

"I... I don't know," Frederico contemplates, rubbing his beard, and now beginning to pace within the room. Motioning toward Angelo, he asks, "How many people are recovering?"

"Why... none."

"None? Not a single person has met the pestilence and lived?"

"The talk is that all who are afflicted will perish with absolute certainty."

"I respect your story, Angelo, I know from your voice that you are speaking the truth of what you heard. I wonder, though, what truth can be found in the voices of those speaking to you."

"A brilliant question," Lord Visconti interjects. "We have wondered this ourselves, and I believe it is accurate to say that some will live. But even if a few live, what world will be left?"

"And what virtue is held by those who are spared?" Another of the stoic men speaks up, "Is it only those who have no sin at all? Then what chance has any of us?"

Silence again.

"Then why are we here now?" Frederico poses.

"To figure out a way to save ourselves, you fool!" argues one of the other men.

"No, no, I mean, if we have been chosen to die the same as the others that Angelo speaks of, then why has it not happened already?"

The men look at each other in a puzzled way.

Frederico continues, "Why are we not suffering right now?"

"Perhaps God is asking something of us, just as he did Noah," one man persists.

"But Noah heard God's word all by himself, as only one man. In our case, the whole city of Milan is not afflicted, so that would mean we are ten thousand Noahs."

"Perhaps our lot is to suffer by watching the deaths of others first," another man postulates.

Frederico counters again, "Of that, we suffer already."

"Perhaps God lacks the capacity to kill us all at once. Noah was given forty days and nights," a third man offers.

"I fear," interjects Angelo, "we are way beyond that time now. From the descriptions of the ships travelling, the pestilence has been taking lives for months."

"Perhaps," Lord Visconti takes his turn, "we have been given an opportunity right now to act in a clever way to save ourselves."

"Only prayer will spare our souls now," continues one of the other men.

"Soon the pestilence will be here in Milan, and we will all be judged at that time," the most vocal man persists.

"Not necessarily," Frederico measures again. "You all speak of the pestilence being spread from one to another. It would seem simple then to avoid all contact with those who have been afflicted."

"Are you suggesting turning our backs on the sick and dying, leaving them all for dead?" one man asks.

"I do not know all of the answers, but I am sharing my thoughts as you have asked me to. If we do not allow for any contact at all, then how should the pestilence find us?"

"Jonah was thrown overboard from the sinking ship!" one man exclaimed. "The other sailors did not wish to kill Jonah, but it was the only way to save the entire crew! God has proven this to be acceptable to Him!" the man persists.

"I do not condone the abandonment of the sick," Frederico replies. "You have asked me for my opinion, and my opinions come from the things I know. If one of my vines is stricken with blight, soon it will grow onto more fruit. So I cut the afflicted bunch away and burn it."

"You sacrifice the afflicted fruit?" a man asks.

"No, not a sacrifice as it is written. My father taught me to burn any afflicted fruit, or even animals for that matter. He told me that diseased things needed to be put back to their earthly form as soon as possible to protect the living.

"So what are you suggesting, Frederico?" Lord Visconti asks.

"When a blight comes to my fruit, it will consume more and more healthy fruit until it consumes it all. But if the afflicted bunch is cut away, then there no longer exists a source of destruction… but with people who are afflicted, I suppose we would need to keep them away from us."

"Wall the city in!" a man shouts.

"Yes, keep the afflicted away from the healthy citizens of Milan!" another adds.

"Frederico, are you sure this will work?" asks a third.

"The only thing I am sure of is that the world has changed today. I would like to see my son please."

"Of course," Lord Visconti opens the door and murmurs to his servant. "Frederico, you are free to go with my best wishes and gratitude."

"Thank you sir. I'll… just take back the grapes."

"Oh yes, that's right Frederico. I shall set the price this year equal to last year plus ten percent more."

"Bless you, sir, and may mercy be with all of you," Frederico nods before departing. The men offer their goodbyes and blessings, but he only hears them as a group murmur while heading out the door.

Outside, Frederico is greeted by a very bubbly Ambrogino who hugs his father around the legs.

"Oh, Father! It is an awesome sight from the tower. I could see the whole city, and even hills in the distance. Did you know there is another castle south of here, and the cows look like ants. Come look!"

"Yes, yes, I know Gino! It is a wonderful sight, but we must be going now. Besides, I have terrific news for you."

"What is it, Father?"

"I will tell you when we are in the cart."

Escorted down the stairs and back out to the courtyard, Frederico and Ambrogino are greeted by the stable boy who gleefully explains the fantastic condition of the horses.

"You do fine work young man," Frederico proclaims. "You will do very well in life."

"Thank you sir."

"You will be wise to heed all that Lord Visconti instructs of you, no matter if you understand him or not."

"Of course sir," the stable boy replies with a puzzled look.

Frederico hoists Ambrogino onto the cart and they move out toward the gate.

"We are in the cart now, Father."

"You forget nothing, my brilliant son. The news I have is that Lord Visconti has made a price for our wine this year, higher than he ever has before."

"We'll be rich!" Ambrogino exclaims as he claps his hands into his chest with a huge grin.

"Yes, indeed."

"That is great news, Father. We will be able to buy a great many things!"

After passing through the gate, and back out into the city streets, Frederico drives the cart, but is fixated in his thoughts.

"What shall we buy, Father?"

Twitching his head toward his son, Frederico comes back into the present time, "Oh, yes, Gino, we will buy many new things... many new things, in fact we shall shop before we leave the city."

"Are we leaving the city tonight, Father? I thought we were going home tomorrow."

"Oh, ah, Lord Visconti already has many guests, so we won't be able to stay with him tonight."

"Then, maybe we can stay with your friend the blacksmith?"

"I don't know, son. We will see."

Chapter 4

As the two ride through the streets, Frederico looks at his city as a completely foreign place. Each stare that he connects with could be the Devil, or it could simply be an innocent child. He doesn't know if he should stop or go, shop or even breathe. Keeping this anxiety from his son is critical, so he decides to make his normal rounds, but a bit faster than usual. Stopping the cart to make occasional purchases, he is looking for warm clothing in all sizes. He never buys finished goods, and always brings home cloth for Margherita and the girls to work with. Ambrogino takes it as odd, but does not question his father's choices, especially since one of those choices is for sweet candy that he has never had before.

Soon, they make their way to the end of the city streets, out to Beppe's blacksmith station. As the evening falls upon the city, most of the other vendors were packing up. Beppe has let his fire burn down and is gathering his tools when they arrived.

"Beppe!" Frederico called out.

"Hi there! Here come the two tradesmen from Como! I told you that you would not find Visconti at home."

"We did!" Ambrogino yells out.

"Quiet, Gino! He is not speaking to you. Be respectful of my ability to talk for myself." Frederico stops his cart, dismounts, and ties up his horses. "Beppe, we did see Lord Visconti, and he gave me a great price for my wine."

"Of course he did. So why do I see you out here at this hour my friend?"

"Lord Visconti was entertaining many guests and had no room for us."

Beppe pauses, not sure of why that would be true. "Then you shall stay with my family tonight."

"You are most kind and gracious, Beppe. It would be a great privilege for us to stay with you and your beautiful family, but I must decline because I have forgotten duties that require my attention back at the vineyard."

"Duties? Surely, your servants and family are tending to all of your needs, Frederico. How imperative must it be that you would take your young son back up this road in the dark of night?"

Ambrogino turns to his father, waiting for the response.

"Your concern for us is dear, my friend, but I have been on this road many times. My horses are strong and smart, and there is a clear night to see by. In fact, Beppe, I have a gift for you before we depart."

Beppe waves his hand and lowers his head in response. "There is no gift you could have for me, Frederico... except your comfort in my home, now that would be a gift."

"Here," Frederico pulls a book from his new stash of purchased goods. "It is called *Ten Tales for Children*. It is a Greek book and has been translated into Latin, of course. I have had a similar book in my family for years, and it would please me for you to have one."

"This is not right, Frederico. This book is of great value, and I cannot accept it as a gift. Especially from a man who owes me nothing."

"Then trade for it," Frederico replies, as he casually lights one of his oil lanterns from the coals in Beppe's fading fire.

"Take whatever you want, for such a gift as this."

"I would like a lock and key," Frederico asks, affixing the lantern to his cart.

"A single lock and key?"

"Yes, that will do. And, please, no more, Beppe. Let us make this trade and be finished."

"As you wish, Frederico. I felt in debt to you before you arrived today, and now I feel even more in debt. You must want something of me in the future."

"Beppe, I wish for nothing more from you than your friendship. I believe there are changes coming to our land, and I fear men will turn against each other. At such complicated times, friendship is the most valuable gift of all."

"Then you have heard rumours from Visconti's palace! You must tell me the details!"

"I have no details. I only know that you must prepare yourself and your family for a time. You must stay clear of strangers, to the point where you may need to lock your family in your home. Please prepare yourself with stores of food, and pray for love and forgiveness as often as you can, my friend."

Stunned, Beppe yearns for more information. "If it is war, Frederico, then please tell me."

"If I told you what has been told to me, I might make matters worse for you. I am not certain if I wholly believe what I have heard myself, so there is no need to repeat half-truths. But I do know there will be a time soon when friends will turn against each other, that is for sure."

"I will never turn against you, Frederico. You are like a brother to me, and I would surely die before compromising our friendship."

"Let's hope it never comes to that."

Frederico gives Beppe a brotherly hug, and then he accepts the book, handing over a lock and key as requested. He steps back and stands quietly while Frederico and Ambrogino manage their horses and cart back onto the road and ride away. Frederico looks back and waves to Beppe as a last assurance of his remarks. The burly blacksmith waves back, and watches the cart slip away into the dusk.

Along the road out of Milan, Ambrogino does not say a word. The cart moves with a much faster pace than the trip into town, as

Frederico takes advantage of his knowledge of the road. A crescent moon begins to provide some light as it rises in front of them, perhaps signaling the duo to head home in this direction as soon as possible.

Frederico reflects on how the moon is so enduring in its place day after day, month after month, and year after year – circling the earth faithfully and unchanging. How is it possible, he wonders, that the land below will soon be ravaged with the end of times. Was it all a ruse back in Visconti's meeting room? It doesn't seem plausible since the men were already gathered. Were the stories so exaggerated as to no longer resemble the truth? Black death, vomiting blood, passing from the afflicted to the well by a mere glance? There have been many instances of sickness in the past throughout history, and Frederico knows of them well, but the scale of this loss tears at his sensibility.

He understands this though: even if the scale is less than told, there will likely be chaos. Chaos that will lead to fighting, looting, and even murder. He fears that mankind has never shown the capacity to deal with turmoil in any other way than with selfishness and greed. His home of Como will be no different.

Perhaps Ambrogino asks no questions because he is afraid for the answers. Or, if he doesn't hear the reason why his father told Beppe that men will turn against each other, then maybe it will never happen.

Frederico is so involved with his own imagination, that he does not consider how little Ambrogino must be trying to make sense of what is happening. He decides not to trouble his boy with unnecessary conversation, and so comforts him with occasional smiles.

A few miles on, Frederico directs the horses down a side road and into a wooded area.

"Where are we going, Father?"

"A safe place I know for the night, son. It is too far a trip all the way home for one night, and it will be better for us to be off the road."

As they continue deeper into the woods, Frederico searches for a spot concealed enough not to be seen from the main road. The cart rumbles over bumps and roots, yet makes very little noise, as the goods on board have been fastened securely.

"This will do fine right here. You can stay in the cart, Gino, and I'll set everything up."

Frederico prepares the cart for sleeping, but leaves the horses hitched. While working, he constantly checks the surroundings for any signs of movement. After a final inspection of the cart, he feeds and waters the horses. Ambrogino is watching his father work the campsite, and sees him turn the lantern down very low and tuck it out of the way. The starry sky is obscured by the thick treetops, covering the Gallinellis in near total darkness

The father and son then open up the food basket to partake in some of the bread and fruit they had brought. It is a very calm and comfortable night, as the air remains warm, and the only sounds come from insects and frogs making their presence known.

Ambrogino's apprehension subsides as his father tells several pleasant stories that the boy recalls from years ago.

After a short trip into the brush, and a few minutes of prayer, the two settle into the cart for the night. Ambrogino is comforted by a new blanket his father had purchased that day, and Frederico is comforted by the fact that they are away from the city. He brings the lantern inside and keeps it covered except for a small bit of room for it to receive enough air and remain lit.

It is a lovely night to be outside, but Frederico is not able to enjoy it. His thoughts fall back into the words that were spoken at Lord Visconti's palace. He keeps trying to make sense of how this sweeping death can be happening. After a short time, he changes his focus. While this may or may not be the end of the world, it will certainly be a test to the most faithful. No matter how the future unfolds, he is certain of one thing – he will find a way to save his family. Already he has a plan.

Suddenly, the sound of a snapping twig grabs Frederico's attention.

"What is it, Father?" Ambrogino whispers.

Frederico presses his index finger over his lips. He then begins moving in slow motion to free himself from the wagon without making a sound, all the while listening for the same.

Back towards the road, he sees the shadowy figure of a horse and a lone rider. Frederico makes his way to the front of the cart, and as the figure moves closer, carefully pulls out a hidden dagger from beneath the seat, tucking it into his belt.

The figure stops moving, and Frederico has now positioned himself between his horses, keeping one hand on each of the mare's bridles so they do not move. He peers up to the road from his camouflaged spot and sees the figure dismounting his horse, and walking towards Frederico's camp.

A moment of truth is coming upon the Gallinellis. Is this a thief who will stop at nothing to take all that he wants? Is this one of the men from Visconti's court who has come to kill a potential security leak? Perhaps he should free one of the horses right now, grab Ambrogino, and make a run for it. Maybe that would take too long. Perhaps he should mount the wagon and drive straight out over the man, running him down in the process. If only Ambrogino were just a little bit older...

Frederico can't wait any longer. He must immediately take control of the situation. Armed with his dagger, he leaps into the cart, removes the lantern, and hops back down pulling out the long brake pole from the side of the wagon.

Turning up the flame and carrying the heavy pole, Frederico exposes himself and marches toward the man with no fear. Ambrogino buries himself in the cart, but keeps one eye fixed to his father's light.

"What do you want?" Frederico calls out quietly, but loud enough for the man to hear.

"Frederico, is it you?"

"Beppe?"

"Yes, it is me."

Frederico lowers the pole and turns the lantern back down a bit. "What in the world are you doing out here?"

"I came to find you!" Beppe replies as the two are now upon each other.

"How did you find me here?"

"I followed you soon after you left."

"Really? But why are you here?"

"You frightened me, with your words about people turning against one another. You can't say those things and leave me! What did you expect me to do?"

"I'm sorry, Beppe, you are right, let's get out of sight of the road. Did anyone follow you?"

"I don't think so."

"Good. Have you eaten?"

"I am always hungry, you know that," Beppe says with a grin.

"We've got plenty, come on over."

As the two men and Beppe's horse walk toward the Gallinelli wagon, Frederico calculates what it means that his friend is here, and how this will now change his plans for a quiet evening and an easy trip home in the morning.

"So truly, Beppe, why would you follow us?"

"I had to, you couldn't leave me with your cryptic words, and just ride out of town. I need to know what you know."

"How can I say this, Beppe? I didn't want you to hear what I have heard. I don't trust the information that was given to me. If it is nothing but lies, then I would be endangering all whom I share it with. I may not know anything at all."

"That's not possible, Frederico. I am a simple man, and you have more knowledge in your little finger than I do in my whole big body. When you tell me that something is going on, I believe you, especially when I can see and sense unrest and secrecy in the city. You weren't the only one to leave the palace in a state of shock today. I know everything that happens in this city. You must tell me what you know!"

"All I know are stories… stories from scared and unfaithful men. Who really knows what is true and what is not?"

"Then why don't you tell me these stories, since I am neither a coward, nor an unfaithful man."

Frederico glances up at Ambrogino and sees his son fixed on every word the two men are saying.

"Gino, you know this is Beppe, and everything is all right?"

"Hello, Beppe."

"Hello, little Gallinelli," Beppe smiles. "I am sorry to startle you tonight, but I have a great desire to speak with your father."

"I know," he replies, and uncovers the blanket from his head.

"Beppe, let's go for a little walk." Frederico takes out a full loaf of bread and hands it to his friend. "We are only going to be a few feet away, son. You can lie down and go to sleep now."

"Goodnight," Ambrogino peeps, and rolls over out of sight.

"So would you have followed me all the way back to Como?" Frederico whispers as the two wander out of Ambrogino's earshot.

"I didn't expect I would have to go that far."

"You knew I would stop here, didn't you?"

"It makes sense doesn't it? You showed me this spot twenty years ago when… "

"Yes, yes, I know… and you call yourself a simple man."

"So tell me what you know, I beg you, and I will leave you as fast as I came."

Frederico looks around to make sure Ambrogino has not gotten up, and then begins his tale to Beppe. The conversation goes entirely one way as Frederico pours over every detail of what he knows the pestilence to be. His head hangs low throughout as he explains the method of death that is ravaging city after city, all the while listening to himself as he speaks, wondering if he even believes his own words.

Frederico further explains all of the questions and answers that he was part of earlier that day, even playing the part of each member of Visconti's trusted circle. The story falls upon Beppe like a giant anvil that is impossible to lift. He slouches in his place and stares at his friend's lips in the dim light.

"Should I continue?" Frederico asks in an attempt to ease his friend's pain.

"It's the wrath of God for sure, isn't it?"

"If it is true, what else could it be?"

"We have been a very sinful people for far too long. We have never been able to change our sinful ways."

"I have the same opinion as you, Beppe, I do. But I will not be convinced there is no hope at all."

"What do you mean?"

"I'm certain that God always has a plan for the most pious, or the least sinful. I don't foresee that He wants to destroy everybody. He never has."

"So how do we save ourselves?" Beppe struggles for the answer.

"I don't know," Frederico confesses, and the two fall silent.

"Well, I have prayed every day since we lost Violeta, Rico. I don't see how any more pain could be inflicted upon me than has been already."

"There are others around you who depend on you, big man. We have had this conversation before, and you know it to be true."

"But it is people like you whom I depend on for answers, Frederico. Without a good explanation, I can offer so little."

"You have more to offer than you know, Beppe."

"So tell me then, Rico. What are you doing out here? Why are you not staying in comfort tonight?"

Frederico contemplates how much he wants to tell his friend the entirety of his plans, and decides that he must provide something.

"I don't trust men when they are confused, Beppe, especially leaders. I thought it would be safest for us to leave the city just in case somebody decided to do something desperate."

"… and what next?"

Not yet knowing the real answer, Frederico offers an immediate one, "Then I will go home, store my food, shutter my windows, and lock my doors until spring."

"You suppose that will be enough, Rico?"

"If there is a plan to destroy us all, then my family will accept our fate without fear and without ever raising up against another man. We will not leave this world flailing and screaming with the blood of other men on our hands when the Lord arrives for us. We will confess of our sins as we always have, and we will cherish the last moments that we have together in peace."

Beppe ponders these profound words, and practices making them his own.

"Then that is what I shall do as well. I am sorry to have disturbed you, Frederico. Thank you for the bread."

"Do you have enough food at home?"

"Not enough for the whole winter, not for all of us... my brother and I always get a wild goat or two the day after Christmas."

"Then take this." Frederico insists as he returns to the wagon.

Opening a small box, he pulls out cloth bundle. Rolling it open, he reveals dozens of gold coins each tucked in their own individual pockets so as not to make any sound against each other.

"There is enough here to buy all the food you need for the winter."

"Indeed there is, Frederico, but I can't take this from you, I am the one who owes you!"

"Then keep this all for me. I do not need any of it. When we see each other again, you can give it all back to me. But if I can count the ribs on any of your children, then I will hate you forever for saving this money. Do you understand?"

"What I don't understand is why you are so good to me," Beppe mutters as he wipes his eyes.

"Our friendship has no price, you big ox. I know you would certainly do the same for me if we were in each other's shoes."

"Oh, Frederico. You know I would."

"Then there is nothing more to talk about. Take this and

stockpile food for your family. Use your skill to bar your doors, and never look into the eyes of the devil."

Beppe accepts the coin roll and embraces Frederico as if for the last time. Without saying another word, he mounts his horse and rides out of the forest in the opposite direction so as not to reveal his location to anyone who might be on the road.

Frederico chokes back a brief feeling of accomplishment, coupled with doubt and fear for what will become of his friend. He climbs back up into his wagon to check on his son.

"Are you comfortable, Gino?"

"My feet are a little cold."

Frederico draws up another blanket to cover Ambrogino's feet. "There you go. Goodnight, son."

"Goodnight, Father."

Chapter 5

Margherita steps out of her house to bathe in the warmth of the morning sun. It's rays knife through the deep reds and purples of the hanging grapes like a painting, and she is sure not to miss the moment, for it is hers. The children rise with no complaints as they are eager to get to work and show their father that the chores are getting done without his attention.

In a short time, Isabetta finishes milking her cow and finds herself looking down the road while carrying her buckets from the barn. "Mama! It's Father, coming up the road!"

Puzzled by the early arrival of her husband and son, Margherita lays down her basket and walks swiftly down toward the approaching cart, trying to hide her concern. To her delight, two happy hands rise up and wave to her.

"Hi, Mama!" Ambrogino shouts from the distance. "We're back!"

Arriving within just a few yards, Margherita smiles, "I can see that, Gino. Is everything all right?"

"All is fine, my love," Frederico assures, as he slows the cart to a stop.

Ambrogino hops out to greet his mother to whom he delivers a big hug.

"I will take the cart in, and Gino will tell you about his trip," says Frederico, hurrying the horses ahead.

Ambrogino is hugged and kissed back by Margherita, and the two begin walking hand in hand up the dry road.

"Mother, it was a fantastic trip. We saw the whole city from a hill, and we went all the way in to the palace, and we met Lord Visconti and everybody!"

"Slow down, Gino," Margherita laughs. "There is plenty of time to tell your stories."

"Best of all, Father got the highest price ever for his wine this year."

"That's wonderful, dear."

"Yes, and I got to go to the top of the tower in the palace, and I could see all around the city just like a bird! Father also stopped to see a friend who was a blacksmith, and he bought a new plow blade."

"It seems as though you had quite an experience, Gino."

"We did, and Father bought some things, too, before we came back."

"He usually does. That is how you have received those gifts over the years."

Ambrogino smiles as he continues to stroll toward the main house swinging his mother's hand along the way. He is wholly at ease and content with his visit to the city, and feels somewhat more important than before he left.

"Here comes the little big man," Bartolomeo proposes to his brother.

"I could have gone to town instead if I had wanted to," Antonio smirks.

"But you didn't, so you have no right to begrudge him," says Margherita.

His three sisters playfully pat Ambrogino on the head and push him around as he passes amongst them.

"It will be a good year for us all," Margherita proclaims. "So let us get back to our chores so we can have a celebration tonight. Gino, I'll help Father, and you can help Isabetta with the milk."

Bright smiles and jovial play come upon the children, even Antonio, as they scatter around the farm. It is a comfortable feeling that repeats itself each fall, and is testimony to the hard work of their father.

When Margherita is certain that all of the children are engaged with their chores, she heads for the barn where Frederico is unloading the cart.

"I expected you much later today, Rico."

"That is because we did not stay in the city last night. We left in the evening and came halfway home. We camped along the road, and came right back before sunrise."

"You camped along the road?"

"We were hidden in a grove of trees, and Ambrogino was never scared. The night was superb, and as you can see, we are unharmed."

"Why didn't you stay at the Visconti palace as you normally do?"

"The Viscontis were entertaining many guests and there was no room for us. I suppose we could have stayed with Beppe's family. We saw him and he offered us room, but you know how I hate to be in any man's debt."

"Oh, how I know," she sighs. "That is why every man we know is in your debt! It seems only fair that you should accept the kindness of others once in a while."

"Maybe you're right, my love," Frederico wraps his arms around his wife. "Next time, we stay with Beppe, I promise. It's so nice to have my arms around you no matter the occasion. You fit so perfectly against me."

Margherita pulls him closer. "It's nice to have my husband and son safe at home."

The two lock into a deep kiss that lasts pleasantly long.

"You seem very happy to be home, Rico."

"I could hold onto you this way forever."

"Well, you could try."

"Maybe I will!" Frederico lifts Margherita off her feet, and carries her toward the main house.

Shrieking with laughter, she playfully protests, "Your chores, Rico! Who will finish your work?"

"The day is young!" Frederico exclaims as he carries Margherita around the yard for everyone to see.

"Hold the door, Isabetta," Frederico effortlessly carries his giggling wife through the door, into the main house and off to their bedroom.

"Did you miss me here last night?" Frederico teases as the two tumble into their bed.

"You know I did, you rotten man!"

"Well this rotten man will make it up to you right now," Frederico says in a devilish tone.

"I knew that's what you had in mind," Margherita giggles as she kisses him all about his face. "But we will see our sons any moment now."

"Of course, you're right, but what a shame it is to let this moment pass."

"The day is young," Margherita says as she stands up and straightens her dress.

"Yes, it is!" he agrees, preparing to head out to the farm.

"Don't work too hard today, my dear, you will need to save your energy."

"It is energy that I have!"

The two then file back out to the yard, where they are immediately greeted by Antonio.

"Father, I have worked the whole day while you were gone, and I was the man of the house, just as you said."

"Hmm, perhaps you are deserving of a gift, Antonio."

"Oh, I am!"

"Then come see what I have for you." Frederico leads Antonio to the barn where the cart is parked.

When they arrive, they see every single item has been unpacked by the other children, each having laid claim to the new gifts they have found.

"What do we have here?"

"They are all looking for things for themselves, Father."

Isabetta interrupts, "No-one has taken a thing, Father. We are only unpacking for you; to reduce your work."

"Then I thank you all for your efforts. Gino, you and Antonio should bring all of the purchases inside for Mother to sort through. Then Isabetta and Allesandra should store the cart and care for the horses. We have much to do today to prepare for harvest, so be patient, and you will all see what was brought for you."

The children all nod in their father's direction.

"Now where is Bartolomeo?"

"He is out in the vineyard with Bernardo," says Maria.

Frederico nods and turns out from the group to head in that direction. He hopes none of his children are making a connection to the reason why he has brought back warm clothing as gifts. It is a bit strange not to see anything fun or different, yet there have been no comments. The children dislike the idea of dressing for cooler weather, so they are most disappointed with this year's bounty.

Remaining calm and collected in the vineyard as always, Frederico greets his workers, and eventually finds Bartolomeo.

"Back to work I see, son."

"Yes, Father," the young man replies. "While the workers have begun harvesting, I have been examining the vine structure for signs of damage."

"Sometimes I sense that you are smarter than any of us."

"Maybe once in a while by luck alone," Bartolomeo smiles.

"Ha, ha, and what have you found, my brilliant one?"

"Almost everything looks very strong, Father, but there is one shoot way back in the ninth row that needs attention."

"I might know the one."

"Goodness, Father, it amazes me how you can know every single shoot in a sea of thousands."

"I could be wrong, son. Is it on the north side of the fifth plant in from the river side?"

Bartolomeo shakes his head with a broad smile at his father's incredible mental catalog.

"So what do you project should be done with that one, son?"

"Well, as you seem to know, the south side fork is strong, and is carrying most of the fruit, while the north side looks okay, but has very small and tasteless berries. I would recommend that the north branch should be pruned out of season, so as to save the south side."

"Interesting. Why not simply pull the entire vine? Whatever has caused the weak branch certainly must come from the root."

"I considered that, but don't deem it to be the case, Father. The remainder of the vine is as strong as the others. There is no reason to forsake the entire plant for the death of one branch."

"But what if there is an infestation, and that one vine spreads its disease to others?"

"Again, not in this case, I do not believe. There was no indication of insect or bird damage. The branch is not altered or strange looking, but withering, as though its water supply has been cut off from the main vine. I suspect this plant has chosen to give up on its north fork, and will support growth on the south side for years to come."

"That is a very good observation and argument, Bartolomeo. I am proud of you. Go ahead and prune as you see fit. Let me ask you something else unrelated to vines, son."

"Yes, Father."

"When you go off with your friends, what things do you speak about?"

"I thought you had no interest in my pursuits away from this farm."

"Perhaps I have resigned myself to the fact that you will not be staying here, and as a result, I should better understand my new son, the man."

Startled at his father's frankness, Bartolomeo ponders, "I guess we most often discuss the university. There is a great interest in laws, and how laws shape the land and its people."

"What else?"

"Um, we talk about women, too. But we keep discovering what

you taught me, that there are many questions... and few answers."

"Few indeed, my son. But what about medicine, do you ever speak about that?"

"Not really, Father. We leave that to the doctors."

"I envision you and your friends as capable as any doctor that I know."

"We look at medicine as something that has already been learned, and that there is nothing to be added. Whereas law is ever changing, and it affects so many people daily."

Enjoying his discussion, Frederico takes it further. "It is hard to trust that there is nothing that can be added to the field of medicine. Surely there is some value to curing the illnesses that afflict people."

"Value, yes, but healing is up to God, and none of us ever questions God's will."

"Then you should not prune that vine, as it will simply be up to God whether that vine recovers or not, right?"

"That's different."

"How?"

"God cares for his people more than he does for the plants."

"I think you are wrong there, son. If God did not care for the plants, then they would all die, and what would the people have to eat?"

"That's true, I suppose, yet it somehow seems different to me."

"But now you can see the similarities, right?"

"I do, Father, but let me give you an example of our discussions."

"Please do."

"If I am in a tree at a neighbour's house, and I fall out and suffer a bruise, it is my problem alone. The medical burden is not shared by anyone. But, if I should fall onto one of my neighbour's chickens and kill it, then what is my liability to him?"

"You should replace the chicken."

"But it was an accident, and not my intention to fall and hurt myself, as my rather large bruise shows."

"Well, you should not have been fooling around in your neighbour's tree in the first place."

"But what if I was asked to go into the tree to pick fruit by that same neighbour?"

"Then you are working for him, and it was not your intention to go into the tree were it not for his demand. Therefore, in that case, you would not owe this man a new hen."

"Correct, Father! These are the things that we discuss. You have changed your opinion of the liability based on the circumstances. We try to imagine circumstances where a man could commit a crime and not be guilty. Or, on the other hand, situations where a man may be guilty of a crime but not know it."

"That is an interesting thought, and I can see how such imaginations can lead to discussions of great length. How about discussions of proper farming techniques? Do you spend a lot of time on that?"

"Too boring. We leave those discussions to our fathers," he smiles.

"Of course! Leave it all to the fathers to provide the food you eat as you relax comfortably in your discussion groups."

"You know, Father, that you have taught us all well, and I know precisely where all of the food comes from. If you should command it, you know I would be willing to work this farm as you see fit."

"Thank you, son," sighs Frederico. "You have my blessings to attend the university. You have become too wise a man to be relegated to only harvesting crops. Your help to me is to speak with me as a man, and for that, I am most blessed."

Frederico places his hand upon Bartolomeo's shoulder and gives him a warm shake. Bartolomeo takes his father's hand in his and replies, "We are all blessed, Father."

He heads off in the direction of the fifth row, where Frederico watches him walk away until he can no longer see him, and then continues to stare at the spot. He wonders if he should go through with his escape plan, and if so, would it even make a difference in any one of their lives. Will Bartolomeo accept his radical idea, or will he leave the family to forge his own way? Will all of his family determine he has gone mad, and not go with him at all?

As he is accustomed to do when nobody is looking, Frederico finds the smallest living thing around him at the moment and begins to pray. He turns his attention to a single grape berry – a tiny specimen in a vineyard of millions. In his mind, he places himself onto this little berry and relates to its insignificance in the world. He reaches out and plucks it, and holding it up for close inspection, he speaks to it. "Little grape, how am I to know what to do? Is this truly coming, as they say? Will any of us survive?"

Pausing to listen for an answer from any direction, he studies the berry more closely.

"If I take you now and place you in my pocket, I can walk out of the vineyard. If the weather were to turn frozen cold tonight, then all of the other thousands of berries would surely freeze and die. But you, being safe in my pocket, would be fresh and perfect tomorrow, and could be made into delicious wine that would last for years. If I only knew that such a freeze was coming, I would try to save as many of you as I could. I would be a fool not to, right?"

Frederico rolls the berry back and forth in his fingers, waiting for a divine response in any form, and suddenly realises he has already removed this berry. What if the freeze does not come? He cannot place this berry back onto the vine! Once plucked, it can never be returned, ever.

He carefully places the berry back onto the spot from where it came. It fits nicely, and looks good for this moment, but he knows, of course, it will never grow again. It will whither right in its own place and die within the day.

After a brief moment of silent pondering and remorse, he takes the berry back, and puts it in his pocket.

Chapter 6

Dinner conversation is unusually light tonight. It is always up to Frederico to lead the conversation, but it is obvious to all that he is deep in thought. The children expected great tales of the trip, and how Lord Visconti came to give their father such a great price. But even Ambrogino does not speak of any details.

"Rico, you're very quiet tonight," Margherita says. "Surely this meal is better than the one you ate last night."

Smiling, Frederico replies, "Of course. It's delicious as usual. Did Maria bake the bread?"

"No, it was Allesandra, and you helped her with the fire. Don't you remember?"

"That's right, I am sorry, Allesandra. It is delicious, and baked to perfection," Frederico pauses, he feels all eyes are upon him. "… I would like to show all of you something," he begins, and takes out the little berry, placing it on the table in front of him.

Each family member looks at the berry, trying to figure out what lesson their father is trying to teach them since it is so obvious what it is.

"It is a grape berry, Father," the matter-of-fact Antonio breaks the awkward silence.

"Exactly, son. It is a single little grape berry I plucked earlier today."

"It is proof of the greatest harvest we will ever have," gushes Ambrogino.

"While that is true, Gino, it is not my point."

"It is a game, Father. And it involves a berry to play it," offers Maria.

"It is not a game, sweet pea, but it is a gamble."

"It is a sample of God's blessing and gifts," says Margherita, in a motherly teaching fashion.

"It is certainly that, my love. But yet not my point."

"Then what is the point, Father?" Allesandra asks.

"Let us wait to hear Bartolomeo's idea first."

Bartolomeo places his drinking cup on the table, folds his hands in contemplation, and begins.

"It's not as simple as it seems. Yes, it is a berry. Yes, it is a gift, and apparently it represents a gamble. But I believe the berry represents the vulnerability of a single person, and that it is best for that person to stay with their bunch."

Frederico smiles in Margherita's direction, "You have raised quite a remarkable son."

"No, you have, Rico. He has many gifts, but wisdom has come from you."

"Well, you are all right. You are all right." He picks up the berry, and holds it up for everyone to see. "But my point is somewhat different. There is something coming that will affect this little fruit."

"A drought?" Margherita asks.

"No, but close. It is a great freeze that will soon be upon us." Frederico stares at the berry and waits for a comment.

"The summer is not over yet, Father. It won't freeze here for… months."

"One would presume, Antonio. But what if I were to say that it will freeze here tomorrow?"

"I would say it would not be true, Father. It never freezes at this time of year."

"So, Allesandra, my oldest and wisest daughter. You fancy that I am crazy to make such a claim?"

"Um, no, but I would guess that maybe you are mistaken."

"How could it freeze so quickly, Father?" Bartolomeo

protects his sister.

"Well, let's consider this," Frederico offers as he puts down the grape. "If I were to say to you that I know without any doubt in the world that the freeze will come tonight, would you heed my warning?"

"I would, Father," Ambrogino jumps.

"I would, too," agrees Isabetta. "You are never wrong about farming. You know when the droughts come, and when it rains, and when it is safe to plant. I would heed your warning, and if it were wrong, then we would be wrong together."

Frederico nods in pride from his daughter's unflinching loyalty.

"Of course, we would follow your direction," adds Margherita.

"Me too," follows Antonio with a smile.

"And me," from Bartolomeo.

"And me," says Maria.

"If you truly believed it to be so, Father, then I would do as you ask," admits Allesandra.

"Thank you all very much. I believe... that there are times when a family must stay together at all costs."

"Is one of those times coming, Father?" asks Ambrogino. "Is that what you and Beppe were talking about?"

"Yes, son. I think we need to stick together now more than ever." Frederico smiles at his precious boy.

"Is that what the berry stands for?" Allesandra asks.

Finally, Frederico begins to open up, "This little berry is not on its vine, but here with us in this room. If we keep it here overnight, and the freeze sets upon the vineyards, then all of the other berries will be destroyed. Except this one. It was safe."

"So the berry was saved because you knew the freeze was coming," suggests Bartolomeo. "Then why not save them all?"

"My gifted son, you have now made my point for everyone to hear."

"I don't understand, Rico, and you are beginning to worry me. I wish you would be more clear," objects Margherita.

"I need to tell you all a story, but it will sound as crazy as a freeze in the summer. I will tell you what I know. But before you heard it, I wanted to make certain you were in the mood to contemplate its consequences, as it is not good news."

With his family as silent as a stone, he begins the entire story of the pestilence that has befallen Corsica. Sparing the most gruesome details, he gives the frightening story enough respect to prepare his family. He goes on to describe how it is now in Genoa, and that the sickness will be delivered to Milan, and from there to Como.

"This can't be true, Rico," shakes Margherita.

"Exactly what I thought when I first heard it myself. I have been examining this story from every possible angle and source, and I am completely convinced of the reality."

"How long before it comes here?" Bartolomeo asks.

"I don't know, but I suspect that the afflicted people who are now coming to Genoa will be able to travel to Milan in as little as a week or so, and maybe one more day to here."

"Why is this happening, Father?" Isabetta's eyes fill with tears.

"It has to be God's will, my sweet, for some reason yet unknown to me."

"Has Florence been afflicted, Father?" Bartolomeo asks.

"I don't know. I guess, I assume… I just don't know. What I do know is that when there is one afflicted person, there will soon be two, then three, then ten, then one hundred. And nobody survives – not the doctors, or even the priests who try to save them."

"I don't want to die, Mama," quivers Ambrogino as he climbs into his mother's lap.

"I won't let you die, son," Frederico counters. "That is why we are leaving."

"Leaving what?" Margherita asks.

"Leaving all of this – the house, the farm, everything."

"When?" Bartolomeo asks for everyone.

"Tomorrow morning."

"We can't just leave tomorrow," bursts Antonio, not appreciating the gravity. "What about the harvest? What about the wine? We are going to make a lot of money this year."

"We will harvest what we can in the morning. We have enough wine to take with us to pay for things we need. We will have plenty of food… but there will be no wine making this year, at least not for us."

"Where will we go?" Allesandra asks.

"I estimate the mountains toward Lucerne would give us the best chance."

"If we will not be safe here in Como in two weeks, then how will we be safe in Lucerne in three?" Margherita asks.

"I don't know if there is any place we can go to be safe. But I know that very few people will be able to get to that land in about a month. The travelling is treacherous even at this time of year, and that is why we must leave now. If we wait too long, then the winter will be too strong in the mountains, and the roads will not be passable at all. If we can make it to the other side before then, nobody else will be able to pass through until spring."

There is a silent moment as each family member ponders the circumstances that their beloved father is presenting to them.

"It's brilliant, Father," Bartolomeo announces, not so much to praise his father, but more to assure the rest of the family. "We will make it to the other side of the mountains before the harshness of winter sets in. Then the mountains will keep the sick and afflicted on this side."

"That sounds like a good plan," states Margherita. "But if the end of the world is upon us, won't other desperate people find any means to follow us?"

"We won't be able to stop them. But you can plainly see those mountains in the summer, and there is plenty of snow on them. No human could survive that journey in winter. Not unless he is a goose."

"But what about the farm, Father, and everything we have?" Antonio begs.

"We take whatever we can. We will need at least four horses

and two mules. We will bring four hens for eggs, and all of the other livestock will stay."

"Stay where? What will become of them, and the crops?"

"I plan to give the entire farm to Bernardo, Margherita. I will give him the farm to care for as his own for a time of three years. He will have the benefit of all of the profits from this season's harvest. At the end of three years, if we do not return, then he can have the farm forever as his own."

"This is too much to bear, Father," Allesandra raises up and paces in frustration.

Margherita is riddled with questions, but chooses each one carefully in order to present a united feeling for her children. "But what if Bernardo leaves the farm just like we are? Surely he will see what we are doing and want to come with us."

"I do not plan to tell him the complete truth of our plans, my love. I don't know for sure what will become of this place, and I do not know if what we are doing is right. But I have to protect my family in any way possible. If we take Bernardo, or anyone else for that matter, then we are responsible for him. I fear we may run out of food as it stands now. We cannot burden ourselves with anyone else – you seven are my only concern."

"Is that why you bought all of those warm clothes, Father?"

"Yes, Gino. I wanted to be sure we were prepared for the worst."

"Rico, I know how much you love this farm, and there is no way you would make such plans if you had any doubt over the course of things to come. We will prepare ourselves, children... not in fear, but in joy. Let's pray together now." Margherita holds up her hands as a symbol for all to join hands. They all oblige, bow their heads, and she begins.

"Almighty God and Father, we thank You for our health, and the blessings of Your wisdom. We believe it is Your will that we prepare to leave this land and save ourselves on the other side of the mountain. We humbly place ourselves in Your care, and we ask You to watch over us on our journey. We know that with faith in You, we have no fears. Amen"

"Amen," the family echoes.

"Come now, daughters, we have much to prepare for," she continues. "There are crates and baskets in the barn; fetch as many as you can so we can pack up our needs tonight."

"Let us be discreet, though, Mother," Bartolomeo suggests. "Let's not alarm the hands so that Father's deal can be made with them."

"Yes. We have plenty of time tonight. We will need warm clothing, food, some utensils, food for the animals, and firewood. That is it. All of the furniture will stay. We will keep this place as whole as possible for Bernardo. Gino, help me to put away the dinner dishes, so Mother can prepare to pack," Frederico says.

Ambrogino rises, and the girls head to the barn. Bartolomeo asks to speak with his father outside.

"Father, I sense Bernardo will easily see that we are preparing, let us go and speak with him now."

"That's a good idea, son. Go and get two loaves of Allesandra's bread to bring with us."

Moments later, armed with sweet bread, the two men march toward the sounds from the vineyard where Bernardo is leading his team. Bartolomeo tries hard to remain relaxed, and lets his father do all the talking.

"Bernardo!" Frederico calls out.

The dark-skinned man with the bushy mustache eases his way toward Frederico, and the three men meet together a few feet from the workgroup.

"Yes, sir!"

"I have a proposition for you, my friend," Frederico says, as he hands Bernardo one of the two loaves of bread. "My daughter just made this bread. Try it, it is delicious."

Bernardo readily accepts and samples, "Mmm, you are right, sir. Her mother has taught her well. Thank you, sir."

"I am prepared to make you a very substantial offer, Bernardo. This offer will require some courage, a large amount of consideration, and faith on your part. Do you understand?"

"It sounds serious, sir. What is it I can do for you?"

"I have been called by the Lord to make a journey."

"A journey, sir?"

"Yes, up over the mountains to Lucerne."

"That is a long way, sir. Are you wondering if I will be able to manage the harvest without you?"

"I have no doubt of your abilities, Bernardo. But it is all of us who are going, my whole family."

"Everyone, sir?" Bernardo stops himself from another bite.

"All of us."

"When will you be back?"

"I'm not certain, my friend. I project it will be in the spring. However, this is where my proposition comes in. I expect this farm to be in outstanding condition when we return, so I will allow you to profit personally from this year's harvest."

"The whole harvest... for me, sir? Are you certain?"

"All of it. I need you to have an incentive to maintain this place, and I would expect you to use the profits to pay the men as well."

"Yes... of course, sir," Bernardo answers, while trying to uncover his master's meaning.

"You will have the run of all of the main house where you can sleep, entertain guests, and do whatever else you please while we are gone."

"Well, I would never let anything get out of place or become ruined. You can count on me, sir, to maintain the farm as you would expect for your return."

"Good. I am glad you feel that way, Bernardo, for there is more to this proposition, so listen carefully. Those mountains are treacherous travelling, and I do not know what lies ahead for us. Should any member of my family not return to this farm in the time of three years from today, then you alone will have deed to the farm forever."

Bernardo stands stunned. "I don't understand, sir. Why would you give this all to me? This belongs to your family."

"I do hope to return, you can be sure. But you are the only one who knows how to care for the crops and the animals as they should be."

"You are so kind, sir... though I don't understand why you would leave this all to me in such a fashion."

"Let me say this, Bernardo – if everything works out the way it should, we will both profit immensely."

"I trust you, sir, and will do as you ask. When do you plan to leave?"

"In the morning."

"Then you need to pack and prepare, sir! Let me help you."

"No, no. You will have plenty to do to prepare yourself. Discuss this with the other men, and collect your questions for later. There is much for all of us to do."

Frederico reaches out his hand, but Bernardo lunges past it, and embraces him with a brotherly hug, finding no words to express himself.

"Okay, my friend, okay. I will draft a document that I will sign for you. Then if anyone troubles you for my whereabouts, you will be protected by this document."

"That is very wise of you, sir. I only hope that a small piece of your great wisdom has somehow rubbed off onto me."

"You are wiser than you know, Bernardo."

"Come, Bartolomeo, let us get to work."

Bernardo watches the two turn and make their way out of the vineyard. When they are almost out of earshot, he calls out, "Thank you for the bread, sir!"

"You are welcome!" Frederico waves the other loaf back and forth over his head.

Bartolomeo also waves, and finally asks his father, "Why did you bring two loaves, and only give him one?"

"Because I want Bernardo to think that maybe the second loaf is for someone else, or for a second plan."

"You wish to confuse him, Father?"

"No, I want him to wonder if there is something more that he is missing. It is just a little guarantee that he should stay on his toes."

"Oh, I expect he will, Father."

"Let us hope so."

Having arrived back in the barn, Frederico finds Ambrogino petting a lamb that he does not recognise.

"Is this lamb one of ours?"

"She is now, Father. A man came by in a wagon while you were in the vineyard. He said this lamb was sick, so I traded the man one hen for her."

"Is that right? And why did you make that trade, son?"

"This lamb is a ewe, so I thought we should keep her and try to make her better."

"But I don't know how we are going to care for it on our journey."

"She can ride in the wagon with me until she's better," Ambrogino insists.

"Do you know what is wrong with her?"

"I think she has eaten something she shouldn't have. With good food, she'll be fine in a few days. Father, what will happen to the rest of the animals that stay on the farm?"

"Bernardo will care for them, and they will be fine."

Ambrogino stares up at his father with a look that a parent can decipher easily.

"What is it, son?"

"I was hoping they could all come with us."

"Why that would be too big of a burden, son. We will not be able to bring enough food with us for so many animals. They will be much better off here with Bernardo and his crew than with us."

"May I care for this lamb, Father. I want to be sure she grows up to give us wool."

"I suppose one extra lamb won't hurt, Gino. I will shear this lamb myself in a year, and we will tell this story together."

"Thank you, Father." Ambrogino motions toward his father for a hug.

Frederico holds on to his son a little longer than normal, and Ambrogino doesn't mind in the least.

Chapter 7

Having slept very little, Frederico's mind is fixated out his bedroom window. He has let the sun climb without him, something that almost never happens. He hadn't even noticed when his wife left the bed. For someone who has the race of his life in front of him, he can't seem to find the right point to start.

The sunrise creeps up over the fields as Frederico observes the spectacular serenity. This past week has been one beautiful day after another. He can't remember another stretch of such pleasant weather in a long while, and begins to question his judgment about the whole trip. If God were truly ravaging the people, how could the skies be so calm and gentle? Then he remembers: the sky must have been perfect for Noah, too, in the days before the dark clouds blocked out the sun.

"Are you awake, Father?"

"I am, Gino."

Nudging his way into his father's bed, the little boy snuggles under the covers. Even though it is morning, and he must get up soon, Ambrogino wants to spend at least one minute in total comfort.

"We should get up and get ready, son."

"I know, Father. But I wanted to stay in bed just for a little while longer."

"Okay, son. It is kind of nice to watch the sun rise, isn't it?"

"I didn't sleep very well last night, Father."

"Neither did I," Frederico replies as he gently strokes

Ambrogino's hair.

"I don't feel very good."

"You will feel much better once we get going. Why don't you go and check on your lamb."

"Okay, Father."

Frederico leaves the bed as well, and notices Margherita in the hallway carrying some clothes. Their eyes meet for a moment, and Frederico proceeds to inspect each room to be sure that every child is up and about. He finds them all empty, and the activities in the house going almost too smoothly. No bickering, no panic, no fear.

In the kitchen, Allesandra and Isabetta are packing baskets with all the food that will fit. Outside, Maria and Antonio are filling the wagons with the provisions that the others are bringing out.

The Gallinellis will be taking three wagons. Frederico expects they will need at least two, so the best way to provide that is to start with three. If something goes wrong with one of the wagons, he can always condense them into two, and not give up any supplies. Plus, three wagons only partly filled will provide more shelter for his family.

"Good work, everyone," he praises. "It's okay if you take something for yourselves you know."

"I have already packed my straw doll," Maria says.

"Can I bring the bocce balls?" asks Antonio.

"Sure you can. Maria, you should pack the wagons in a way that there is an aisle in the middle. Then we can access each crate if needed. Here, I'll show you," Frederico hops up into the wagon and begins shifting crates to the sides. "Then you can even lie on them if you want to rest."

"Father!" comes a yell from the barn doorway.

Frederico jumps down and races over.

Antonio points toward Ambrogino who is sitting on the ground near a stall. Frederico sees his youngest boy cradling the lamb in his lap.

"She's dead, Father," he whimpers.

"I'm so sorry, Gino honey," Frederico comforts and sits down beside his son. "She was already sick, and you did your best."

"Not a very good trade," mocks Antonio.

"Be quiet, Antonio!" Ambrogino yells.

"Antonio, go help your sister now. Come on, son. Let's go bring her out to the fire pit."

"Okay," Ambrogino says as he gingerly gets up while holding the lamb.

"She must weigh almost as much as you, son."

"I've got her," he replies.

Frederico guides his boy outside, and looks up to see his other children gathered to witness the events. Antonio keeps laughing as he joins his siblings, whereby Allesandra fails to see the humour and slaps him on the shoulder for being cruel to their little brother.

Around the corner now, Ambrogino lays down the limp animal in the fire pit. "Can we say a prayer for her?"

"Of course we can, Gino. Shall I get the rest of the family?"

"No, only you and me."

"That's fine. Shall I start?"

"Yes, please," Ambrogino says as he bows his head.

"Dearest God, our Lord and Father... we offer today the soul of this little lamb back to You. She came into our family only yesterday, but as such she earned her rightful place as one of our own. We ask that You accept her into Your Heavenly Kingdom, and that You provide for her the greenest of pastures, the warmest of days, and the comfort of others like her. Amen."

"Amen," Ambrogino whispers.

Packing the wagons goes easily, but solemnly, and within minutes, the family is ready to go. Frederico and Bartolomeo complete their deal with Bernardo over the dining table with paper and ink. For Frederico, a quiet anxiety for what is being left behind is replaced by one for what lies ahead: not so much for the difficult travel, but for the helplessness that may face him soon.

For the first time in days, clouds roll in from the west as the wagon train eases its way from the courtyard. Frederico turns back to the men on the farm and blows them a kiss of affection, reassuring them of his honesty and sincerity. Within a few minutes, the caravan is out of sight, and the Gallinellis are mobile for the first time in their lives. Bernardo stands at attention in his spot to make sure that it was all not some odd test from his master. A half hour goes by, and he retires back to the field.

Up the road to the Alps, the twelve wagon wheels roll over the dusty earth as twenty-four hooves pound the ground in an erratic pattern of strokes. The first mile of travel is quiet, as the children do not wish to break the silence, set the mood, or be the first to find complaint. They stay vigilant and alert, and wait for their father's directions.

Frederico understands this mood, and remains silent himself. He wants to get as many miles underway as he can before the family engages in conversation. If they remain close to the farm, then there may be pressure to turn around or camp closer than they should later tonight. The last thing Frederico needs is fear or dissention, so he looks over at Margherita, asking with his eyes if everything is okay.

"Everything is fine, my love," she smiles, placing a comforting hand on his thigh and rubs his knee. "We are all in this together now, no matter what."

"Isn't that right, Gino?"

"Yes, Mother," he replies.

Margherita then looks behind to the other children and gives them a small wave. Each of them returns the wave indicating that all is well so far.

Although they have passed several farms along the way, none of the children have expressed an observation. Had this been a vacation, they would have been shouting, pointing, and laughing.

After about three hours of travelling, Frederico looks for a spot to break. He sees a small grove of trees at the crest of a slight hill, and decides it will serve his family's needs. Upon approaching the spot, he signals to the others with his left hand straight up in the air, and he begins to slow his two horses.

Behind him, Antonio and Bartolomeo slow their wagons and follow their father's lead. Frederico guides his wagon under the trees, followed by the other two. They can see a farm up ahead on the other side of the road, but at the moment, there is no activity by men or beasts at this spot.

"This is a nice place to rest, Father," Bartolomeo proclaims as he tethers his horses to one of the trees.

"It will do for a short while, son."

"It's about time. My rear end is killing me!" Antonio barks and lightens the mood.

Margherita has already laid out a couple of blankets, and has brought out some bread and cheese for lunch. "Come rest your sore behind over here, Antonio, and have something to eat."

Each of the children gradually relax and partake in the delicious food, except for Ambrogino, who remains in his place.

"Are you feeling any better?" Frederico asks.

"Maybe a little."

"Do you need some help to get down and have something to eat?"

"No, I'll have some bread, but I'll stay here."

Frederico obliges his son's request, hands him a piece of sweet bread, and kisses his boy on the forehead. Not sensing anything seriously wrong, he turns back to the rest of his family, produces a map, and lays it out for them to see.

"This is a map of Milan, and it shows all the way to the mountains. This is Como, and this area over here is where our farm is. We are on this road right here, and right now we should be somewhere in this area," he points out, and circles his finger around a broad area at the edge of the map. "I feel that we need to get up to this lake here by evening and set up a camp. If anyone asks, we are vacationing in the mountains before turning back home after a couple of weeks."

Nobody questions their father's plan. In one sense, they don't want to know if there is any doubt in his mind. And secondly, it is easier to digest the uncertain future of their lives if they just wait for instructions.

Margherita has completed her preparations of lunch, and now turns her attention to Ambrogino in the wagon.

"How are you feeling, Gino?" she whispers.

"Okay, I guess."

Margherita places the back of her hand on his cheek. "You feel warm, dear. Are you sure you want to stay under this blanket?"

"My feet are cold."

"Let me get some stockings for you. How about something to drink?"

"Yes, please," he mutters.

Margherita quickly produces his stockings and casually draws a cup of water from one of the kegs. She hands them to her son, and gives him a long kiss on his forehead. Smiling to her boy as she glides away, she takes Frederico's hand and walks him away from the rest of the children.

"Gino is ill."

"He'll feel better in the morning."

"I hope so, Rico. But I'd be able to care for him better if he were at home."

"Are you suggesting we abandon this journey?"

"What if we go back and then head out again when he is feeling better?"

"Truthfully, my love, I suspect we are already out of time. I know it bothers you to see him lying in the cart like this, when you know we could be back home by sundown. But we have food and medicines, and he can rest all day. It will be enough, you will see."

"I understand. I guess we shouldn't go back... but it's just not fair that he should fall ill right now."

"But maybe it's best for Gino that we are on the road now.

"Perhaps if he became sick two days ago we would not have left when we did, and we all would have been in danger. We should never question God's will, and accept that whatever happens is meant to be. Gino will be fine in a few days, we'll be high up in the hills with the fresh clean air, and we'll all be safe a year from now because of this journey."

Wanting every word to be true, Margherita wraps her arms around her husband and holds him tight. "You are right, my love. Everything will work out. Plus, I would rather be on the road living in a wagon with my family, than huddled in a lavish house waiting for the Devil to arrive."

"Thank you, my sweet beloved wife. Let's go comfort the children, lest they imagine we are making secret plans."

"There is plenty of cheese, Father," Allesandra offers as Frederico and Margherita rejoin the group.

"Thank you, my dear," he replies as he takes the food from his daughter's hand. A brief moment of clarity falls over Frederico as he notices the way in which his oldest daughter is caring for the family, however so briefly, in this spot.

"Sandra... "

"Yes, Father."

Searching for the words to describe his immense joy in how confident and capable his child has become, he stumbles, "... this cheese is your work, isn't it?

"You know I make most of it, Father," she smiles.

"I'm sorry not to have appreciated all that you do for the family these past few years."

A bit startled by her father's frankness, she replies, "I'm only trying to do my share, that's all."

"You have many gifts and talents, my sweet," he offers, and delivers a quick kiss to her cheek.

"Thank you, Father."

Margherita has listened to every word, and is warmed by her husband's extraordinary respect toward women: the kindness that so few men have, and that she grew to love so many years ago.

"Has everyone had their fill?" she asks.

The children nod all around while they continue chewing on their lunch.

"Good. There is no need to rush. We will make our destination with ease. Let's take a moment here in this lovely spot to enjoy each other's company."

"I'm enjoying not doing any chores today," chimes Antonio.

"You don't do any chores anyway," fires a playful Maria.

"Neither do you!"

"I do more work by sunrise than you do in a whole day!"

"Ooh, bake bread with Sandra, that's a lot of work."

"Mother, do I have permission to beat Antonio?"

"Not until we have made camp tonight, then you can beat him with the biggest stick you can find."

Margherita finds comfort in the fact that at least these two are behaving normally in the face of the unknown dangers ahead, and she has no desire to stop the arguing.

Meanwhile, Isabetta has gone to check on Ambrogino and is seen leaning against the wagon beside him. Frederico makes his way over as well, and his footsteps cause her to turn around face him.

"He's sleeping, Father."

"Good," he whispers back. "He needs his rest."

Frederico puts his right arm around his middle daughter's shoulder and holds her firmly against his own.

"Do you feel he has the same illness that Maria had, Father?"

"It looks that way. She started out with a high fever, too."

"Yes, but she was in bed for over two weeks before it broke. Do you think Gino is going to be okay out here?"

"Oh, I'm convinced of it, sweetheart. He'll be very comfortable and warm in the wagon, and we'll have warm fires and hot food every night. It will be as good as being at home, but more fun," he smiles into his daughter's brilliant hazel eyes.

She looks back down, but hugs her father tightly, "I hope so."

"Why don't you try to find Bartolomeo. I haven't seem him."

"Okay, I will," she replies, and releases to show her father a faithful smile before heading off into the trees.

Frederico stares lovingly at her as she walks away. He judges that Isabetta is the one daughter of the three who is most like Margherita. Thin as a twig, but strong as a tree, she is the first one to check on Gino, and the first one to come up with positive ideas. Allesandra and Maria are both wonderful in their own way, but in Frederico's eyes, there is something extra special about his Isabetta.

There is a path that leads up to another clearing, and Isabetta finds Bartolomeo sitting on a rock where the sun has broken through the leaf cover.

"What are you doing?" she asks her brother.

"I'm writing," he holds up his book and his ink.

"What are you writing?"

"It is the instructions of how to operate a successful vineyard."

"Why would you write something so boring?"

"Because our grandfather taught our father how to do it, and he taught us. But no-one has written it down."

"That's because you'll tell your children, and I'll tell mine."

"We might not have any children, and you may not marry a farmer."

"Well, it makes no sense to write anything like that."

"Maybe not to you, but we may not come back to the farm for a couple of years, and I don't want to forget anything.

"Whatever you say. I'll tell Father where you are, since he was asking."

"Did he need me?"

"No. He was wondering where you were."

Isabetta eases her way back down the path, stopping to look at the flowers along the way. Stepping a few feet out from the trees now, she notices a cloud of dust coming from the road behind them. She is slightly higher up than her family, and she realises they may not see this dust yet.

"Father!" she yells.

Frederico looks up to his daughter about 50 feet away. Isabetta points down the road toward what she sees. Frederico now takes a few steps in that direction and peers down the road. Within a few seconds, the rumble of racing horses can be heard as the cloud of dust moves closer.

Frederico indicates to Isabetta that she needs to go back into the grove and remain out of sight, and stands over by the wagon closest to the road, prepared to meet the riders if need be.

Appearing over the road horizon is a single man on a horse travelling at the horse's top speed. However, there is more dust being kicked up than a single rider can produce. Moments later, three more riders come up behind the first, all at top speed as well.

The rider races upon the Gallinellis, and without even a glance in their direction, he flies on by. Dust swirls around Frederico, and his watching family.

Soon after, the three other riders, one of them a young boy, dash on by as well without any curiosity towards the Gallinelli party. While they are travelling equally as fast, they do not seem to be chasing the first rider, but instead might be together, if there were such a thing.

Amidst the choking dust, Margherita has made her way beside her husband.

"What do you make of that?"

"I don't know. One was a boy, maybe 12 or so."

"I saw that, too. But it didn't look like they were chasing the first man."

"I was thinking the same thing. Maybe we should get moving."

"Good idea," she nods, and turns back to gather up the picnic.

By now, both Isabetta and Bartolomeo have come down from the grove and see their mother gathering things up. They help her without her asking, and the other girls take the feed buckets from the horses. Within minutes, the family is on their way again.

Chapter 8

It's been two days since the Gallinellis left their world behind on their farm back in Como. Camping overnight along the road has gone without incident. With no complaints other than Ambrogino's fever, they have crept to the foot of the impressive Alps towards a town that Frederico knows as Bellinzona.

Cooler temperatures have descended into the valley, and the snow covered peaks ahead no longer loom, but are right on top of them.

"What is that castle up ahead on that rise, Rico?" Margherita asks.

"I don't know who it belongs to, but I recall there being several large castles in this area."

"Why so many?"

"Much like the towers and walls back home, they were made hundreds of years ago to protect Italy from invaders through the mountains. They were once part of the great Roman Empire back in a time when lawlessness ruled the lands outside of Rome. Savage people would attack the farms and pillage the homes."

"It doesn't sound too different from just a short time ago," Margherita sighs.

"All the more reason to have good fortifications, dear. One never knows what the future will bring."

"There's another one over there."

Low rolling clouds separate enough to unveil another grand castle on a hill many miles away.

"It gives a sense of comfort, doesn't it?" says Frederico.

"It reminds me of war. I don't know why men must always go to war. Why can't people leave each other in peace to farm the land?"

"Because it's always about wanting what the other person has, my dear."

"Well, I don't want anything that anybody else has."

"Perhaps that's because you have all you need, my love."

"I'm not talking about coins, or livestock, Rico. I am content to have nothing at all, as long as I have my family's love."

"What about the people who don't even have that? Those are the ones who are easily convinced to go to war. When one is truly desperate, and has nothing to eat and nothing to lose, then what choice does that person have?"

"You are talking like you condone such a thing."

"Not at all. I try my best to understand it. Then, if it ever happens, I'll have a better chance of defending myself – and you. Besides, there is a ruling man in Milan right now who has brought years of peace to our province."

"I suppose that's true about Visconti, but it feels so temporary, with war looming on the horizon at all times."

Frederico turns to look into his wife's eyes. "My darling... nobody is at war right now. We have all we need with us. We have not been shown any hostility all along the way thus far, and we'll make it to the other side of the mountains with ease."

Margherita senses her husband's attempt to console her, and realises that Ambrogino can hear all of their words.

"Of course, you are right, Rico. Where do you suppose we can camp tonight?"

"Maybe we can stay in one of these castles," he smiles.

"And how would we accomplish that?"

"We have the most valuable currency in the land with our wine, Rita. It has opened many doors for me in the past."

Frederico shouts back to the other two wagons, "How would you all like to stay in a castle tonight?"

"As long as they have soft beds!" Antonio bellows.

"I would like that, too!" returns Allesandra.

"But how, Father?" poses Bartolomeo.

"Leave that up to me." Frederico replies. He wants to keep some mystery and pleasure on a journey that is growing in anxiety for everyone.

"You always seem to have a plan, my husband."

Frederico then slides his head closer to his wife and whispers, "I'd give all the wine we have, if it meant good medicine for Gino."

"It would be nice for all of us to be out of the damp air for a night."

A few minutes later, the wagon train approaches the bottom of the hill where perched atop is the ancient, but magnificent castle. Massive running walls spread in both directions, gently curving around the topography of the hill, showing menacing teeth all along the top edge.

Antonio and the girls stare up in awe as the wagon train comes to a stop far below the gigantic structure.

"How do you get up there, Father?" Isabetta asks.

"There must be an access road around here somewhere."

"We should keep going and forget about the castle," Antonio protests. "We can set up another camp tonight."

"We have nothing to fear, son. I promise you there are no dragons or evil spirits in there. It's just a form of protection to keep people safe from wars of many years ago. Normal people just like you and me live here now. Let's keep going around until we find the road, okay?"

"Okay, let's go," Isabetta states for everyone, even though Antonio remains unmoved by his father's assurance.

Slowly, they start again around the base of the hill, but as soon as they get lined up again, a full wagon with two drivers comes straight toward them from around the bend. This wagon, piled high with kegs, is being easily pulled by four muscular stallions.

"Good man!" Frederico calls out to the drivers, holding his

right hand high up in the air.

There is no response to be seen from them.

"Good man!" yells Frederico again as the two wagons are now almost upon each other.

The wagon of kegs slows down, and Frederico lowers his hand now that he has caught their attention.

"What is it?" the driver on the left asks.

"My son is ill, and I was looking for a place to bring him for the night. We are coming from Como, and do not know anyone in this village."

"Why didn't you go to Milan? It would have been much easier travelling for you," one of the two men says.

"That's true, sir. But we are trading on the other side of the mountains, and are only going in this direction."

"You know it's not the best time to be going through these mountains right now," the other driver suggests.

"That is why I was hoping to spend a night in a place such as that castle up there, where my son could find comfort."

"The Montebello castle? You would have better luck at the inn with the apple trees about three miles ahead."

"So the castle accepts no visitors?"

"Oh, I didn't say that, I am certain you will have a poor chance of getting inside. I mean, who are you and your children? I do not know you. Adel, do you know these people?"

"No, I don't know them," the other driver replies.

"So there you go, travelling man. Good luck with your son."

They snap their reins, and the huge horses put the heavy cart back into motion.

"I thank you," Frederico waves his hand to the men.

Margherita turns to Frederico, "What do you take from their advice?"

"I think they are two drivers of little intelligence, and they don't expect anyone to be welcome at Montebello because they are not welcome."

"I agree, let's try to get in anyway."

"I'm glad you feel that way, my love. If there are any good doctors in this village, they surely will be associated with this Montebello."

Margherita looks back at Ambrogino and adjusts his blanket. He has eaten almost nothing today.

"How are you feeling, my little cabbage?"

"My feet are cold."

"You've got to keep them under the blanket dear. You keep poking them out. Aren't you hungry just a little bit?"

"Not really."

Margherita places the back of her hand against Ambrogino's cheek, much as she has done a hundred times in the last two days. His face remains hot, while the boy continues to shiver.

"We're going to stay in a castle tonight, Gino. There will be a warm bed for you, and maybe even a doctor."

Ambrogino nods in agreement, and rolls back under his blanket. Margherita carefully tucks him in, especially around his feet, and turns back to her husband. She leans against him and grabs onto his arm around the shoulder.

Frederico stares straight ahead, and keeps the horses moving. The road continues to bend to the right, and the castle walls continue to follow it. Flowing serpent-like along the hill and up ahead, it moves closer to the road. The more they travel, the closer the wall gets, and within a few hundred feet, the monstrous castle wall comes right up to the edge of the road, where a gate is now visible.

"Look at the wall," Antonio calls out to anyone who will listen. "Look at all the colours that make up the wall – black, brown, grey, and white."

"That's so interesting," Maria chimes in. "It looks all grey from far away, but now you can see the different coloured stones."

"It must have taken years to build it," Allesandra adds.

"Visualise trying to attack these walls with simple swords and arrows," the academic Bartolomeo poses. "How quickly would you expect to get inside?"

"Probably never!" shouts Antonio.

"That's why it was built," Bartolomeo completes his short lesson to his siblings.

Stopping at the front of the immense gate doors, Frederico marvels at its sheer size and durable features. He imagines his friend Beppe gushing over the quality of the iron reinforcements. His attention turns to a stationed guard who is paying only slight attention to the Gallinellis. Frederico drives his wagon up, and approaches the guard.

"Good man. My family and I are travelling through this area and we are looking for comfort for my son who is ill. Do you think the owner will allow us to stay in his care for a night?"

"This is not an inn," he replies. "There are other places for you to stay in the village."

"Yes, but we are seeking the best of care for my son. Certainly, the Lord of this castle would enjoy the exceptional wine we have made especially for magnificent men such as he."

"Lord Rusca has all of the wine he needs."

"Then I'm sure Lord Rusca would appreciate hearing vital news from Lord Visconti of Milan."

The guard looks Frederico in the eye.

"I will ask him," comes his cool reply, as he turns in through a small door and closes it behind him.

"Are you going to tell him, Rico?" Margherita asks.

"I don't know."

A minute or so passes, and the guard reappears.

"Bring your wagons in through the gate and off the road."

As the two doors of the main gate squeak and lumber their way open, Frederico motions his team forward. They drive all three wagons into the courtyard, and the magnificence of the interior appears like a magical garden.

"Stop your carts right here. Dismount and tie your horses. Lord Rusca will see you."

Feeling confident now, Frederico smiles back at his family so as to make them feel comfortable with the guard's instructions.

Activity in several places around the courtyard draw curious attention from the children. There are gardeners working the landscape, and masons working on some steps that lead from one of the doors into the main building. The main building itself is more of a fortress than a home; robust and imposing, it seems indestructible. But before the family can make a comment, three men and a woman emerge from the center door.

"Who seeks me today?" cries out the pudgy man in the middle who steps out in front of the others.

"I am Frederico Gallinelli of Como, Lord Rusca, sir. I am travelling with my family, and we are seeking the most hospitable place to spend a night where my ill son can be best cared for."

"What is this important news that Lord Visconti has for me, and how is it that you have come to speak for him?"

"Sir, I am a regular trader in Milan, you see, and my wine has the highest favour of Lord Visconti. As such, I see him directly, and at times I share in his confidence."

"Is that so? Go on."

"I am happy to do so, but since my fine wine seems to hold no favour with you, my information is all I have. So I would require some assurance that we can take comfort in your castle tonight before I divulge Lord Visconti's secrets."

Laughing, the rotund ruler replies, "You are in no position to demand any assurances from me. Montebello is mine, do you hear me? Visconti would never send any word to me with some sorry group of children!"

The other folks in the group join in the laughter, while the Gallinelli children nervously look at each other. Bartolomeo eases himself forward and stands beside his father.

"You will give me your useless information right now, or you will leave. That is your choice, Frederico Gallinelli of Como."

After a brief moment and a glance into Margherita's eyes, Frederico begins.

"There is a pestilence, your Lordship, on a biblical scale, that is consuming hundreds of souls who live in the cities of the

Mediterranean. It has fallen upon Genoa, where innocent people right now are dying by the hour."

Rusca stares at Frederico for a few seconds of silence.

He roars with laughther, "That is very valuable news! Thank you very much, Mr. Gallinelli!"

Howls and amusement erupt again from Rusca's people, as they flap their hands at Frederico and walk back toward the main building.

"This is not a joke!" Bartolomeo defends. "My father is not a liar!"

"Yes, young man, I agree with you. He is crazy, that's all. Now, away with you all!" Rusca shouts, his laughter turning into contempt, as he waves his hand in disgust and walks away.

"Tell him, Father!"

"No, son. It's okay. Let's go."

Crestfallen, the Gallinelli family follow their father's lead, load up, and depart. Their caravan retreats back through the main gate and onto the road where behind them, they hear the loud clank and thud as the castle doors are closed and bolted.

"Why did you let that man humiliate you, Rico?" Margherita asks.

"Because if he did not believe me right away, then he would have never believed me, and besides, I did not trust him. I have heard of that man, and I remember Visconti granting him that castle. It should belong under the control of Milan, so reconsidering now, it is good we did not stay in his care tonight."

"But what about Gino?"

"We will have to care for him the best we can."

"So where do we go now?"

"We'll find that inn up the road, and we'll pay for some proper beds. Gino will be as comfortable as he can be, and we'll assess his strength when we get there. It's best that we stay anonymous, Rita. Rusca reminded me how much influence Visconti has around here, and I don't want any word getting back to him what we are doing. He could easily overrun us with soldiers and then close off the mountain pass. If that were to happen, we'd be doomed like everyone else."

"But he's your friend, Rico."

"Not in crisis, he's not. I only trust one man in Milan."

"Beppe?"

Frederico nods, "I should have taken them with us, Rita."

Margherita reaches back again, and feels for her son's hand. She takes it in hers and kisses the back of it.

"We should take care of ourselves," she says.

"And take care of you I will, tonight, at this comfortable inn."

"Did you hear that, my sweet cabbage? We're going to get a nice warm bed for you tonight."

"Yes, Mother," he sighs.

Progressing up the main road into the bustling village, Frederico notices a good deal of activity, but is fixated on a singular mission to find this inn. Normally, he would be full of ideas, and would be making commerce from the wagons, with his children as his business partners. But at this moment, he knows his entire family is depending on him to produce a comfortable place where Margherita can care for their precious boy.

Although this entire journey is more of an escape from impending horror stories of death and destruction, incredible scenic beauties abound all around. The towering mountains frame the wide green valley, with countless houses and farms dotting the hillsides. One spectacular castle dominates their sight, while another, even larger one, is visible a few miles away. In their highest points, the mightiest mountains on earth push up into the sky with bright white snow spilled upon them, as if each peak had pierced a heavenly sack of flour.

Although all of these amazing sights are unfolding, Ambrogino sees none of it.

Chapter 9

Precisely as the keg drivers had told them, the inn with the apple trees has come into sight. It is a working orchard with an oversized house, and the sign out front simply reads 'Inn'. There is little effort to keep the properties' repairs in order, as though the owner decided that if a traveller were desperate enough, he would accept anything. Clearly, Frederico could show this sloppy owner how he could better care for his building and the surrounding land.

As the wagons approach, small children become evident in the yard. Circling, laughing, and playing, these children obviously have no chores or responsibilities, and even though Margherita smiles at their exuberance, she feels these children should be working on chores for their parents.

"Is this the place?" Antonio asks from behind.

"Yes, it is," Frederico replies. "Let's keep the wagons on the road until I speak with the keepers."

"We'll be spending the night here, right?"

"I will see about that... you will be staying where your mother and I see fit."

"I'll go with you," Margherita insists.

While Frederico has no need for his wife to accompany him, he does not object, and the two approach the main house, walk up to the doorway, and ring a bell they have found next to the door.

It makes a loud clang. Oddly, though, the young children playing in the yard pay no attention to it, and have chased each other into the barn, acting like the Gallinellis are not even there.

A short time passes, and Frederico shakes the bell again. There is no response from inside the house.

"Maybe those children know where their parents are, Rico. I'll go and find them."

"We'll go together."

They turn and head across the courtyard over to the barn. About midway there, Frederico spots a figure moving toward them from the amidst the apple trees. It is a woman, and she is carrying two baskets of freshly picked apples. She is walking very briskly, and handling the heavy weight of the baskets with ease.

"Woo-hoo! I'm coming!" the woman wails.

Frederico looks around to see who else might be coming from another direction. It is only this one woman.

"Hello! Hello!" the woman calls out as she draws closer to them. "Let me put down these baskets! I'll be just a moment!"

The diminutive woman closes the distance and hoists her two baskets at the same time up and over the edge of a large crate that is almost completely full of apples. Next to the crate sit six others which are all empty.

"You know... you can carry more with the help of a mule."

Smiling back at Frederico, the woman smacks the dirt off her hands, and wipes them clean on her colourful, but very dirty, dress.

"We have a wonderful mule, but my husband has her way in the back. So I pick from the friendly trees closest to the front here."

"It seems to me the husband should be doing the heavy hauling while the wife enjoys the purpose of the mule," he continues.

"Well, that's probably true, hoo, hoo," the woman responds in a happy giddy way. "But my Dario has only one working leg, and he doesn't get around very well, you see. So he gets the mule to help him get something done, ha!"

The woman's ultra enthusiasm makes Margherita laugh, and she checks herself with her hand over her mouth.

"You can laugh, lady. It's okay. I know I'm a bit of a loony bird. My name is Guendalina, but everyone calls me Guenny!"

"One would guess it would be Lina," Margherita attempts.

"You would assume so, wouldn't you pretty lady? But I think it has something to do with me being half-crazy. It seems to fit me just right, ha!"

Frederico looks at Margherita and rolls his eyes.

"So… Guenny… my family of eight is looking for a few warm beds for the night. Do you have any?"

"We can take twelve, and right now there's nobody else here."

"How surprising," Frederico smirks.

"Sir, I know it's not much here. But since Dario broke his leg last year, I've had to do most things myself. I know the place needs work, but you'll be happy with the price!"

Margherita whispers to her husband, "It's good enough, Rico. We need a nice bed tonight for Gino."

"What do you say, Rico?" Guenny offers, having overheard.

"We'll stay, you crazy bird," Frederico half smiles to Guenny.

"You're alright, Rico. I like you! He's a good one, lady. You're lucky!"

"I know," Margherita smiles as she places her hand on her husband's back and rubs it up and down. "I know."

"Well then, let me show you folks around the place. We've got some good sized rooms for everybody."

Frederico looks back at the wagons where his children are waiting, and catches Antonio staring at him. The impatient boy raises both arms up, asking his father if they can please get off the wagons. Frederico smiles and waves to his son with a motion to come on down.

"We're staying!" Antonio shouts to the rest as he hops down and leads the horses to the hitching post.

Frederico and Margherita follow Guenny over to the house.

"Now!" Guenny barks. "Before you go in, here are the rules!"

"We'll abide by all of your rules, Guendalina," interrupts Frederico. "But we have one concern. Our youngest son is sick, and he needs the most comfortable bed you have."

The crazy smile drops from Guenny's face. "Where is he?"

"He's lying in our wagon," Margherita answers.

"Let me see him, please."

Both Frederico and Margherita go out to the road to fetch Ambrogino. Margherita pulls out her son, tightly wrapped in a blanket, while Frederico gets Ambrogino's things.

Guenny is not far behind them, and sees them coming toward her. "Hi there, little man," she offers in a peaceful voice, not at all similar to the one she has been using up to this point. "Are you feeling sick, my precious?"

Ambrogino has his head hanging over his mother's shoulder while she holds him like a sack of grain.

"Let's get you inside, and see what we've got, okay?" Guenny says to him, comfortable and confident in her ability to do so.

Margherita carries him inside where Guenny leads her to the first bedroom from the kitchen. It is warm, quiet, and conveniently located. Guenny pulls back the top blanket from the bed, and fluffs the pillow. Margherita places her son down as easily as she can, and the boy sighs in relief as he sinks into the soft bed.

"What's wrong, little honey bee?" Guenny asks him as she sits down on the bed.

"I don't know," he murmurs.

"Are you hungry?"

"No."

"Thirsty?"

"No."

"Achy?"

"Yes."

"Where?"

"Everywhere."

"Let me see, honey bee," she says she reaches under the blanket and begins to probe his body for the source of his pain.

Margherita is strangely comfortable with Guenny's examination, as there is something about this crazy woman that is almost familiar.

"Does this hurt?"

"A little," he replies.

"How about over here?"

"No, not really."

This assessment goes on for a few minutes as Guenny asks, probes, and asks again. Ambrogino does not seem to mind the questions, because he can feel his parent's attention watching over the inspection.

"Do you know of a good doctor in this town?" Frederico asks Guenny.

Guenny looks up and smirks.

"You don't want to see any of the doctors in this town, Rico. They nearly killed my husband when he broke his leg. The only reason he can stand at all is because I fixed the leg myself."

"What do you think is wrong with Gino?" Margherita pleads.

"He has the measles, I reckon. We'll know for certain in a few more days."

"Oh, but we're only staying this one night," Frederico states.

"This boy is ill! He'll need to be cared for, for at least a week, don't you see?"

"I can see fine, thank you," Frederico protests and walks out.

"If you can't afford to pay for the week, we can work something out," Guenny offers to Margherita.

"Oh, we can afford your price... but my husband and I will have to talk about how long we can stay."

"You go do that. I'll make up some medicine for your boy. You just leave it up to Guenny."

"Thank you so much for your kind hospitality."

Margherita gives Ambrogino a kiss, turns away to find Frederico, and help the others unpack the wagons.

Like dutiful soldiers, Isabetta and Allesandra feed and water the horses without being asked, and Bartolomeo inspects the wagons for any needed repairs. Maria and Antonio carry baskets and other provisions from the wagons at their father's direction.

"Rico? Can't we stay here for a while, and take care of Gino right here?"

Maria overhears the question as she walks by, so Frederico takes his wife by the hand and leads her over toward the apple crates.

"What if Gino doesn't have the measles, but the pestilence instead? What if he was given the sickness from that travelling man who traded him the lamb? Don't you see? We could already have amongst our midst the very thing we are fleeing."

"But Guenny said it was the measles, and I trust her. Besides, those stories from Lord Visconti tell of the pestilence killing within hours, and all those sickening details of the blackness and the buboes and the vomiting. Gino has none of those things."

"Maybe not, but we have never actually seen it, so how can we know for sure?" He holds his wife by the shoulders, looks her straight in the eye, and begs for her understanding. "I have to ask God what he is telling me to do. I know He told us to leave, but now it seems like He wants us to stay. I don't want to go across those mountains any later than tomorrow, but I will never forgive myself if Gino's sickness gets worse."

"Can't we spend two or three extra days here, Rico... and then travel through when he's feeling stronger?"

"I don't know, I just don't know. I need to think about it."

"And pray about it... as will I."

As if on cue, Bartolomeo approaches his parents. "How is Gino?"

"The woman here is certain he has the measles." Frederico replies.

"Is it bad?"

"For the measles, it's not bad at all," Margherita takes over. "We won't know for certain for a few more days."

"Does that mean we are going to stay here for those days?"

"That is what your father is contemplating right now. Why don't we leave him alone for a while."

"No, he can stay. It's not a secret. Bartolomeo, let's help this women with her apple harvest, so we can earn our stay. We'll talk as we pick.

Frederico grabs the two baskets Guenny had brought from the orchard, and hands one to Bartolomeo. The two then head into the trees in the same direction where Guenny first appeared.

"Son? What do you conclude about the wisdom of this journey we are on?"

"I don't question your judgment for one second, Father."

"You are so loyal, Bartolomeo. But you can answer my questions freely. Your intelligence has great value to me."

"I don't question your judgment, Father… but I do wonder what is ahead of us: where we will end up, where we will live. I trust you have a good idea with all of your experience, and I have no fear."

"I have but one fear – I don't know if leaving when we did has somehow put Gino's life in danger. If we were home, he could rest in comfort, and be well soon. But on this rough road, we can't care for him very well."

The two continue to stroll among the bountiful trees.

"So you gather that Gino's health is a test of your conviction to put your family through this journey."

"The decision to leave everything behind based on some stories of doom is a test enough, so I don't know why God is testing me again. Maybe He is trying to convince me now that I have made a grave mistake."

"You have always told me, Father, one should never try to understand God's ways, as they are beyond our comprehension."

"I said that because I knew I would always be there to protect you from your mistakes," he smiles at his son. "But now there is nobody here to protect me from mine."

"How about God Himself? How about simply trusting God, doing as your heart tells you, and letting Him protect all of us?"

Frederico stops. He puts his hand on Bartolomeo's shoulder, and nods, "Of course. What else are we to do? It's so simple, perhaps I just needed a wise son to remind me."

Ken A. Gauthier

The two men smile and turn the corner of the path they are on. They hear the sounds of a mule braying, and walk toward it.

Cutting between the trees, they come upon a man picking apples and loading them into baskets hanging from either side of the beast. A pair of little girls are plucking clovers beneath the tree, and they stand up to look at the two Gallinelli men.

"So you must be our guests for the night," the man replies in apparent pain as he stiffly turns around.

"I am Frederico Gallinelli, and this is my son, Bartolomeo."

"I am Dario Malatesta, and this is my orchard," he motions with his hands. "These are two of my daughters, Caterina and Angelina."

He grabs onto a branch from the tree above him and makes a shifting motion to strengthen his balance.

"What happened to your leg?" Frederico asks.

"I had the misfortune of slipping from one of these trees while I was pruning it up high. My leg got wedged in at an awkward angle when I slipped, and I was trapped between two branches, hanging four feet off the ground. I grabbed a lower branch to untangle myself, but it was too late. I knew it was broken when I looked up and saw the bottom of my foot!"

"It sounds painful," Bartolomeo adds.

"You have no idea, son, I never thought I would walk again. But I have my wife to thank. The doctor wanted to cut the leg off, but she wouldn't have it. She fixed me up good. Now I can get some real work done out here... but a little bit slower."

"Does it still hurt?" Bartolomeo asks.

"No. I can hardly feel a thing anymore. That's what makes it so hard for me to walk."

"You are a courageous man to endure such pain, and to laugh about it today," Frederico praises.

"What choice do I have?" he smiles. "I trust Guendalina has shown you the rooms?"

"Oh, yes, she has. They are fine and they will suit us well, thank you."

95

"Good, then. Thank you for collecting those baskets for me. The children must have left them out."

"Oh no," Frederico replies. "We have taken these to the orchard with us to help you with the harvest."

"So… you don't have any money?"

"Not at all, Dario. We have the money to pay for our rooms. Your wife, Guenny, said you were out here, so we wanted to help you."

"We have a farm back in Como," adds Bartolomeo. "We are very comfortable around such work."

"Then shouldn't you be harvesting your own crops?"

Bartolomeo looks to his father.

"We have hired men working right now," Frederico responds.

"Oh, I see now. Then cheers to you, my good man."

Not wanting to seem above Dario, Frederico delivers his story, "My family and I are on a journey on which we believe God has sent us. We wish of nothing more than to help you with your harvest. Your wife has been most hospitable to my family, and especially my youngest son, which matters a great deal to me. For that, I am at your service, my dear Dario."

"A journey... from God... whatever suits you, Frederico. It's not my business."

"It will be soon, I'm afraid."

"What's that?"

"I'm sorry, never mind," retracts Frederico.

Conversation turns into labour as the three men pick until the baskets are full. They share stories about growing crops, raising livestock, and soon discover a warm friendship. Frederico is now feeling more relaxed in the orchards of this rundown farm than he did at any moment within the walls of the lavish Montebello castle.

As they approach the barn and begin to unload the harvest, Dario asks, "So how long will you be staying, Rico?"

"Until my son is well enough for travel, perhaps a week, if that is okay with you."

"That's fine with me! We could use the money."

Bartolomeo looks at his father with favour, but Frederico does not look back. He knows the decision has now been made, for better or worse. They would be staying until Ambrogino is better. Whether that puts the entire family in jeopardy remains to be seen.

"May God bless you for helping me with these chores."

"He already has, Dario."

Joining the rest of the family in the main house, the men connect with the activity as the Gallinelli family is preparing themselves for the evening. The smell of baking bread and spiced apples fills the air.

"They'll be spending the week, Guenny!" Dario yells out.

Margherita, who is sitting with Ambrogino, looks up for her husband.

"Is that true, Mother?"

"We'll see, Maria. Please stay here with Gino for a moment."

Margherita steps into the greeting room to see Frederico and Bartolomeo settling in. She looks at him and asks by raising her eyebrows. Frederico nods his head, and Margherita smiles with relief. A heavy load has been lifted from her, as her youngest son will now be cared for in a very comfortable place.

The sun sets earlier deep in this valley, so a quick dinner is a welcome sight for the Gallinellis. It is served with very simple foods served in very delicious ways, as Guenny's use of spices and flavourings match any recipe Margherita knows. Maria and Antonio dig in to their meal with zeal, while the three older children prefer to savour the food in a more civilised fashion. The Gallinellis are enjoying themselves thoroughly in the rustic inn, even though the accommodations are short of what they would have been in the castle.

"I have a medicine for your Gino if is proper with you, my lady," Guenny offers to Margherita as the two work on their meals.

"What is it?"

"It's a combination of root remedies that gave comfort to Dario when he broke his leg. It won't cure, but it will ease pain and suffering."

Margherita looks at Guenny, and nods her head.

"Great, let me show you, dear."

The two women dispatch to the pantry and prepare the remedy by grinding roots, and boiling water. Guenny is pleased to be showing off her knowledge to such an upstanding woman of means. After several minutes of boiling and steeping, Guenny pours the resulting potion from the pot into a cup. On the top, she sprinkles a pinch of cinnamon.

"For the taste," she smiles.

Margherita brings the cup to Ambrogino and lifts up his head to help him to drink. He accepts the medicine with no hesitation, as he allows the fullness of his mother's nursing.

"How much should he take, Guenny?"

"The whole thing, as soon as he can."

"Did you hear that, sweet cabbage? Do you feel you can take some more?"

Ambrogino nods, takes a few more sips, and lies back down.

"I'll drink some more later, Mother."

"Does it taste terrible, honey bee?" Guenny asks from across the room.

"No, it's okay."

Margherita caresses Ambrogino's head and face. She gives him a long kiss on the cheek and tucks the blankets tightly around him.

"I'll be back in a minute to help you finish the medicine," she whispers to him.

As Margherita stands up, she notices Frederico has been peeking in from the hall, so she goes to him.

"How is he doing?" he asks.

"Guenny's medicine should make him more comfortable. I think he's happy to be in a bed, and he'll sleep well tonight."

"Good. Once everyone gets settled in for the night, we'll relax outside."

Margherita places her hands flat on her husband's chest and tip-toes up to give him a kiss on the cheek.

"I would like that very much, my husband."

Later in the evening, with the children in their beds, Frederico and Margherita retreat outside to where Guenny and Dario have made a fire in the pit. Frederico carries a carafe of one of his choice wines. It is not from a keg that he uses for trading, but one that he has kept for his family. Margherita carries four drinking cups and two small wedges of cheese.

Around the fire, Guenny has one of her daughters snuggled away and asleep in her lap, as she gently rocks her and hums a melody.

She looks up to Margherita and notices the four cups, "Oh, you are very kind."

Frederico pours without hesitation or asking, and hands out his offerings of friendship.

"Thank you very much, Frederico," Dario accepts. "So how do you find our accommodations?"

"They are perfect, Dario."

"You are lying, but I will not stop you," Guenny adds.

"I have been in grander buildings that were steeped in richer furnishings," Frederico states. "But your farm is a home indeed."

Dario looks over at his wife, Guenny, where their eyes meet and share in the compliment. They silently toast each other and drink their wine.

"Fantastic, Rico. Your wife is right about you. This is excellent wine!"

"Thank you, Guenny."

"How soon before we know if Gino has the measles?" Margherita asks.

"If not tomorrow, then the next day for sure. You shouldn't worry, dear."

The conversation stops for a moment, as the warm fire crackles in the evening air. Sparks pop out of the flames and escape skyward as fast as they can.

"Let me ask you, Dario," Frederico begins. "What do you know about travelling through these mountains?"

"Well, I don't go over them very often. Most of my trading is done in Lugano, and I have relatives in Locarno. But we have everything we need right here... except of course now I will be trading in Como to get more of this." He holds up his cup of wine, bringing a smile to Frederico's face.

"I hope to be there next year for your visit," Frederico holds up his cup in a toasting gesture.

Confused, Dario raises an eyebrow at Frederico, looks over at Margherita, and then back to Frederico, not quite understanding what he means.

"Back to the travelling advice, Dario, surely you have some?" Frederico presses.

Dario lowers his cup and turns it in both hands, "I would focus first on the care of your animals. The roads are very rough, full of stones, and the switchbacks are steep and tricky. If your horses are weak and tired, you will be spending several nights."

"That's good advice, thank you."

"Of course, you'll need plenty of food, too," Guenny adds. "If you get a broken wheel up there or get slowed down, you don't want hunger messing up your decisions."

"We're pretty well stocked."

"Well, even if you aren't, you will be when you leave here," Guenny replies.

"Thank you," Margherita whispers through her soft lips.

"Well, this little one's asleep," says Guenny shifting her daughter to her shoulder. "I'll bring her in and check on the others. I don't hear a peep anywhere. Your team must be asleep like a litter of puppies."

"I'll go with you."

As the two women disappear into the house, Frederico fills up

Dario's cup again, and the two men enjoy the last of the fire, each lost in his own thoughts.

Chapter 10

Every morning there is always an amount of hunger in any working man. Large round red apples can fill an entire hand, and make a meal in itself. While this delicious fruit can be baked, chopped, boiled, dried, peeled, stewed, jellied, or juiced, there remains no substitute for eating them right off the tree. The moment of first bite is an orchestra for the senses. A pop through the skin into the apple's flesh releases an eye-twitching tartness followed by the sweet aroma of goodness and a taste that was meant to be.

Frederico chews on the mouthwatering fruit with the joy of a child, as its sweet juice runs down his wrist. With his other hand, he continues to fill up his basket, softly placing each red treasure down inside without bruising.

"Gino, come and try one."

"I've already got one, Father!" he replies, and holds up the half-eaten specimen for him to see.

Today is Ambrogino's first day out of bed, and it has prompted the family to prepare for their departure.

Margherita and her other children, along with Guenny, are restocking the wagons and hitching the teams, when their attention is drawn toward four strong horsemen rumbling up the road in formation.

About halfway between the road and the orchard, little Angelina Malatesta is trying to feed some clover to an apprehensive rabbit. She looks up to see the four men making conversation with her father and the Gallinelli family. While she can't hear them, she sees much hand gesturing, concluded by her father pointing out to the orchard where Frederico is picking. All four men stop talking and look out in that direction.

Unaware, Frederico and Ambrogino continue to stock up on apples out in the orchard. Suddenly appearing between them, Angelina interrupts by pulling on Frederico's trousers.

"What is it, my little dear?"

"There are men here."

"And what do they want, my sweet?"

Without saying a word, the little girl points directly at Frederico. Not wanting to upset the girl with any of the thoughts racing through his mind, he lowers her hand, kisses her on the forehead, and smiles to her. He brings his basket over to Ambrogino and leaves it at his feet.

"Stay here, Gino."

Marching back to answer his call, Frederico is met halfway by his noticeably anxious wife who stops him before he appears.

"They're Rusca's men, Rico. What do they want from you?"

"I'm going to find out."

Margherita plants her hands on her husband's chest to keep him from continuing. "They said they only want to speak with you, and that you had no choice but to meet them."

"I am going to meet them, everything will be fine, don't worry, Rita."

"What if they detain you, Rico? We can't be without you!"

Frederico holds her by her arms and assures her, "Bartolomeo and I have worked out some code words in case of such an occurrence. We knew that anything could happen, but we didn't want to upset you or the other children. Just make sure he is nearby so that I can talk to him."

"He was already talking to them when I came out here."

"Good. Try to look as calm as possible, and continue doing what you were, like there is nothing bothering you. If we wait out here too long, they might become suspicious, so let me go."

She takes in her responsibility, nervously nods, and steps aside.

Frederico continues onward, and finally approaches the men. They are unfamiliar, but bear the colours of the Montebello castle.

"Are you Frederico Gallinelli?" asks the bearded man in the front.

"I am."

"Lord Rusca asks for your presence immediately."

"Then why did he not accompany you here?"

"Do not question his Lordship, lest you face the consequences, Gallinelli," he barks.

"I am under the protection of Lord Visconti of Milan, and I am standing on his ground."

"You have nothing to fear from us, Gallinelli," smoothes the oldest of the four horsemen. "We only require your company for a brief time, after which you are free to go."

The bearded soldier rolls his eyes at the courtesy, and then stares back at Frederico showing his willingness to attack at any moment.

"You go and tell his Lordship that he had my presence in his hands four days ago, and ran my family out in disgrace. I will not be subject to such ridicule again. If he wants to see me, I shall be right here waiting for him."

"We did not come here to bargain, Gallinelli," the older soldier continues with a smile.

"That's good," Frederico holds his ground, but does not raise his voice. "For if we were bargaining, then I would be offering something, which I am not. I will not go with you now, or tomorrow. You will need to take me by force, and I assure you I will not go easily.

All of the activity in the yard has stopped, as the eyes of Guenny, Dario, Margherita, Bartolomeo, and the other children are focused in fear and anticipation.

The bearded man laughs, "Surely you are not pitting the four of us against your hobbled friend and your women and children?"

"Not at all. Just me."

The smile drops from that bearded man's face at this curious response. Bartolomeo resists the temptation to add his name to the fight. He is waiting to hear the code words that his father has prepared, and so far – nothing.

"Stand down, Gallinelli. No blood will be spilled over this conversation today. You are taking your chances with Lord Rusca's patience, and will suffer the consequences of his decision when we return empty handed. I can see that you are leaving, and you can be assured that whichever road you take, your wagons will not outrun our stallions. May God have mercy on you."

He pulls his horse around, and the other three follow his lead. Stopping only a few feet later, he turns back to Frederico.

"Are you certain that you have no desire of a large financial reward from his Lordship for your cooperation?"

Realising the situation has been diffused, Frederico relaxes his position.

"Thank his Lordship for his kind offer, would you please?"

Disgusted, the older horseman smiles in feigned delight, and moves his team out for good. When they have left the sight of the group, Margherita turns to her husband. "What are you thinking, Rico? Those men could have killed you on the spot!"

"There is no way that soldiers such as them would have slaughtered women and children over such a petty squabble, Rita. You know that."

"But you alone couldn't take on those four, either!"

"Precisely! Four soldiers would never have fought against one man. That's how I avoided any fighting at all."

"I don't understand."

"Mother," Bartolomeo interjects. "If there were four men rising up, then they may have fought us. But to attack a single man is a cowardly act, with witnesses no less. Father's life was never in danger."

"I hate men and their fighting ways," she sighs.

Frederico consoles her again, "My fears are greater than those men, Rita. They are hired to protect a slob of a man who means nothing to us. Let's get back to our business and be on our way."

"But they said they would catch up to us if they wanted to, Rico."

"That's a good question then," Frederico ponders out loud to the group. "Will they have the desire to come after us?"

"They must have found out something about the pestilence, Father," Bartolomeo reasons.

"What pestilence?" Dario questions.

Realising the family's secret has now been broken to the Malatestas, Bartolomeo tries to recover.

"Oh, I mean there was just some story... something that isn't true that... we don't really know... "

"You are a terrible liar, son," Frederico shakes his head, but not in disappointment. "The truth, Dario and Guenny, is that we have directly heard of a horrible pestilence that some are calling a great death."

"A great death?" Guenny listens more carefully.

"It's a ghastly story that I don't even want to repeat, and do not even know if it is completely true."

"But you believe it well enough to abandon your farm with your whole family."

"You are correct, Dario," Frederico surrenders.

"What are we going to do?" Guenny ask her husband, but looks at Frederico.

"Please don't ask me, Guenny. I am tormented enough."

Margherita steps into her husband's arms to show her faithful support to everyone.

"We could go with you!" Antonio enthuses.

Margherita looks into Frederico's eyes, waiting for the answer, when Guenny saves him.

"No, we won't."

"Why not?" her husband demands, ready to take control of his wife. "Don't you believe him?"

"I do," she softens and moves closer to Frederico. "And I imagine that he is doing anything he can to protect his family, and we will not get in his way."

Realising Guenny's sacrifice, Frederico offers, "We can take the two of you with us, Guenny... and Dario."

Margherita does not care about the outcome, and might enjoy the security of two more in their party.

"No, no, Rico. This is how it will go," she delivers. "You will go today as planned, and we will stay. If those soldiers come back, then they will find Dario and I preparing to leave also. When they ask where you went, we will point in your direction. Those fools think they are so smart, they will insist we are lying, and will take the other road. Trust me on this, Rico. It will happen. The other road has so many forks, they will be hunting for days. Plus, they wouldn't consider that anyone would be crazy enough to choose your road anyway."

Frederico chuckles at Guenny's honesty.

"But what about you two?" Margherita asks.

"Well, my lady... " Guenny resorts back to formality. "If we don't see any more soldiers for about a week, then we might follow you anyway. You'll be far enough along that we won't be exposing you, and the road shouldn't be snowed in yet."

"Thank you, Guenny."

"Oh, Rico, we should be thanking you, hoo, hoo!" she waves her finger at him with a smile.

The Gallinellis resume their loading and prepare the animals. Before long, hugs and kisses are exchanged like a dance between the two families who now share a strong friendship.

"You take care of each other now," Guenny instructs.

"You, too. Goodbye," Margherita waves.

Filled with fresh food and supplies, the Gallinelli wagon train rolls away from the comfort of their home for the past few days. For the first time on their trip, Ambrogino is sitting up in the wagon. He did not have the measles after all, but his illness has improved well enough for him to travel. To Frederico, he seems alert and on the road to recovery, but to Margherita, who keeps her fears to herself, his health remains tenuous.

"It's nice to be able to see out, isn't it, Gino?"

He nods in agreement. "Where are we going?"

Frederico realises he has kept his children in the dark over this specific route they will be taking. "This is the road to Lucerne. It will take us up and over the mountains, and all the way down into beautiful valleys below."

"It looks cold up there, Father."

"It is, son. But this roads cuts through the mountains at the low points. We aren't going to the top of any of these peaks."

For this leg of the journey, Maria is driving the second wagon. Frederico has realised after spending a week with Guenny, the time is right to empower his youngest daughter. While driving a wagon is a boy's job, Frederico is showing the rest of the family that everybody will need to be ready and capable from here on.

Out from the Malatesta's Inn, the road is well travelled, and they are making comfortable progress. Only in spots does it take on a few small inclines, and it follows beside a strong river. They ramble past small farms, tiny cottages, and groves of harvested trees.

From the time they left their own farm, Frederico has not cared at all what others thought of him, or how his family appeared out on the road. He knew he held a secret knowledge, and in that secret was power. But now, since a week has passed, even the occasional glance from a child in a field leads him to believe his secret has been revealed, and now the whole world knows of his foolish plan to flee his home at the most bountiful time of the year.

Within a few miles, they come upon another small village. Each successive town that they enter now is a bit more remote than the last, and a bit more curious to the sight of this entire family with three wagons going up into the mountains.

The river flows effortlessly nearby, and soon Frederico sees a good spot to halt the wagons and give the animals a rest.

"We can probably go a bit further," Margherita suggests.

"The horses will need more regular rest. This road has been increasing in grade, and the horses have been working harder than the distance would show. They will need to be in the best condition for what lies ahead."

Conceding in silence, Margherita hops down to instruct the others. Below the road, the path to the river has steep banks, and there is no way to bring the horses to its edge without unhitching them.

After checking their brakes, Bartolomeo begins bracing the wagons' wheels with large stones. It is more of a gesture of ingenuity, than one of necessity, as the incline in the road at this spot is not that severe.

"Good thinking, son!" Frederico calls out, as he brings one of his horses to the rear.

Bartolomeo nods.

"I was about to do the same thing!" Antonio hollers.

"Sure you were," Allesandra retorts.

Frederico, Allesandra, and Bartolomeo take two horses and a mule down the rocky path for a cool drink. Even though the day is getting long, there is no rush to push the animals. Heeding Dario's advice and his own better judgment, Frederico is making sure that animal care is the top priority.

"How is it?" Margherita calls down to the river.

"Very rocky, but the water is great," Frederico calls back. "Go ahead and feed the others. We'll be back up in a few minutes."

While the animals drink, Allesandra removes her sandals and walks out onto the generous boulders that make up the river bed. She gathers her dress in her hands to better hop from stone to stone, being careful no to fall in. Eventually, she finds a comfortable spot, sits down, and dips her feet into the water.

"Whoa!" she screams.

"Cold, isn't it?" Frederico laughs.

"It's freezing!"

Bartolomeo lowers himself to scoop up a drink to test the temperature himself.

"Aw, it's not that cold," he fakes comfort with the frigid water.

Smiling at the playfulness of his oldest children, Frederico enjoys a brief respite of joy from this unnerving expedition so far. He looks down at himself and becomes captivated by the incredible clarity of the mountain water. Sparkling and ice cold, it flows over and through its bed of boulders and between the lush green riverbanks. It runs in dazzling contrast to the rugged barren mountains above, and is a spot of magnificent beauty. If only the circumstances were different today.

Margherita, Antonio, Isabetta, and Maria feed the other animals the worst of the apples from Guenny's farm. The better ones, they will keep for themselves.

Within an hour, the other two horses and mule have switched places, enjoyed the food and rest, and are back under harness. Frederico inspects all of their shoes, one by one, cleaning out small stones and dirt. Although it is a job any one of his children can do, he keeps control over every detail himself so he alone bears the burden of blame in the event of failure.

"Do they look good, Father?" Antonio asks.

"They look great, son. You and Maria are doing a fine job."

"How much further until camp tonight?" Bartolomeo asks.

"It will all depend on the horses, son. We move when they are able, and we rest when they do. That will be camp."

Frederico climbs back aboard the first wagon, and the caravan heads up the road again. The family begin to notice they have put some elevation below them, and can see back down into the valley.

"There is that castle that threw us out," Bartolomeo points from the rear.

Chuckling, the others begin to make their own observations.

"You can see all of the castles."

"I only see two."

"Way over to the right."

"And that water you see to the left is the far part of Lake Como," Frederico teaches.

"That's Lake Como?" Margherita asks.

"I know it's hard to imagine, but it's a very long lake. It is as long in length as the distance we have travelled so far."

"That's amazing," says Allesandra.

Continuing onward, the family is almost enjoying their exodus from the valley. Although somewhat cooler, the weather has been manageable, the teams have been strong, and the road has been easier than expected.

The time has come to begin the search for a camp site, and Frederico's attention is now refocused. He will weigh the proximity to the river, the distance from the road, and the size of the space needed. Fortunately, there are plenty of options.

Before Frederico can pick out a spot, the wagon train comes upon a fantastic stone arch bridge leading them up to their river and crossing to the other side.

"Wow, what a spectacular bridge," announces Margherita. "It almost looks like it's grown out of the rocks by nature."

"It's another remnant of the ancient Roman builders."

"I can't believe how sturdy it is, Rico."

"It's because they had large armies who were always on the move, so it needed to last. But I agree it's amazing that it remains standing with such strength after hundreds of years."

The width and easy grade of the stone bridge handles the Gallinellis with no effort at all, and it deposits them back on the other side without a care. Frederico notices a side road meandering back along the river banks, and decides to take it.

Around a corner and out of sight from the main road, the three wagons are able to park in a column near the river. This location is surrounded by woods except for the break from the river on the opposite side of the road. Behind and above them towers a steep rocky cliff with a skirt of fallen stone around its base.

Studying his position, Frederico is captivated by the dazzling pops of red and gold colours that have settled onto several nearby trees. Yet again, he is presented a sight of splendor so great he can only shake his head. He wonders why God is making him realise so much breathtaking beauty in His world at such a frightening time.

"It's a lovely spot here, Rico," Margherita offers.

"Of course it is."

In almost no time at all, Margherita and the girls have begun preparation of tonight's meal of pasta with heavily spiced tomato sauce and eggplant. Included is Frederico's favourite borlotti beans that have been soaking all day. Bartolomeo has already set up a small fire from the lantern flame, and hidden from view of the main road. As soon as he is able to push two cooking rocks around it, Margherita sets a kettle on top to boil. Eating well will be no problem tonight.

Even Ambrogino participates in the camp activities, carrying water from the river, and feeding hay to the horses.

"Thanks for helping, Gino."

With a simple nod, he accepts his mothers' praise and continues about until he runs into Antonio.

"What are you doing?" he asks his older brother.

"I am going to get us a rabbit for supper."

"But Mother has supper almost ready."

"Yeah, with no meat. So it's up to us men to go out and hunt something."

"You'll never hit anything with that sling anyway."

"Well, there's plenty of rocks around here, so I have a lot of ammunition."

"Why don't you leave the animals alone, Antonio? We've got plenty to eat."

"You're too young to understand, Gino. When you get older, you'll see how men are meant to kill. It's a matter of survival."

"But we can survive fine on what we grow."

"Yeah, but there's no fun in that! There's satisfaction seeing another living creature die at your hand, and know you have won the battle."

"Some battle – a rabbit against a stone."

"The rabbit can win by running from the stone."

"Maybe, but I like seeing things live. It's more fun to play with a sheep than it is to eat it."

"Like I said, you'll see what I mean when you get older," Antonio gets the last word in as he sneaks off down the riverbank.

Ambrogino continues to care for the animals, especially the mules who are mostly ignored by the others.

Beneath the colourful canopy of a twisted mulberry tree and the setting sun, the campsite is an idyllic setting away from noisy villages and bustling harvests. Only the soothing sounds of the river and the occasional songbird break the cool mountain air. The tranquil dinner is served, and the day slips into evening as though the entire world has become the Gallinelli's home.

Late for dinner, Antonio the mighty hunter appears from woods and into his family circle. He has nothing.

Chapter 11

As day breaks, Frederico wants to get the family on the road as soon as possible, since every moment of daylight is valuable. They are all hustled into work details to take down and gather up the campsite.

"Hey, look at Antonio!" Maria points out.

Having refused to sleep on the ground, Antonio slept in a wagon and had lain his face in such a way as to leave the imprinted lines of a crate against his cheeks.

"He looks like a crate today," Maria continues her amusement.

"So, Maria, you look like a chicken everyday!" Antonio fires back.

"Stop it, you two," Margherita scolds.

"Yes, let's get everything put away so we can get moving."

At their father's command, the children get on with their business, and the camp is emptied. With the six powerful animals back in position, the wagons work their way back up onto the main road again. Today, it is Antonio driving the middle wagon with his two closest sisters, Isabetta and Maria, while Bartolomeo brings up the rear with Allesandra. Travel is much the same as it has been the previous day, with crisp clear weather, and few obstacles in their path.

After another brief water break for the animals, midday is almost upon them, and Frederico's attention is broken by the sight of a single man in a mule-drawn cart, heading toward them. His travelling is relaxed as one who has all the time in the world.

Margherita offers a kind wave to the man, who now slows even more. He peers at the Gallinellis through a gravel face with small dark eyes. His hair hasn't been cut in what must be years, and he shows very few teeth while he chews on a piece of straw. He has much more clothing on than the Gallinellis have seen so far.

"Hello," greets Margherita.

"You folks got some wine?"

Frederico, who has now positioned his wagon to the side replies, "We do."

The man stops his mule.

"All I've got are these apples," he offers to Frederico.

Frederico gazes down at the apples, which are much poorer quality than the ones the Gallinellis already have on board. Looking up at the man, he asks, "Do you travel this road much?"

"All the time. I come up and down this road all year long."

"Then perhaps you can keep your apples, and lend us some advice on making the trip up and over to Lucerne."

"Lucerne? That's all the way. You'd be better off waiting until spring."

"Thank you, but suppose we want to get all the way through right now? I will offer to fill your wineskin there in exchange for your expertise."

"I accept. What do you want to know?"

"What markers are there to tell us where to go?"

"Well, the road used to be marked with stones, but they've all disappeared over time. But stay on this road here that follows this river. Even if it looks like it will be better to take a fork, don't. And don't listen to what anybody else tells you along the way. I'm telling you the fastest way, and that's what you need, with the youngsters and all. Just stay with this river as long as you can. You'll come to your first pass in about two days. It'll be steep and cold, and you may want to dismount and pull the horses through... or at least the mules for sure."

"Will these carts make it through?" Margherita interjects.

"Oh yeah, they'll make it. It'll be steep though, slow and

115

narrow as Hell. You don't have to fret much about the first pass. Once you get through that, the land will flatten out a while. There's a lake there, and you'll be feeling pretty good; feeling like you've done something. But don't get all full of yourselves. You've just started."

Bartolomeo has already reached for his writing book and his quill. He is writing down as much as he can.

For Frederico, he already knows the road will be steep and narrow. He also knows that it will be difficult, and at times dangerous. All he wants to hear is some local advice on how to best thwart the dangers.

"Go on."

The man pauses, and double-checks, "You say you've got wine?"

"Yes, of course," Frederico replies and looks back to catch the eye of Isabetta.

She is sitting closest to the wine kegs and takes direction from her father's nod. She dismounts and steps up to retrieve the old man's wineskin for filling.

"It is my own. And I trust you will find it to be very fine."

"I'm sure I will," the man continues. "When you are on the plain, try to make time. If you get stuck there in a big storm, nobody will find you for six months, 'cause you won't be able to get out either forward or backward."

Margherita looks back at the family, smiling half-heartedly to soften the man's perilous words. She sees Bartolomeo with his head down, dipping and writing.

"When you get across that plain, it'll be another two or three days, depending."

"Depending on what?" Frederico asks.

"Depending on anything. Then you'll get to the double pass. The second one you will get through fine, 'cause that means you've made it through the first one, which is going to give you fits."

"Here you are, sir," Isabetta hands over the filled skin to the man.

"Bless you, my child."

"Go on, please," Frederico persists.

"Where was I? Oh, that first pass after the plain is all rock. It'll be cold, windy, and they'll be nothin' behind you and nothin' ahead of you, so you've just gotta do it."

The man now looks over the wagons and animals with more scrutiny.

"If you're gonna take these three wagons through that pass, you'll have to go one at a time. There won't be any riding. All the people gotta go on foot, and guide the animals. You'll need to lock the back wheels, and go one cart at a time. You gettin' that boy?"

"One wagon at a time, on the first pass after the plain," Bartolomeo calls out, without looking up.

"Smart boy. Now, when you take these wagons through, one at a time, you want to get them going in a zigzag fashion. You don't want to get pointed straight down hill if you can help it. Oh, and if you've got something essential in any of these wagons, then you best carry that on your back. The valley below is full of wagon wrecks."

Margherita lets her anger show at the man for his continued embellishments. Realising that there are children listening, the man softens with a smile.

"'Course, you folks will be fine, I'm sure. Remember, just get through that first squeeze after the plain, and the last one will be easy. In about one and a half more days of riding, you'll get to a small village of about three families. The one with the waterwheel has a cabin for rent if you need it, and if it's been snowing, you'll pay handsomely for it. After that, it's a lot like what you're riding on right now, and Lucerne will be another two or three days after that."

"Well, it sounds like we've got some adventure ahead of us! I thank you very much, my good man, and I hope you enjoy my wine."

"Oh, bless you, sir, I will," he replies, and reaches back for one of his apples, and tosses it in Ambrogino's direction. "Here!"

The athletic boy catches it easily, and examines it.

"That's for you, little man."

"Let's go!" Frederico orders as he snaps the reins of his team.

As soon as the old man is away from them, Margherita whispers to her husband, "Do you think that man knows what he's talking about, Rico?"

"I suppose he knows as much as any man up here, and we would be smart to heed his words and be thankful we met him."

"Then perhaps we should better plan the days and nights. These snow covered peaks are getting closer and closer, and I'm worried about our comfort at night."

"You are always wise about such things, my dear. I know there will be fewer and smaller villages as this road climbs higher. But I anticipate the people along this way will be more and more receptive to visitors, as they must not get many this high up."

"You think they will be more receptive?"

"Yes, they will be happy to see fellow vintners, and will take us in for the night if we need it."

"Then you are more trusting than I am, Rico. I believe our opportunities will be fewer, and we'll have a greater chance of sleeping on the side of this road in the middle of nowhere."

"We'll see."

Plodding along at a measured pace, the animals continue their march up the ever increasing incline. The wagons wheels and axles join the sound of the hooves by creaking and squeaking in different spots. Unsure of the real confidence he has in his own plan for resting and sleeping, Frederico studies the road up ahead for any hints of opportunity. As it climbs before them, it emerges in and out of view, and tightens to the river as it continues between the growing mountains.

"I can see why you would be uncomfortable with a gamble each evening, my dear. Perhaps we should take the very first occasion to camp each day once we are past midday, and well before the sun begins to set."

"I don't want to be the one to slow us down. We can always

make do someway, somehow. But the nights are getting colder, and there won't be many good spots for campsites once we're above the trees."

"All of what you say is true, Rita. Please leave it all to me. I will find the best camp sites, and I will bargain for better shelter when the need arises. In fact, I will guarantee covered shelter this very night, if that is what you desire."

"How can you make such a guarantee?"

"Because we will be staying at that vineyard up ahead."

"Where? I don't see anything up there."

"Do you see the hillside on the right?"

"There are two mountainsides. Of course I see those."

"Look at the second one, down on the low side. There's a pattern to the colors. That, my dear, is a vineyard."

"A vineyard? Up here?"

"Yes, that is definitely a cultivated area. I can't envision anything else that would be growing in such a fashion up here."

"Do you know the owners, Rico?"

"I may know of their winery when we find out who it is, but I can't say for sure."

"What makes you presume they will be friendly toward us?"

"Well, how would you feel if we were home, and a travelling family of winemakers stopped by our farm?"

"I suppose I would welcome them in, as we would have much in common."

Not feeling a need to complete the conversation, Frederico quiets himself and lets time manage the debate.

Ambrogino, who is sitting close to his parents, has been listening to this conversation, but has not participated, as his faith in his parents' decisions is firm. He has finished his apple and is nibbling at the core, pulling off the smallest pieces of juicy white flesh. When Frederico looks back and their eyes meet, Frederico holds out his hand to receive the core from his son.

The boy smiles and hands it over to his father, not knowing why he would want such a thing. Frederico takes the core, faces forward, and hurls it high up over his head, backward toward the two wagons behind him. It clears the middle wagon and comes down on the back of one of Bartolomeo's mules.

"Hey, you hit Fifi!"

All of the children are now smiling and paying close attention to the response.

"I wanted to make sure you were all awake," Frederico shouts back.

"Of course we are!" Antonio replies from the middle.

"Good! Then be on your best behavior!"

Trekking their way up the narrowing road, the animals carry on with their burdens; their strength and fitness proving well, as the Gallinellis close in on the orchard.

Coming in the opposite direction, there appears to be another wagon heading toward the party. Such little traffic has been encountered thus far, that Frederico sees another person as a welcome sight.

As the approaching wagon comes upon them, Frederico must manage to the right side of the road in order to let it pass. His sons do the same, and the road is clear to the left. The oncoming wagon is driven by a man and his young son. It is overloaded with straw, and it sticks out of both sides.

The foreign driver glances at the ends of his straw load as it passes the Gallinellis. The straw tips tickle and distract the Gallinelli animals. However, the man pays no attention to Frederico or any other person in the caravan. He seems content that his wagon has passed without incident, and that his payload is unharmed.

Once he has passed, he resumes a path in the middle of the road, and his son looks back over his shoulder at Frederico. With no words exchanged, Frederico looks at the boy, and they both stare far longer than normal, trying to figure each other out.

Unfazed, Frederico then turns his attention up to the sky, and weighs the air for possible changes in the weather. He notices a faint ring around the midday sun, and he slaps the reins of his two horses to quicken their pace. Stopping at the orchard will provide some much needed rest for everyone.

Close enough for details to emerge, Frederico sees that it is indeed a vineyard of ripe grapes. The vines are terraced upward into the hillside in parallel rows, and Frederico nods at the precision of the cultivation. He stops off the road and a few yards short of the property.

"I will seek out the owner, and the rest of you can stay with the team."

Margherita slides over to the middle of the seat while Frederico dismounts and dusts himself off. Bartolomeo does the same, and ties up the mules, leaving Antonio to follow the actions of his brother.

"Hello there!" Frederico calls out as he approaches the main house.

There is no answer, so he makes his way inside the compound and sees a very slender old man approaching. He stops and waits for the man.

"What business do you have with me?"

"My name is Frederico Gallinelli, and my family and I are on a journey to cross these mountains."

"Heck, that's a pretty dumb idea," the old man remarks as he spits to the ground.

"Maybe so, but we are on our way just the same."

"What're you running from?"

Stunned at the man's insight, Frederico hesitates, "Running? We're not running from anything – or anyone."

"You're lying, winemaker."

Again, Frederico is taken aback by the man's lightning quick observations of his character.

"Do I know you?"

"Never seen you before in my life."

"Perhaps not," Frederico grants, and gets right to the point, "I have stopped here hoping for rest for my horses and mules, and

I'm looking for overnight accommodation for my family."

"I got no rooms here, this ain't no boarding house."

"We don't need much, sir. Any space with a roof, even in the barn would be fine."

"Nope, the barn is full."

"Look, sir, we have money to pay."

"No, you look! About five more miles up the road there's a village," he spits again. "All they do is sit around and drink all day. They'll be happy to take in you runaways. Now get out of here!"

Knowing a losing battle when he sees one, Frederico decides not to waste daylight trying to change the man's mind.

"Thank you so much for your hospitality," Frederico glares.

Turning back around, the old man waves a silent hand of good riddance. Frederico straightens his coat and hat, and returns to his family.

"What did he say?" Margherita asks.

"He said his rooms are full and we would find more comfort in a town about five more miles up the road."

"Can we make five more miles on this road before sundown?"

"If we have an ample place to rest when we get there, then, yes. Let's give the animals a quick drink, and I'll check their shoes."

"Bartolomeo already has, my dear."

"Excellent then... that's good. So we are off now"

Frederico accepts Bartolomeo's quick work with a nod back to him. He returns to his spot in the lead wagon and whips the reins. Almost as quickly as they arrived, they are gone.

Remembering his guaranteed shelter, Frederico elects a quicker pace now, and the labour of the horses in noticeable. The wagons creak and squeak much more, as considerable dust is kicked up into the air. Perhaps it is the wind from the faster pace, but Margherita begins to shiver at the dropping temperature. She looks back at Ambrogino, who is being bounced around by the swaying wagon.

"Bundle up, dear. It's getting cooler."

Ambrogino pulls a blanket up, but does not make any attempt to warm himself.

Frederico turns back to see the other two wagons behind him. Antonio and Isabetta are focused and keeping pace with their father, while Maria rides along, huddled down inside the cart.

At the end of the line, Bartolomeo and Allesandra are falling back. They have the two mules who are now becoming more difficult to manage at the faster pace. Bartolomeo waves up to his father to suggest that everything is fine, and to keep going.

"What did that old man say we should be looking for, Rico?" asks Margherita.

"Nothing specific. He said the village further up will be able to provide better comfort for us."

"They had better, because you – "

Suddenly, Ambrogino lunges for the side of the wagon, and vomits over the rail.

"Gino!" Margherita yells.

Frederico brings the horses to a stop, and again Ambrogino vomits his apple and everything else he has had this day. His body convulses each time with all the energy he has.

Margherita jumps into the back to hold and comfort her boy. Over and over again, Ambrogino heaves with much distress, sweat now pouring from his brow.

The second cart arrives, and stops behind them. Margherita sees her startled family and yells to them. "Get me some water!"

As most of the children hesitate about who has the water, Isabetta appears from nowhere with a bucket and a cloth right next to Ambrogino. She hands the bucket to her mother and awaits further instruction.

"Thank you, Betta," Margherita sighs as she takes the cloth, dips it in the water, and cleans Ambrogino's face.

The third wagon finally arrives, but the violence has stopped. Ambrogino hangs his head over the side in complete exhaustion.

"How is he, Mother?" Allesandra cries out, and leaps from her cart to be near.

"We've got to get off this godforsaken road, Rico."

Frederico is upset by the words, but he figures there are over three miles left, and they won't be leaving this spot for at least a few more minutes, so he walks around the wagons, and inspects them for wear.

"We'll need to be in that village in less than two hours," Frederico says to Bartolomeo, who has blocked all six rear wagon wheels.

"I understand, Father. This road is getting more difficult by foot. I think I'm going to vomit next."

Frederico smiles at his son's attempt at making light of the situation and pats him on the shoulder. He then turns back and heads up to see how Ambrogino is doing.

"Is the ride getting a bit too rough?" he half-heartedly asks his tired boy.

"It's not only that," Margherita replies for her son. "There was something wrong with those medicines he was given back at Guenny's."

"But that was days ago."

"Whenever it was, it was not right for some reason. We need to get somewhere, or set up camp soon."

Frederico walks right up to Ambrogino's face, and puts his hand on top of his sweaty head.

"Gino, honey, can you ride for a little bit more?"

"I think so," he whispers to his loving father.

"That's my big man."

Margherita mutters a few words to herself, and the family assumes their previous positions to start out again. Once more, the pace is quick, and the animals continue to perform. Frederico has already calculated that the family only needs four animals to make the entire trip, so if two should falter or become injured, he knows their loss will not affect the mission's success.

Chapter 12

The wonderment of the scenery is no longer a topic of discussion, now that the Gallinellis have become a mountain family in only a few days. With the steep slopes and rock outcroppings all around, the snow covered peaks above, and the deep drop-offs below, it is all ignored but for the few feet in front.

While there are several hours of sunshine left in the valley at this time, the sun setting close to one of the peaks shortens the day. Combined with the increasing clouds, Frederico suspects he may have miscalculated the amount of daylight left. Without realising, he's been lashing the reins harder to pick up speed.

"Slow down," Margherita begs.

"We're fine."

"The mules can't keep up, Rico. Bartolomeo may lose us."

"He'll keep up. Where else will he go? He can't get lost; there is only one direction to go!"

Margherita glares at her husband, not wanting to question his reasoning, but fears he has become bull-headed about racing ahead of the last wagon. The family needs to stick together so they don't end up with two problems.

Frederico senses her uneasiness, but does not let up. He will get Ambrogino some place safe tonight, no matter what. He trusts Bartolomeo will deliver himself, his sister, and their wagon with ease.

Onward they fly, thundering along the rocky road, while the horses begin to labour ever more. They begin to slip on some larger stones, but each time they do, Frederico strikes at the reins to push them on. Margherita climbs back into the rumbling wagon to pull Ambrogino close to her, while looking behind to see that Antonio is staying close, but Bartolomeo has fallen out of sight.

"Slow down!" Margherita pleads again.

All of a sudden, Frederico slows right down, and stops. Dust swirls up around the wagon, and Margherita looks up and around.

"What is it?"

"A bridge."

Margherita climbs back up to her riding seat. She sees the road bending to the left and going back over the river that they have been following. This necessary bridge puts the road on the other side of the river where the terrain is more suitable. But this bridge is very narrow and wooden, and the largest of the Gallinelli's wagons, the lead one, will barely fit.

It is not so much the difficulty of the bridge that is of concern, but the penalty for a mistake. Below the bridge is a drop of about seventy feet to the churning river below. The cliffs are steep, rocky, and almost impossible to climb out of.

By now, Antonio has caught up to the first wagon, and he slows to a stop behind his father. Bartolomeo can be heard trudging up from behind. When he finally catches up, he finds his father down on foot, studying the situation.

"Everybody dismount," he orders. "We'll lead the animals across by hand. And listen! If anything goes wrong, let the wagon and the horses go. Don't try to save anything and get tangled up yourself. Coats and boots can survive a fall, but you can't."

Margherita and the children don't say a word.

"Do you understand?" he yells.

"Yes," they all reply and drop out of the wagons.

"Good. Allesandra, Maria, Isabetta, go over right now with your mother and Gino."

The three daughters comply, and join hands as they glide to the other side.

"Bartolomeo, you take your wagon first. Take your time, and

focus on keeping the wheels centered."

Bartolomeo brings his team around to the front.

"Here," Frederico takes three apples from his wagon. "Use these to keep the beasts focused straight ahead. You don't want them milling around and looking down."

"Good idea, Father."

Waving the apples in front of their noses, Bartolomeo gives each mule a nibble. Now holding the treats higher, he leads the team up and onto the bridge. Watching his wheels, he steers the animals in a straight line. Whether they are very brave or very hungry, Bartolomeo does not care. The mules behave, and deliver the wagon without trouble.

Once on the other side, Bartolomeo hands the reins and the apples to his waiting mother, who praises and feeds the two animals for their work.

"Father!" Bartolomeo yells across. "Let me come back over and take Antonio's wagon."

"He can do it! You need to keep your wagon where it is, and keep those mules under control. I don't want them coming back."

Frederico's insistence that Antonio bring his own team over magnifies the moment. While it would make sense for Frederico to take turns bringing both wagons over himself, he wants his son to accomplish this goal. This will be Antonio's time to help the family like a man, and put his childhood behind him.

Frederico focuses his boy's attention. "Look, son. The bridge is sturdy, and will bear the weight with ease. Just keep moving, and control the team. If you were in the vineyard, harvesting with these same two horses, you would not put up with any rude behavior from them, right?"

"Except there's no hundred foot drop to my death back on the farm."

Frederico laughs, "That's true."

Without hesitation, and to Frederico's amazement, Antonio calls his horses to come, and leads them straight towards the bridge.

"Keep them steady, son."

Antonio continues straight ahead, giving the horses no choice but to follow him, and marches them right over to the other side. Bartolomeo is there to help, but Antonio shrugs him away, and moves the team all the way up past the mules, and back into the second position.

"Well done, Antonio!" Margherita calls out to her son.

When she looks back, she sees Frederico already on the bridge and moving the last team across.

"Very good, everybody," Frederico calls out, now about halfway.

Just then, a small boulder that Isabetta is standing on dislodges and rolls out from under her feet. She falls down unharmed, but the boulder tumbles toward the bridge, and rolls out onto it with a big bang.

One of Frederico's horses whinnies and jumps up to his hind legs.

"Rico!" Margherita yells, and runs toward the bridge.

Frederico jumps up to grab his frightened horse by the bit.

"Easy does it," he calls to his young stallion. "Easy… easy!"

He doesn't realise it, but the horses have moved to the side, and as Frederico struggles to gain control, he is only inches from the side of the bridge.

"Look out, Father!" Bartolomeo yells out.

Frederico looks around and sees how close he is to the side. Clinging to the horse, he is out of position to provide any leverage to pull him forward. He has ignored his own advice, and is hanging on for his life where another jump by either horse could easily cast them all over the side.

Frantic and figuring his next move, he feels the horses being pulled back to the middle of the bridge. In an instant, he finds himself safely standing with plenty of room, and the horses have settled down. Margherita had leaped into action, ahead of her sons, and grabbed the bridle of the second stallion. She pulled them both to safety and brought her husband back with them.

"What took you so long?" Frederico asks his hero.

"I had a stone in my shoe, so I stopped to get it out first," she jokes.

They soon collect themselves and complete the crossing. Isabetta is waiting in tears.

"I'm sorry, Father," she sobs.

Frederico hands his reins to Bartolomeo, and embraces his daughter.

"You didn't know that boulder was loose, did you?"

"No, I swear I didn't."

"Of course you didn't, I know. You have no fault at all, my sweet girl. Everything is fine. You see, it was me who tried to jump over the edge, only Mother wouldn't let me," he offers to make her laugh.

Instead, she reaches up and wraps her arms around her father's neck.

Frederico looks up from his hug and calls out to his family, "Watch out for loose boulders!"

"Loose boulders! Got it!" shouts Antonio with a smile.

"Let's get going!" Frederico brings everyone back to the task at hand.

Walking ahead with his daughter under his arm, he offers to her, "Why don't you ride up front with me. Gino needs some looking after."

Isabetta nods her head, wipes her face with the shoulders of her dress, and proceeds with her father. When everyone is loaded back up, Frederico starts them out again at a much slower pace. The shadows are now gone as dark clouds have rolled in, and Frederico knows he must cover the next two or three miles tonight, as good camping along this exposed road seems impossible to find.

The long drop to the valley below is now noticeable since crossing the bridge. Bad judgments, or spooked animals from this point on could prove disastrous. Up ahead, there awaits another steep test for the team, as the road's grade makes a hard climb over a very short distance.

Frederico stops his wagon, and calls back, "Keep about five wagon lengths between each of us. It gets very steep ahead, and we don't want to pile up, if one of us stumbles."

Antonio waves in acknowledgement, as does Bartolomeo from the rear. The two boys let their father move up ahead, and when the distance has been achieved, Antonio starts his horses. After waiting for a similar gap, Bartolomeo begins the mules.

Upward they go, climbing at a steeper angle then at any time so far. The horses strain, but don't fight, as the weight of the wagons resist at twice the burden as being on level ground. Frederico feels they are very close to the limit of their ability as they pull forward.

"Keep going!" Frederico calls out. "Don't stop. Keep your momentum!"

They snap their reins harder and faster, again and again. Forward they push as the grunts and groans of the animals become louder than the wheels. Frederico sees the breath of his horses now steaming from their mouths, as the coldness has come upon them in a very short time. The altitude change is dropping the temperature as fast as the dwindling daylight.

"Just a little further. Keep going!"

Up ahead, relief is in site as the road begins to plateau. Frederico keeps his speed and continues so that the other two wagons don't slow down on the heavy grade.

"Keep it up! You're almost there!"

"We're coming!" Antonio shouts up to his father.

Frederico finishes and begins to slow on the more level ground. Antonio then follows, and they both relax their animals as Bartolomeo comes over the crest to join them. A smooth plain awaits them now, and it is a welcome sight. Frederico dismounts.

"We need to continue, but the animals need a break, so let's water and feed them."

Bartolomeo picks out a few heavy stones to block the wheels.

Antonio kicks them in tight, and the girls begin to care for the animals.

For a brief moment, Frederico stops to admire his family. Bartolomeo is more valuable to the family than three hired men. He is strong, bright, and more than ready for his own family soon.

Allesandra and Isabetta are skilled and obedient, and only question authority when it makes sense. Otherwise, they work exceptionally hard without complaint. They each have all of the skills a woman needs, and perhaps for the first time ever, Frederico sees Allesandra as being nearly as capable as his own wife.

Margherita has raised all three of the girls to be clever and tough. They all share so much in common with her; each in her own right as adorable as a woman can be. Although other friends of Frederico hold their wives in little regard, Frederico can't help but to feel awe and admiration for how hard his wife works, and how much he depends on her. He wonders if it has been too long since he has told her this.

Maria and Antonio seem to fight and complain without end, but it is only because of their intelligence. If these two were ignorant or dim-witted, they would have nothing to fight about.

Then, of course, there is the sweetest and most cherished child of all, Ambrogino – the boy who possesses all of the finest qualities of his five siblings, rolled into one. He sees the entirety of the world, and questions it all. He works so hard at everything he does, and even makes clever observations that adults would miss. Perhaps he is the perfect combination of both Frederico and Margherita. Handsome and intelligent, Ambrogino completes the family like an exclamation point.

Margherita pulls out a basket from her wagon. "Who's hungry?"

"Me!" Antonio shouts first.

The girls also find their way over, while Bartolomeo continues to inspect the wagons with his father.

"There is a new crack in this wheel, Father."

"Yes, I see."

"Perhaps we can move some weight from this wagon to my own?"

"You know son… when I put this particular wheel onto this cart about six years ago, I noticed that it was a bit warped. I knew it was strong, but I also knew that someday it would crack and begin to fail. It's actually lasted longer than I thought it would."

"I guess its strength must have compensated for its crookedness."

Frederico runs his rough hand over the smooth wheel, gingerly feeling for its longevity.

"Let's move some weight as you suggest, son. The travelling from now on will require more strength than speed, so we'll use more of your wagon with the mules."

"Rico!" Margherita's voice shouts out.

Frederico does not reply, but hastens up to where the call came from.

"Gino is not well at all."

Frederico rushes over to see his son shaking his head back in forth as he clutches his midsection. The grimace on the boy's face tells Frederico what he needs to know.

"It's going to be alright, son. We'll be in the village soon, and everything will be okay."

Margherita rummages through her crates, and produces a small container. "Gino, take some of these seeds."

Ambrogino slowly reaches for them and does as he is told.

"These will help your stomach," she says as she covers up his feet against the cooling temperatures.

"We need to keep going, Rico. Right now."

"We won't be going anywhere if these animals drop dead, Rita."

"The mules can make it, Father. You and Mother can move on with them, and the rest of us will stay here until the horses are ready."

"No, Bartolomeo. We stay together no matter what. Once we

get separated, then who knows what would happen next."

"We can stay here, Father," Allesandra steps forward. "We can easily manage by ourselves for a few hours… and you can leave us a trail to follow."

Frederico is surprised by the conviction of his oldest daughter's words, and for a moment he believes them. "I have no doubt about your willingness, Sandra. But your strength alone may not be enough in this foreign place. Who knows what lies around the next bend? An army of thieves? A pack of wolves? The thought of losing any one of you on this journey is more than I can bare."

"We can fight off thieves and wolves," Antonio says as he waves around a stick in a sword-like fashion.

"Excellent," Frederico smiles. "If they come, then we will put you and your stick out in the front."

Antonio freezes with his stick in mid-motion. "On second thought, I think we should stay together."

"We'll rest here for a little longer, everyone."

Frederico looks up into the sky again to gauge the weather.

"It smells like snow and it's not even winter yet," Maria mentions aloud.

"You all have warm coats and boots in the last wagon if you need them," Frederico reminds his family.

Margherita pulls out a coat for herself, and one for Maria.

Isabetta remains occupied with wiping the sweat from the animals. She has always been quick to notice what they need, and to care for them without direction. She doesn't even look up during the conversations, as she knows that work needs to be done, and somebody has to do it.

"Maria, go help your sister," Margherita points over to Isabetta.

"Yes, Mother."

Margherita then turns her attention to Frederico. "How long will we rest here?"

"Not long, my dear. The cloud cover will make it dark soon, so we need to get going. I don't know how far we need to go, but I don't want to be on this crazy road with lanterns.

Margherita pauses, and comes closer to her husband. They are now far enough away for the others not to hear them.

"You know, Rico, I don't know if that Guenny woman cured Gino at all. I think she gave him some medications to make him feel better only for a short while. He's very sick, and I haven't spent any time caring for him. I'm worried, Rico."

Frederico pulls his wife close and wraps his arms around her. "Don't worry so much, my love. The boy is strong. Maria fought off this sickness, and so will he. You will see. There is no way God would take that boy from us, as He would surely take you or me first. Our Gino is special, and has much service to his family remaining in his life. I have complete confidence that he will be fine. You should, too."

Margherita does not reply, but turns her head to the side and rests it on Frederico's chest. He allows her this quiet moment of relief and holds her tight.

"Let's get back to the children," she releases herself. "They might suspect we have abandoned them."

Frederico smiles at his wife's selflessness.

The two head back to the family and tend to the needs of the moment, and after their short rest, all three Gallinelli wagons are moving again.

A long stretch of flat terrain waits in front of them, and a sheer rock wall to their left amplifies the sounds of the creaking wheels and grunting animals. The family is quiet, and few other noises are heard.

In the distance, the road disappears around a bend. Frederico is hopeful that this is the entrance to the village he has been longing for. He prays to himself that this will be the spot where the family can find comfort for the night.

The wagons approach with a smooth speed, and what is now becoming visible in the twilight is something Frederico has never seen before.

"What is that, Father, up on the mountain?" Antonio yells out.

"That's our road, son."

"That's the road? It looks like a wall or something."

As the clan draws near, they begin to take in the spectacle. It is indeed the road they are on, and it zigzags in huge swinging sections as it works its way up the sheer side of the mountain. The size and proportion of this vision has left the whole family speechless.

"Those are switchbacks in the road. It looks steep from here, but it will be easy when we get there," Frederico calls out.

"If you say so," Margherita replies, fixated on the terrain.

"We've been on a couple of these already. Only they haven't been as noticeable as those up ahead."

"Or as dangerous."

"It's perfectly safe, Rita. This road is designed for wagon travel. There is no need to worry."

As the family focuses on the vertical sight in the distance, Isabetta calls out, "I see a village."

"That old fool was right!" Frederico gushes. "That's the village for sure, and plenty of daylight left. Ha! We did it."

A dozen or so houses nestle into a small group at the base of the switchbacks. Smoke rises from several fires to form a low thin cloud that creates a foggy division between the comfort of the valley, and the uncertainty of the mountains.

As the wagons get closer, citizens are becoming visible; most working in some way, filling carts, gathering hay, or tending to animals. Frederico feels confident now that he has made the right choice for his family. This place is ideal – far from home, but peaceful and right on time.

Grassy fields now open up on either side of the road. Combinations of stone walls and wooden fences meander around the countryside, indicating comfortable living. On the right lies a small clear lake. For the first time this day, Frederico relaxes. "Let's stop at that lake ahead."

"Finally!" moans Antonio.

Margherita turns her attention back toward Ambrogino, "Gino honey, did you hear Father? There is a lake up ahead with cool water." The weakening Ambrogino nods as his mother caresses his face and forehead. "I can even smell the pure clean water," she whispers. "It's simply delicious. Mmm... I can't wait."

Just a few yards ahead, there is a break in the road, and a short path leads to the wide shoreline.

"Keep the teams hitched, everyone. We'll bring them buckets to drink from."

Frederico stops his wagon, dismounts, and watches as Antonio and Bartolomeo do the same. The girls then take out several empty buckets from the middle wagon and head to the water.

Staying with his first team, Frederico strokes the neck of one of his stallions, and encourages him. "Good job, Rocco, you big wonderful boy. We've got some good fresh water coming for you now."

Rocco's younger teammate rocks his head up and down, anxious for his turn.

"You wait your turn, Forty-seven," Frederico admonishes. This horse he often calls by the nickname given soon after its premature birth due to its extreme light weight. "You would have died if it weren't for me. Your water is coming, don't get all excited. I won't let you run dry."

Allesandra comes up straight away with two full buckets and places them on the ground in front of the horses.

"I'll let them drink this down, and I'll refill them again," she replies.

"Okay, we'll need to get them into one of these fields for grazing, but I want to be welcome first. Tell Maria to get the apples, and we'll feed them those for the moment."

"Yes, Father."

A few moments later, she returns and grabs the two empty buckets. "She's coming with them right now, Father."

"Excellent," Frederico exhales as he keeps stroking the two horses.

Just as Maria comes over with the bushel of apples, Allesandra returns with two freshly filled buckets.

"Hand feed them one at a time, Maria. I don't want them to fill up on apples, but I want them to feel satisfied until we can get into one of these fields."

Then he approaches his older son. "Bartolomeo, Maria has apples for the animals to snack on until they can graze. Let's take a look at that wheel again."

"I was able to watch it on the way up, Father, and it does seem to be wobbling a bit more than when we looked at it last. Maybe we can get it replaced in the village."

"Perhaps, but let's take it off and soak it in the pond here. It won't fix it, but it will keep the wood from drying out and getting worse."

"Should we try it now with the horses tied in?"

"No, I think… "

"Rico, there is somebody coming," Margherita calls out.

He looks up to see two men on horseback riding toward them.

"Bartolomeo, come with me."

The two Gallinelli men walk out from the wagons, and back onto the main road to await their greeting party.

Two very plain looking men in very plain clothing arrive, remain mounted, and look down upon the travellers with contempt. They appear to have been disturbed from some other activity, since they are carrying little equipment. Frederico detects a strong odour of beer.

"You there, are you lost?" asks the older, stringy haired man.

"No, we are not lost."

"Where are you going then?"

"We are going through this pass to the other side, to Lucerne."

The two miscreants turn to look at each other and smile. The second man, more filthy than the first, speaks, "You takin' that family up and over this pass when it's about to snow?"

"How do you know it's going to snow?"

"Oh, it's going to snow alright," he chuckles.

"Well, we certainly weren't going to go up tonight," Frederico steals a glimpse skyward. "We were hoping to trade with you folks for a place to stay until morning."

"What do the lot of you have to trade? Maybe that young one there might be a good place to start," the dirty man chortles as he points toward Maria.

Frederico steps forward with his fists tight at his side. "I have the finest wine in the valley, right here. I'm sure you will find the value to be quite high."

"We can find the value in any wine," laughs the dirty man.

Old stringy hair laughs out loud at his partner's joke, and shifts his horse right up to Frederico, causing Bartolomeo to move even closer to his father.

"Look, wine man… "

"My name is Gallinelli, my good man. Frederico Gallinelli," he stands taller.

"Look, Gal'nelli… we don't want anybody staying here. You can go on, or you can go back. You can even go to Hell for all we care. The toll to pass tonight is two whole kegs of your wine."

"Two kegs? Just to pass?"

"That's right, mister!" the dirty man rips in.

"You chew on that, Gal'nelli. And if you wait too long, it'll cost you a keg to turn around and leave the way you came." The men laugh out loud, exposing several missing teeth.

Frederico is unafraid of these two bullies, and feels quite comfortable taking a stand, but his thoughts are with his family. He knows the next words out of his mouth could change all of his plans, and the future of everyone he loves.

"Thank you two good men for your offer. My animals are tired, and I will only take the time that they need to graze. When I come up to see you, whom should I ask for?"

"You can ask for me," the first man says.

"And what is your name, good sir?"

After a pause, the man replies, "Frederico Gal'nelli."

"Thank you very much… Mr. Gallinelli. I look forward to seeing you soon," Frederico nods with a smirk, and tips his cap to both men.

He then turns toward Bartolomeo, escorts him around by the arm, and the two head back to the wagons.

"They were looking for a fight, Father."

"Those two were as drunk as two men could be, son. They will be useless by sundown. We have nothing to fear from them."

"Should we go into the village and look for others who would be more hospitable?"

"Not yet. Let's take the time to care for the horses and ourselves for the moment, and we'll study the situation."

Margherita is standing guard waiting for her two men to return the short distance. "What did they say?"

"They want us to pay two kegs of wine for toll passage," Frederico shakes his head.

"But what about our roof for the night?"

"They did not offer that as an option."

"Not an option? There must be somebody up there besides those two that would take us in."

"Precisely your son's opinion, my dear. I believe that to be the case as well. So I have secured us ample time to rest the team and graze them here. After that, we'll enter the village and see what we can make of it."

"But it will be dark by then, Rico."

"Then we'll go in right before dark."

"What if we can't find a place to sleep? Will we wander around in the dark, up here in these frigid mountains?"

"We will find a place. Don't you worry about that. Don't worry at all. Gino will rest comfortably tonight, right beside you and me."

Margherita pauses. "All right, we'll wait, but then we're going in. Bartolomeo, take the teams out from their harnesses, and assign one person per animal. "Each of you take your animal into the field by hand and walk with them as they graze. I don't want them getting loose."

Moments later, all four horses, and the two mules are out in the fields grazing, each with a family member. Frederico is now left alone with the wagons, and Ambrogino. He walks over to find his precious son asleep. He strokes his exposed shoulder and whispers to him.

"How are you doing there, sweet bean? Everything is going to be perfectly fine, you know. Don't you worry about a thing. Father has a plan for you, my sweet little boy. Father has a plan."

Chapter 13

About an hour has passed, and Bartolomeo is getting nervous that they have been left unattended for the entire time. Many of the villagers continue about their business, occasionally stopping to point at the odd family.

"It's about time to go in, son," Frederico says to him. "I want you to keep your wits about you and try to avoid conflict wherever possible. We will have no chance fighting with these people."

"I understand, Father, but we shouldn't be made fools of either."

"And what if we are? What will become of us if a handful of drunks who will never remember us have some fun at our expense for one night? How will it matter to us and our journey?"

"We will have lost our dignity in the eyes of many, and amongst ourselves."

"That is where you are wrong. Your dignity is never lost until you give it away. These drunks who challenged us have already given up theirs. We are a strong family on a mission from God Himself. We will stick to our plan, and we will move on. We can't win or lose anything with these people. They are but one more obstacle on our journey, just like the bridge, and just like the cracked wheel."

"And just like the snow, Father?"

Frederico is tapped back from his lecture to realise that tiny snowflakes are beginning to fall around them. He looks over at the lanterns to see the delicate drift of more flakes in the light.

"Yes, Bartolomeo, just like the snow indeed... let us please stick to our plan, and let God guide us."

"Are we ready?" Margherita asks for all to hear.

"We are ready. Let's move."

The family mounts their wagons behind the now fresh animals, and they begin their advance with the extra light from the lanterns illuminating the road ahead.

"It's snowing out!" Antonio says.

"You're a genius," replies Maria.

Frederico focuses, "A little snow is not going to slow us down, children. Just stick to the plan."

Margherita turns back to Ambrogino who is now sitting up somewhat and watching out at the village ahead. She knows that tonight is a turning point for him, as he is very weak from not eating. "I'm looking forward to a warm night's sleep tonight, aren't you Gino?"

Ambrogino nods with a quick glance to his mother; his eyes sparkling in the lantern's light, and speaking a thousand words to those who know how to hear them. Margherita's thoughts drift back to their farm in Como, and all she had back there to keep her boy safe and well.

Filing up the grassy road, the wagons rumble across a short bridge over a soft section of ground where a thin creek trickles through. At this sound, several villagers begin to appear carrying candles and lanterns of their own. The houses in this small village are packed together and situated very close to the road. There is a definite smell of meat cooking somewhere.

"Hello!" Frederico yells, with his hand raised high.

There is little response, only more folks beginning to gather. When the wagons are nearly upon them, one man moves forward from the group.

"What is your business here this evening?"

Frederico measures the man, as he is not either of the two men who came out to them earlier. This one is taller, and much more dignified. His dress is neat and clean, and appears to be a leader of some sort.

"My good man… we are travelling through these mountains to Lucerne, and we would gladly pay for a place to stay this evening."

"What have you to pay for your stay here?"

"I have the finest wine a man could ask for."

"Well then, present it to me."

A bit surprised, but not wanting to seem unwilling, Frederico looks back to Bartolomeo and makes a hand gesture for him to bring forth a carafe with a cup. Bartolomeo rummages through the crates, produces the items, and walks toward the demanding man to present it as matter-of-factly as he can, all the while, never taking his eyes off the man.

"We'll see about this," the man says, and pulls the goods from Bartolomeo's hands.

Bartolomeo steps back, while Frederico dismounts in anticipation of the man's request for more. He reaches into his own cart and pulls out a drinking cup for himself. Just then, the tall man inverts the carafe over his mouth and chugs a mouthful.

Frederico stops in his tracks, shocked that this man would be so bold and uncouth. The brutish man turns his face to his people, showing his cheeks full of Frederico's wine, and shakes them while looking up in the air and judging the wine's quality. In a complete twist of expression, he spins his head in disgust and spits out the wine onto the ground. Laughter erupts from the on-looking villagers.

"Disgusting!" he barks.

Frederico knows the man is simulating disgust only to gain a bargaining advantage. He has seen this type of ploy used before, and has too much knowledge of his craft to be fooled by such a display.

"I'm sorry you do not find it appealing, but it is all we have."

"So you are asking for one of our cottages to sleep in tonight? A warm fire I suppose, too? Maybe a hot meal? And all you have is this putrid wine?"

Fearless, Frederico walks right up to the man and says to him alone, "The amount you have spit out would sell for five lira in Milan. Even you can calculate the value of an entire keg, and use it for other trading, if indeed you are so disgusted by its taste."

The villagers strain to listen to Frederico's words. By being so quiet, Frederico has removed the disadvantage of being made fun of again.

"It is you, vintner, who can see the predicament you have put your family in tonight. You are at our mercy if you are to find any warmth tonight."

"We are quite capable of setting up a very comfortable camp of our own, my good man. We require nothing, but would prefer to trade for better accommodations if there is one among you who is willing. Do you know of anyone here who might be willing?"

Impressed with Frederico's confidence, the man pauses. Suddenly, a chilling gust of wind blows hard into the two men, whipping up some ever-increasing snow into Frederico's face. He stands firm and unaffected by it, showing that he is not bothered at all by the weather.

"Why don't you stay with me!" the tall man exclaims for everyone to hear.

Without missing a beat, Frederico asks, "What is your price?"

"Why, four kegs of your overrated wine, of course."

"Four kegs?" Frederico protests. "That's robbery."

"No, my good man, I assure you it is not. If you are unhappy with the price, I'm certain you will find great comfort in your little camp back across the bridge and out in the field with the goats."

Frederico ponders the prospect of paying too high a price for one night's stay versus the idea of making camp out in the cold meadow, especially with snow falling.

"While I appreciate your so generous offer, I feel it is too dear. We will make our own camp, and bother you no more this evening."

The tall man loses his smile. "As you wish. Oh, and by the way, you may want to camp close to the road."

"Why is that?"

"This snow… " the man looks up into the cloudy night sky, "It may not seem like much now, but don't be surprised if it is over your wagon wheels by morning."

Frederico doesn't know if this is good advice or more posturing. "Thank you for your advice, sir," he replies, and turns back to his family.

There is a silence from both parties as the conversation ends with the men turning from each other and walking away. Then Frederico turns back to the tall man, "Oh, my good man! How much for two hens for our dinner?"

"One keg."

"I'll take them."

A bit surprised at Frederico's quick acceptance of the deal, the man motions back toward one of the villagers to produce the birds. Bartolomeo brings forth the keg, along with an empty crate. When a woman appears with two clucking hens, the peaceful exchange is made, and Frederico, with his son and his new hens, returns to the wagon train.

Each family member anticipates the good news from the meeting, but without a word, Frederico climbs into his wagon and turns his team around back over the bridge.

When they have cleared the bridge, Margherita lets go, "Why aren't we staying in the village tonight?"

"The price was too high."

"Too high?" she gasps. "We have plenty of wine to trade. Look at this weather, this is going to be an awful night to be outside! What about Gino?"

"Precisely! That's exactly what I am considering most!" Frederico replies, but keeps his voice down.

"Then why are we going backward, to camp in the fields?"

"We're not camping in the fields!"

"We're not?"

"Please wait a moment until we can pull off the road."

"So we are staying in the village after all?"

Frederico stays silent until they have travelled out of view of the village, and then pulls the team off the road. He dismounts, and motions the other two wagons up along side.

"Everybody down… " he calls out, "… except Gino."

The family obliges, dismounts, and gathers toward their father. Bartolomeo holds the reins of both the mules and Antonio's horses. Margherita holds the reins of her two horses, and they wait to hear what is coming next.

"We're not staying out in this field tonight."

"You have a plan, Father?" Antonio asks.

"Yes, I do."

"We'll be staying in the village, right?" Margherita tries again.

"No, not quite."

"We're turning around?" Allesandra asks.

With his face as firm as a stone, Frederico states, "No. We're going up and over tonight."

"Tonight? That's crazy, Rico! We have no chance on that road at night."

Remaining quiet, Frederico lets everyone absorb his decision.

"We should be settling down for the night, not travelling," Margherita pushes again. "We didn't stay at the farm, and now we're not staying here… after you promised Gino a warm night's stay indoors?"

"Why can't we wait until morning, Father?" Isabetta asks her beloved father.

Frederico stays quiet, and looks over to Bartolomeo to see what he has for a question. Much to his surprise, his son does not have a question, but an answer.

"We have to go tonight, everybody," he says. "We have to go tonight because of what the tall man said."

"We are going tonight because he doesn't like the wine?"

"No… " Bartolomeo continues on behalf of his father. "… because of the snow."

"It's because of the snow that we should stay," Margherita argues.

"That was my first thought too, Mother, but we need to go before the snow gets too deep. If it is so deep that the wagons cannot travel, then we will be left on this side of the mountain all winter. We'll never make it to Lucerne, or any town on the other side. We will then have no choice but to return to the valley. We haven't come this far only to turn around now and head back to the pestilence. I know we can't spend the winter here in this village, or any other place behind us so far. As hard as it is to say, there is no other choice."

"We have a lot of choices," Margherita interjects. "We can stay here and go tomorrow, when there is plenty of daylight."

"But, my love, what if the snow is too deep?" Frederico returns to the conversation.

"What if it isn't?"

"That would be great. But if it is, we can't make it up this pass, and we might as well go all the way back to Como."

"That's fine with me," she fires as she drops the reins she has been holding and stomps away.

"So you are happy with all of us sitting down and waiting for the end of days to fall upon us? That is what you have for a plan? That suits you?" Frederico calls to her.

"What is so magical about the other side of these mountains that will protect us against a sickness that is predetermined?" she returns to fight. "Do you actually think that God will not find us in Lucerne?"

"God has already found us, my love. He has given us this chance. He has given us the wisdom to survive. He wants us to live, and that is what we are fighting to do right now. We are not risking death going over this pass at night in the snow. We would be risking death by not going. Consider the entire series of events so far. How was I fortunate enough to learn of the pestilence when I did? Why did we leave our home when we did? What caused us to spend exactly the right amount of time with the Malatestas, fool

Rusca's soldiers, and then leave? And how did we get to this spot right now? We have a chance right now to make it. Had we arrived tomorrow, just one more day later, we would not have had this very chance before us. The fact that we have been put in this place, right now, this instant, is not a punishment or misfortune, but true grace."

"It's just so crazy… this whole journey, Rico. How do you know that this is the plan. How do you know?" She implores into her husband's dark eyes.

"I can't tell you how I know, my dear. But I have every certainty that this journey is precisely what we need to do. There is no doubt in my mind or my heart at all."

A teary Margherita sinks into her husband's chest, and he returns the gesture by wrapping his arms around her.

"It's freezing up here," she says to him.

"Then it's time to go. Listen to me everyone, we will be going straight through the town, at a quick pace, and we will not stop. No matter what anybody says to you, we will not stop. Does everyone understand?"

They nod in silence.

"Then we are off."

The children mount their wagons in the light of the lanterns. Each wagon has a solid working lantern, and there are four more on board as back-ups with plenty of oil. The plan that Frederico is unfolding seems more and more absurd, but for certain, the family is prepared and well stocked. It's as if Frederico had long ago understood every obstacle that would be placed before him, as was ready for them.

Into the snowy night they set out, back over the short bridge, and into the village. Several villagers scurry around at the commotion, and soon the man who scoffed at Frederico's wine reappears.

"So you have changed your mind I see," he pleasures.

"No, sir," replies Frederico without slowing. "We will not be needing any services tonight."

"State your business then."

"We have no business!" Frederico retorts as he is now moving past the man. "We are just passing through."

"Passing through? Now?" He looks at the smiling Bartolomeo who is now even with him. "Why, you're all mad! You... you've been drinking too much of your own wine!"

The wagon train keeps moves along, as instructed.

"We'll find your bodies in the spring!" the tall man now screams out to the whole family. "You haven't got a chance!"

Margherita is concerned with how her children are hearing these words, and is compelled to discredit the man. "You're a crook!" she shouts. "Keep your advice for yourself!"

Frederico looks over at her, and knows what she is doing, so he doesn't try to stop her. Soon, all three wagons have cleared the village, and the road ahead is made visible with the light from the lanterns. The snow has begun to stick and offers the benefit of illuminating the ground.

"How long will the lanterns last?" Margherita asks her husband.

"We have a few more full ones, and enough oil for all of them for two full nights. I hope this will be the only night we have to travel."

"We'll probably find a few farms here and there up over this pass, right?"

"I expect so, Rita."

Within a short time, the road makes a sharp turn to the left and begins a steep, but manageable incline upward.

"Slow and steady!" Frederico calls out to his crew. "Keep them moving... slow and steady."

They are on the modest climb of the first switchback they saw from a distance earlier that day. The grade is fair and constant, and the animals march forward in rhythmic fashion.

As the snow continues to fall, the lanterns catch the flakes and expose them for a brief moment before they hit the ground. The sounds of the wagons creaking combine with the slight hissing sound of the snow hitting the ground to create an odd sense of silence.

"How much further?" Antonio calls out from the middle position.

"I can't see much further away than you can, son. Concentrate on keeping the horses slow and steady."

Frederico knows the road switches back to the right sometime soon, but it seems to be taking forever. With so far to go, he worries that his family will lose their ambition very soon, so he begins to sing.

"I once knew a lady who was most fair... "

"No, not this one," Antonio cries out to his father.

"With olive skin and long brown hair... "

"Somebody stop him," Antonio calls out again.

Then Margherita chimes in, "She worked all day in the golden sun... "

"... then she became my chosen one," Maria finishes her father's song.

"You remember!" Frederico howls, happy with his daughter's participation.

"No, I just wanted to finish it before you did!"

Allesandra and Isabetta laugh at their sister's mocking. It's the first sound of laughter that's been heard since they left Bellinzona.

"I once knew a road that was so steep... " Bartolomeo calls up from the rear.

Now the game is on to make their own songs, and Bartolomeo's siblings eagerly wait for his return line.

"... that a whole family turned into sheep."

The girls howl with laughter, and Margherita's heart is warmed by the sounds of joy coming amidst a formidable moment.

"I once knew a horse that smelled so bad... " Antonio tries his hand at the game. "... that he just wanted to feel so glad."

"What?" Isabetta laughs out loud.

"That doesn't make any sense," Maria also laughs at her brother.

So Allesandra begins, "I once knew a boy who could not rhyme… "

"… so he made no sense almost every time."

Laughter comes from all three wagons, even from Antonio at himself. The perfect put down by his older sister leaves him unwilling to try another.

"Who's next?" Margherita calls out, wanting to continue the game.

"I once had a father, brave and strong… " offers Isabetta.

Not knowing where this is going, there is a brief moment of silence.

"… who drove up a mountain all night long."

This time Frederico leads the laughter. "… all night long!" he replies in the same musical tone as his daughter.

Defending her husband, Margherita quips, "I once knew a girl who slipped on a stone… "

"… and her father's cart was nearly thrown."

"Ha, ha!" Antonio revels in his sister's put down by their mother.

The others cover their giggles so as not to hurt Isabetta's feelings.

"Well, this is turning into quite a game," Frederico proclaims. "And I was just singing a little song to myself."

"I once knew a father who sang too loud… " Maria tries.

Silence follows as she does not know how to finish her thought in a funny way.

So Allesandra helps out, "… but he thought he was good, so he stood and bowed."

Laughter erupts from everyone.

"Alright, alright, that's enough," Frederico bellows at his family. "You're all very funny. Well done. I think it is leveling off up ahead."

Within a few more feet, the road does begin to flatten. Frederico crests the hill and pulls forward to give the others room to fit in the open area.

"We've made it!" Antonio calls out.

"We're at the top already?" Maria asks.

"No, no, not even close," Frederico answers. "This is the first switchback. The road goes up again from here." He points in the opposite direction where the road turns back to where it climbs even more steeply than before.

"Goodness, it's a lot steeper here than it looked from the valley," says Margherita.

"We'll have to rest here for a moment," Frederico decides.

"How far to the top of this one?" Antonio looks for relief.

"We will need to take it one at a time. But we can't wait too long, or the snow will pile up."

"I say let's go right now."

Frederico turns toward the voice that is obscured by darkness and snow.

"How are your mules?" he calls back to Bartolomeo.

"They are fine. Let's get more of this climb behind us."

"Okay. Let's go."

They line back up and head up the next leg. The snow remains steady, and swirls in all directions from the wind, but the road is visible and they can manage.

"Look down below," Margherita calls out. "You can see the fires in the village."

"They're like stars below us, like the world is upside down," Allesandra points out.

"It's hard to believe that we were way down there."

"That fire sure looks warm," Antonio pines on behalf of the whole family.

Imagining himself toasty warm, his thoughts turn to his brother, "How is Gino?"

Frederico realises they haven't heard a word from him since they left the village.

"He must be sleeping," Margherita states.

She turns back to him to see him curled in a ball under several blankets and a dusting of snow having blown in upon him. She pulls back the blankets and reaches her hand under them in the darkness. A small hand reaches back and softly connects with her.

"Are you hungry, my sweet?"

"No, thank you," Ambrogino can just get out the words.

"Are you warm enough?"

"My feet are cold."

Margherita climbs back under the canopy and fishes out another pair of stockings for his feet. She removes his shoes, puts the stockings on his feet, and wraps them up in an extra blanket. Looking into her son's eyes for approval, she gets a small smile and a nod, to which she warms his forehead with a long kiss.

The Gallinelli caravan trudges along, higher and higher, while the road is wide and smooth enough not to cause any alarm. The snow, however, is now deep enough to leave tracks behind them, and the animals create small puffs of snow as they step.

"How is everybody else doing?" Frederico shouts out.

"Good from the back," Bartolomeo replies.

"We're okay," Antonio responds.

"Do you need Allesandra to relieve you?"

"No, I'm fine," Antonio replies.

"We need to keep up our momentum, and keep moving. We can stop at the turns when we need to."

"Can you see the next turn, Father?" Maria asks.

"Not yet."

Frederico gauges the grunts and groans of the horses, as they navigate the unknown road beneath them. He never wants to be in a situation where he does not have complete control, yet that is exactly where he finds himself. In the middle of these steep switchbacks, on this forlorn road, in this foreign land, he has no choice but to continue upward.

Crack! A loud noise pierces the night air from the rear.

"What was that?" Frederico yells.

"It sounded like a spoke on the cracked wheel," Bartolomeo calls backs.

"Are you moving?"

"Yes! It's a little wobbly, but it's rolling."

Frederico turns toward Margherita, "Keep the horses moving," he orders, handing her the reins and jumping off.

"I'm coming back there, just keep moving."

Antonio's wagon quickly comes upon him.

"Keep moving, Antonio, everything's all right."

Bartolomeo's wagon arrives, and Frederico moves alongside it, trying to get a good look in the poor light. Bartolomeo's lantern hangs out in front for the mules, and does Frederico almost no good at all.

"Keep going, son, I'm going to feel for it."

"Okay, but tell me if we need to stop."

Walking along with the wagon as it goes, Frederico feels the outside of the wheel while it remains in motion. Amidst darkness, snow, cold, and a difficult incline, he is able to make a perfect assessment of the situation by the feel of his hands alone.

"It should be fine until we get to the next turn. It's on securely, even with the wobble."

Frederico decides to stay on the wheel, and keeps his left hand on the top as it goes. He is now scraping the snow with his palm as the wheel turns.

"How long are you going to walk like that, Father?"

Before he can answer, Margherita calls out, "We're here!"

"There is your answer," replies an equally relieved Frederico.

Moving up to remove the lantern from Bartolomeo's wagon, which has now finally stopped, Frederico weighs the situation with a closer inspection. Through the falling snow, Bartolomeo hops down and also walks around his wagon in search of the problem with his father.

"There it is. One of the spokes is split from end to end, but it's staying in its place."

"That's not so bad," says Frederico, handing Bartolomeo the lantern. "We can wrap it with some rope. Find some and take care of this."

"Easily, Father."

"How bad is it?" Margherita asks.

"It's not bad at all," Frederico replies. "It's split, but not broken, so we're going to strengthen it with rope, and it will be the strongest spoke on the wheel."

Satisfied, Margherita then shuffles around for a bit of food, and pulls back a covering, causing the two new hens to begin clucking.

"Ooh, I forgot about you two," she says out loud.

"Can we have them, Mother?" Antonio asks. "I'm hungry."

"Everybody is hungry, Antonio," Frederico interjects. "When we get to the top, we can make camp and cook those birds."

"It'll take forever to get to the top, Father. Let's make camp here."

"We can't, Antonio," Isabetta defends. "We need to get up this road before the snow is too deep, or else we'll get stuck right here. Don't worry, you'll live."

"Your sister is right."

"The wheel is all set, Father."

"Excellent, let's get going again," Frederico announces, and moments later, the family is on procession again.

This time, though, a strong wind slaps into their faces. Coming up on the last leg, it wasn't felt because it was on their backs.

"Where did this wind come from?" Antonio calls out.

"Soon, it will be on our backs again, so don't worry," Margherita comforts.

For the first time since leaving the village, the travelling is becoming difficult for the family. Frederico has already had to fight off animal trouble, wagon trouble, weather trouble, and almost everything else. Now he and his family must tolerate stinging windswept snow blowing right into their faces.

"Keep your wagons to the right as you go!" he instructs out loud. "If the animals can't see well, you'd rather go off the road to the right."

Frederico's point is clear. A tumble off the road to the left would be deadly for sure. Suddenly, Frederico feels shaking under his seat. He doesn't know if it is the road, or the wagon, but shaking is coming from somewhere. He looks around in the dim light to see what it might be.

"Gino!" he cries.

Margherita leaps into the back and reveals a convulsing Ambrogino.

"He's having a seizure, Rico!"

"Stop!" Frederico calls out. "Allesandra!"

"I'll block the wheels!" Bartolomeo reacts immediately.

Allesandra already has the lantern from the middle wagon and is in the back of Gino's with her mother.

"Give him some space!" Margherita cries as Allesandra draws the light near.

"Easy, my baby... easy. It's alright, sweet honey," Margherita moans as she caresses Ambrogino's head. He is uncontrollable and has pushed all of the straw away from himself, kicking like a newborn colt.

Allesandra moves away heavy objects as she hovers over her brother to protect him from the wind and snow blowing in.

"What does he need?" Frederico asks of his wife.

"Your prayers, Rico... your prayers."

After a few moments, the seizure subsides, and Ambrogino lies motionless and exhausted, his eyes closed and his hands holding onto bits of straw.

"Heavenly Father!" Frederico begs up to the snowy sky, "Give us a chance, please!"

Maria begins to cry, and is quickly held by her sister, Isabetta.

"Rico," Margherita calls to her husband. "We need a camp, and we need it now."

"We have to make it to the top, and we're over halfway there now. There is no way we can stop right here; it's too dangerous. We'll press on as fast as we can."

Feeling helpless now, Margherita gives her husband a look of defeat, lies down, and curls herself around her little boy. Allesandra mirrors that effort on Ambrogino's other side. It is all in Frederico's hands now, good or bad.

"We're going on now and we don't stop until the top! Isabetta, you ride with Antonio. Follow my light, and stay to the right. When we make the turn, stay to the left. Watch my tracks, and call out if you have trouble. Let's go."

With determination for their brother, the able children regroup, prepare the wagons, and push ahead with the charge of finding a suitable camp site as soon as possible. That means taking on this impossible road at an even faster speed than before.

Frederico has his horses on twice their previous pace, and he looks back every few seconds through the snow for the two lights behind him. Inside, he prays that strength be given to his children and also to keep two lights in view.

In all the action, though, Frederico hasn't noticed that the snow is increasing in depth. While it is not snowing any harder, it must have been snowing up here earlier, or perhaps the wind is creating deeper drifts. His eyes are fixed on his own horses' hooves as they kick up snow with every step. Making out the details of the road is almost impossible now, as the light from the lantern doesn't give much definition. But, it is obvious that the hillside is to the right, and the drop-off is to the left. Other than that, it is all the same.

"We're good!" Bartolomeo calls out from the rear.

"What was that?" Frederico calls back.

"Keep going, everything is good!"

"Okay!"

The wind is blowing side to side as well as straight at them, causing snow to whip in all directions, and the dim lights of the lanterns are becoming less effective with every step. Frederico keeps snapping the reins of his team to push them harder. He knows there is much further to go, so he must make good time. Abruptly, the hillside on the right disappears, and the road turns back to the right.

"Thank goodness," Frederico says to himself, as he steers his team around the corner. But to his dismay, within about fifty feet, the road turns back again to the left.

"Quick turns ahead! Stay - in - my - tracks!"

Skyward they go, with the four horses and two mules heaving exhaustive breaths into the snowfall. The steepness of these switches provide no breaks. This abominable road turns back and forth like a march straight into the belly of a monster.

A horrible thought now falls upon Frederico: It might be possible that the family does not make it to the top. The snow is alarmingly high, and is almost at the axles of the wagons. A few more inches or so, and the strain will become too difficult for the animals.

At one point, the turn is so severe, Frederico can look almost straight down and see the light of Bartolomeo's wagon coming up in the other direction.

"Keep going, Father! The mules are slow, but they're strong!" Bartolomeo calls up, as he too can notice his father's change in direction by the sounds above him.

"I'm watching you, Bartolomeo. Keep calling out to me! How about you, Antonio?"

"I'm staying in your tracks, Father. The horses have it figured out."

"Are you warm enough?"

"My feet are like ice, papa."

"Then take your boots off and wrap your feet in two layers of the sheep skins. Then keep rubbing your feet together."

Isabetta takes her father's idea and helps her brother do exactly that while he keeps control of the horses. She then snuggles in tight to him and puts her feet in with his.

Maria is huddled down into Bartolomeo's wagon, much like her sister and mother in the first wagon. All six animals pull and groan their way up in pain and fatigue.

Frederico isn't sure how much further it is to the top, or how many more times the road will turn. He does know that his horses have a limit, and when reached, they will be stopped right there, no matter where that is.

He contemplates abandoning one of the wagons and then hitching three animals on each of the remaining wagons. He shakes off that idea and then envisions dropping one wagon, giving the two mules the lightest, and then hitching all four horses to the other fully loaded wagon. Or perhaps he should put all six animals on one wagon carrying just his family and almost no provisions. These perplexing thoughts of strength, stamina, distance, snow depth, and his animals' well-being consume him.

"We're good!" Bartolomeo shouts out.

This time, his voice is much further away.

"Okay!" Frederico yells back.

This gap is not good, and it is one more thing for Frederico to agonise over. Perhaps, Bartolomeo will perform fine even though he is far behind. Besides, he will have the wagon tracks to follow, and Frederico will wait for him with a warm fire at the top.

Then the road turns back again.

"Thank you," Frederico cries out loud again. "We are getting closer, my dear."

Lying still in her protective hopelessness, Margherita does not respond.

While they indeed are getting closer, Frederico has no idea how long it will be. What he does know is that this journey of salvation is turning into a nightmare. All of the people who said Frederico was crazy for taking his family into these mountains may have been right all along. He wonders now if there was a better route through these mountains. Did he wait too long at Guenny's Inn back in Bellinzona? A thought that rips into Frederico's heart like a dagger is how much easier this trip would have been had they just started one single day earlier. Maybe his selfishness caused him to misunderstand God's word for him and his family. Maybe this planned escape will cost more lives than it will save.

Maybe he is mad after all.

A sudden burst of wind and snow hits Frederico directly in his eyes, and he dodges his head down to protect himself. Blinking to relieve his eyes, he refocuses his vision on the road out in front of the wagon, and in the soft snowy lantern light he notices a short rope dangling over the front of his wagon.

"Ropes," he says to himself. "We should be roped together."

"We're stopping at the next turn!" he shouts to Antonio and Bartolomeo.

Wind and snow whip into Frederico's face with more and more ferocity, and it's difficult just to keep his eyes open. He fears that it must be worse for the animals. Now that he has a plan in mind with the ropes, the next turn seems to take forever. Maybe the thought of tying themselves together has come too late, and what if there is an accident right before he gets them tied up?

With fortune on his side, Frederico reaches the next turn spot, and maneuvers his wagon on the uphill of the turn and stops his team.

"Allesandra," he calls out to the pile of blankets behind him. "Come out and hold the team for me."

She emerges from the coverings, with the light of their lantern now shining out. She is careful no to let any of the snow inside.

"Are we at the top?"

"No, I'm going to tie the wagons together so we are sure to get there."

Antonio is soon up behind, and Frederico is now down on the road to meet him.

"What is it, Father?"

"I am tying the wagons together, son."

"What shall I do?"

"You and your sister can get down deep and cover up!" Frederico finds himself yelling now through the oppressive wind, even though he is only a few feet from his son.

The snow and wind continue to increase as though it were assigned the wicked task of punishing the family. After tying the first two wagons together, Frederico now plods to the back and awaits the arrival of Bartolomeo.

"Keep coming, son! We are waiting for you!"

"We're coming!" comes the return yell.

To his surprise, Bartolomeo's team is much closer than he thought, and the faint light of his son's lantern grows through the storm, as the shapes of the mules and Bartolomeo's figure start to emerge.

"Why are we stopping, Father?"

"Because I want us all to be tied together! This way, if the animals get confused or lose the trail... "

"... they won't go down the mountain," Bartolomeo finishes.

"Right! Hand me the reins."

Guiding the mules up behind Antonio's wagon, he ties them to the back, and completes the unification amidst the swirling snow.

"Son! Why don't you come up to the front and ride with me? Then Maria can huddle down with Antonio and Isabetta."

"But nobody will be riding in the last wagon, Father!"

"The mules won't care, and we can save some lantern oil."

"Good idea, Father."

Having contained the wagons in their new system, the two men now mount the first wagon and begin the ascent again. Behind them, Margherita and Allesandra are covering Ambrogino in their wagon. The second wagon now has Antonio, Isabetta, and Maria all covered and protected under covers. The mules are tied at the rear with only their rider-less wagon behind them.

Freezing winds and blinding snow have enveloped the wagon train, but the Gallinelli's push on. It is now a test of will for Frederico, as he will soon find out precisely how much punishment his family and their animals can take.

Chapter 14

Perspiration glistens on Frederico's forehead as he guides his burdened mule to the pressing room for unloading. Bartolomeo empties the baskets and smiles back at his father, nodding with satisfaction at the yield.

"Do you see what hard work and a good sense of pride and dedication can do, my son?"

"Father, you always seem to have the best crop no matter what the conditions."

"I am only doing what my father taught me, and that is why I teach it to you. Don't you know you can run this farm every bit as well as me?"

"Your attention to detail is greater than anyone's, Father. You can tell by smell which bunches to use, and I cannot."

"That's because most of the time, I am not judging, but rather enjoying."

Frederico hoists up a handful of the plump ripe grapes. Holding them up to his nose, he pulls in the sweet fruity aroma that qualifies his life in this world. As he fills his lungs, he is shocked by a frozen sensation ripping into his body. He pulls the grapes away from his face and sees solid chunks of ice covering the fragile fruit. Snowflakes whiz around his hands and swirl the scene into a blizzard of chaos and confusion.

"Father!" comes a cry. "Father!" Bartolomeo continues.

Frederico looks up to see the snow covered face of his son, and is now aware of the cold and wind himself.

"Were you asleep, Father?"

"I'm awake. I'm fine, son."

"The road has straightened out, and we are going flat now."

"Good! We will find some shelter to make camp."

"But it's hard to see anywhere at all."

"We'll feel for the wind, Bartolomeo. When there is a break, we'll know we've found a sheltered area."

"It feels like the wind is getting worse though."

"Let's go another half-mile or so, then I'll go out on foot."

Softened by the powdery snow, the grinding of the wheels is imperceptible, and the wagons creak straight through the pass. Every step from the horses presents difficulty as the road is now undefined, and the only indication they have to guide them is the narrowness of the road itself. Any false turns, and the horses are met with boulders, fallen logs, or the uncertain footing of slushy creeks that have yet to freeze over.

In what has seemed like an eternity, the steep incline has flattened out, and the frozen family no longer has the fear of a treacherous fall from the alpine road. It is a small consolation, as they are only on the climb up, and have the equally difficult descent to follow, but for now, the worst is over. Shelter for the night is all they need, but Frederico fears that time is running out with the animals. They have used up so much energy to get this far, they might drop at any moment.

"Should we begin looking now, Father?"

"Not yet, son. We are too exposed."

"But it might continue on this way for miles. Everybody is starving and freezing."

"Bartolomeo, if we make a fire, and the wind and snow put it out, what good is it? Everyone has eaten today, and will certainly live to see tomorrow."

"What about the horses though? They're barely able to walk."

"If we stop in an exposed area, they will be the ones to suffer most. This flat travelling right now is a welcomed break for them after what they've endured. When they rest, they will need to rest out of this wind."

"Do you think there is a farm up here somewhere?"

"I don't know if we will find a whole village or a single house, or anything at all for the next few miles. But if the horses can keep pressing on, then we should too."

"The cold is getting unbearable, Father."

Frederico does not want to verbalise his concerns, nor does he want to check on his youngest son with any frequency. But perhaps in the quiet of the night, and with the time that has gone by, Ambrogino's condition has improved.

"Why don't you check on Gino?"

Bartolomeo consents, and moves back into the wagon where his mother and sister are huddled around the young boy. He carefully lifts up the coverings so as not to disturb them.

"How is Gino doing?"

"He won't eat, and he can't even stay awake," Margherita delivers with the defeated sentiment of a doctor. "We are in the middle of nowhere, with no way to care for him, and we have too far to go to save him."

Absorbing the reality of what his mother is telling him, Bartolomeo fights these thoughts in his mind, and calls to his little brother.

"Gino! Can you hear me?"

Ambrogino remains motionless against the sound of his big brother's voice.

"We're going to make it, Gino! Can you hear me? We will find shelter for a fire soon, and we'll roast those stupid hens. Okay?" Bartolomeo reaches for his brother's shoulder to comfort him.

Margherita looks up to her grown son with love and smiles at his passionate concern. He can see in her eyes that his mother has already cried, and has now resigned herself to the fact that only a true miracle will save Ambrogino now.

"He's going to make it, Mother. You will see," Bartolomeo asserts with great conviction.

"Of course he will, Meo," Margherita agrees, using her

favourite pet name for her oldest son.

Bartolomeo searches for something else to say that will make great sense, or make his mother feel better, but he would rather scream at the top of his lungs in anger. If he's going to do any good for his brother, he will help his father find shelter for everyone, right now. So he slips away and creeps back up to his post at the front of the wagon.

"Father…"

"I know!"

"You know what?"

"I heard you. I heard everything!" Frederico fires back at his son.

"Mother doesn't think that…"

"I said I know! Didn't you hear me?" Frederico now thrashes at the reins to punish the horses' slow pace.

The exhausted animals can barely muster a lumber in the deepening snow.

"Let's go, you loathsome animals! Get moving, or we'll be eating you all for dinner!" Frederico flogs the beasts even harder as the horses fight the weather, their own fatigue, and now their master.

"Easy, Father. They can't take anymore."

"Don't you give up on me now, son! I need you to stay alert."

"I am alert, Father!" Bartolomeo fires back through his welling tears. "Everything is perfectly clear to me!"

"Then take the reins. I'm going out on foot to find some shelter."

Frederico leaps from the wagon in disgust that his horses can't move any faster.

Bartolomeo obliges while Frederico trudges back to grab the lantern from the second wagon. He powers through the snow with newfound strength. He passes the first cart, moves further up the road, and abruptly turns to his right. Bartolomeo stops the caravan and watches the dancing lantern move around in the darkness. Further and further it goes away from the road and into the night.

Bartolomeo is losing its sight now in the distance, but he is reasonably sure it has stopped. He wonders if his father could have found something.

"Bartolomeo!" Frederico's voice cries out from the distance. "Do you see that?"

"See what?"

"There is a light up ahead!"

"I can only see your light, Father!"

"There's a light in this direction! I can see it!"

Bartolomeo sees his father's lantern begin moving once again as it grows smaller and dimmer.

"Do you want me to come with you?" Bartolomeo offers as loud as he can.

There is no response. Frederico's light has now disappeared. Unsure of what to do now, Bartolomeo wonders if he should follow his father and make certain he is alright, or stay with his wagons since he is now the oldest man there should anything happen.

Frustrated and confused, he sits where he is, and decides to stay. If his father sees a lantern or a fire, he will be back to get the rest of them for certain, and he would have asked Bartolomeo to come along with him in the first place if he wanted him to.

"Mother, Father has seen a house, or something up ahead. We might be saved."

She does not reply.

Far away from the wagons, Frederico kicks through the snow with vigour toward the light up ahead. Keeping his head low, he looks up every third or fourth step, as the wind continues to blow sideways across his face.

"Dear God," he prays out loud to the snow. "I have been Your humble servant all of my life, and I have never asked You for anything. I have only paid You homage at every opportunity. If there is ever a family deserving of Your sympathy, please, please, give me the strength now to reach this house and to save them. I beg of You, Lord. Please."

As he presses forward, he now sees the light higher above him, as though suspended in the air. He wipes his eyes and continues on while holding his lantern now beside him so as not to obscure his view.

He sees it now, and it is not a house at all, but a stone formation. Obscured in the swirling snow and darkness, he sees a stone wall up about twenty feet high, and the light is coming up high from behind it.

"Another castle," Frederico says to himself. "Of course. How else could anyone survive up in this area?"

But he can't find a door, so he yells up at the formidable castle wall, "Hello! Is anybody there?"

Frantic, he can't make out which direction he should go to find a way in, so he calls out again, "I need help, please! Anybody!"

"I can help you," a gentle voice falls upon Frederico's ear.

Whipping his lantern around to his left, he sees a dark figure standing alone.

"Oh, dear God, thank you! My family is back at the road, and my son is very sick, and we desperately need shelter for the night."

"We will be more than happy to take your son inside and care for him."

"Thank you, my man, thank you so much. We have plenty of money to pay you." Frederico cries as he maneuvers his lantern to get a better look at the figure.

"No pay will be necessary, sir. We will cure your boy, no matter what ailment he has."

"Are you a doctor?"

"Oh, I am not, but we have doctors here."

"Fantastic, thank you. Let me go and get him right away!"

"That is a good idea, since time is not on your side in this weather."

"You're right about that! I can't believe we even made it this far. I'll be right back with everyone!" Frederico announces with overpowering joy as he turns back in the direction of his footprints.

"Wait! We only want the boy, and no-one else."

"What? I have my whole family, and we are freezing to death!"

"The rest of your family should be capable enough to reach safety."

"What are you saying? That is heartless of you, man! How can you abandon the rest of us like this?"

"We are not abandoning you at all, my friend. We will be able to cure your son, and I will guide you to safety further down this road. Isn't that what you wish for?"

Bewildered, Frederico tries to understand what he is hearing.

"So, you have another place for us to stay? And how long will I have to wait for you to cure my son?"

"You don't understand. The boy will stay with us, permanently, and you and your family will have to leave."

"What? We aren't just going to leave him here! What kind of people are you? What kind of fool do you take me for? And how dare you take advantage of us while we are in such distress!"

"It is quite the opposite, my good man, as we are offering to save your son's life. Isn't that what you want?"

"Why? I don't understand why," Frederico begs.

"You see, we need children up here. Most of us are very old, and we need the young so we can carry on for the future, as we are unable to produce children of our own. Do not be afraid though, I can direct your family to safety for the night, and we will make your son a part of our family. He will go on living with us up here, protected and isolated, and he will flourish."

Falling to his knees in the snow, Frederico strains to make sense of his predicament. "Why is this happening to me, Lord? Why?" he weeps, "I can't give up my Gino."

"Sir," the shadowy man tenders some comfort. "If he stays with you, you will all suffer."

Frederico is now sobbing like a child himself. He has brought his family into this horrible blizzard, at the expense of his most beloved child's health, and now the only way to save him is to gamble by leaving him here forever. It is an evil paradox that consumes every ounce of Frederico.

"Can't one of us stay as well?"

"I'm afraid that's not possible."

"What are you people… some sort of monks or something?"

"You might say that. But the overriding point is that your son will become a king with us. You have nothing to fear for him. He will be hailed and loved more than you could ever imagine. This is a glorious day for him, and you should not let your feelings take priority over the sensible thing to do."

Having his life's energy sucked out of him, Frederico sets the lantern down in the trampled snow. He thrusts both hands into his hair, pulls back on the hood that is covering him, and releases his full face up to the sky to feel the full brunt of the wind and the snow. As if reaching the limit of human suffering, the snow and wind have subsided.

"You will make him a king, you say?"

"Truly."

"And we are not allowed to stay even one night to be with him, or to stave off the cold?"

"After you bring your son here, you will need to continue on your road for about two more miles. There you will feel the road tighten as enormous boulders encroach upon you, leaving only enough room for a single wagon to pass. Before you go through, you will park your wagons and bring whatever provisions you have up the hill to your left. There you will find shelter in a large cave with enough room for your family and your animals. You should find plenty of firewood stacked inside."

Straining to remember these details, Frederico replies, "And then I shall return to here in the daylight to see that my boy is well."

"I am sorry, but that is not possible. Should you return here, we will not recognise you or any other member of your family, so we will not let you in. I apologise for these conditions, but that is the only way for us."

"The only way… "

"Yes."

"… and he will be a king with you."

"It will be done."

Absorbed in his own grief, Frederico stops fighting. He stands up, picks up his lantern and heads back to the road. Retracing his footsteps, Ambrogino's fate weighs on him like a thousand pounds. As he reappears from the night, and is now near the caravan, he is greeted by a bounding Bartolomeo.

"What did you find, Father? Is it a farm?"

Frederico does not even look up at his son, and keeps trudging forward.

"It is a castle of monks, and they can cure Gino," he sighs.

"That's fantastic, Father! You did it!"

Now Frederico looks up into his son's eyes to see the unbridled joy on his face.

"It is not that simple, my son."

"What do you mean?"

Frederico does not say anymore, but just keeps moving toward the wagon where his wife and youngest are lying. Upon reaching them, Bartolomeo announces the news with unbridled joy.

"Father has found a castle with doctors!"

Margherita is sitting up with all of her children around. They are covered in blankets, and there is a single lantern in the middle showing Ambrogino's quiet face.

Turning to her husband, she asks, "Is that true, Rico?"

"I met a man," he begins, and pauses. "He lives with others in a castle off in the distance," he continues with his head down.

"Then let us go there right now!"

Frederico looks Margherita straight in the eye, "They only want Gino."

"What?"

"He says they can cure him, but none of the rest of us are allowed."

Margherita shakes her head in disbelief, "So we are not allowed inside as they care for him?"

"No, we have to leave him there with them… forever." Frederico chokes.

"Leave him? Leave him?"

"But they will cure him, and he will be better, my love!"

"I'm not leaving him!" she announces.

"But Rita, we have no choice! Look around. What more can we do for him now?" Frederico explains, feeling that time is running out.

With her heart torn from her chest, Margherita picks up her son's limp body and begins to sob uncontrollably. She cradles him tight in a blanket and rocks him back and forth like an infant as the tears flow from her eyes. The other children too begin to weep for their brother.

"They will love him, and care for him, and they said they would make him their king."

"But why must they keep him, Rico?" Margherita pushes through her tears.

"He said that most of them are older, and they need young ones… that is how they are able to continue."

"But how do we continue?" she sobs.

"Look at him, Rita. He won't live this way! This is his only chance! Don't you see?"

Her husband's pleas fall on top of Margherita like the massive mountains that surround her, and the thought of leaving her child is more than she can bear. She continues to rock Ambrogino back and forth, nuzzling her face into his with kisses upon kisses. Allesandra strokes his hair over and over, while Isabetta and Maria, hold onto eachother, crying without end.

Keeping his tears inside, Bartolomeo is standing by his father, as he knows it would be easy to make him out to be the one at fault. He knows his father is torn to shreds inside just like everyone else.

"Let me take him now, Rita," Frederico pleads as he holds his hands out to her. "I swear to you that I will come back for him someday. I swear to God I will, my love."

Margherita nods as her sobbing continues, and she takes Ambrogino and leans him toward each of the children for a kiss goodbye. First, Allesandra, and then Isabetta and Maria take their turn to show their love and affection for their baby brother. Antonio sits in the back with his knees pulled up to his chin.

"Antonio," Margherita insists. "Come and say goodbye to your brother."

Shaking his sunken head in defiance, he feels that maybe if he doesn't see Ambrogino leave, then it won't really happen, or maybe he doesn't ever want to remember his brother in this condition. Either way, he cannot bring himself to this moment and say goodbye.

Margherita accepts the finality, and hands Ambrogino over to her husband as Allesandra wraps her arms around her mother and pulls her in tight. The two women's tears are muffled into their heavy woolen coats. Frederico covers up his son from the cold and turns toward Bartolomeo.

"When I get back, we will continue for about two miles to a cave for safety."

Bartolomeo takes a lantern and walks alongside of his father as they turn away from the wagon and back up the path toward the castle.

Margherita can't bear to watch, and holds on to any of the children she can grab. They comfort each other, and wait for the empty-handed return of their father and older brother.

Over their heads, the clouds begin to break apart, and a few stars appear in the sky; the family has been granted a small moment of peace at the end of the most dreadful experience they could ever imagine.

Margherita stares out of the wagon to see the night sky. She no longer feels the hunger she has carried all day. The grueling exhaustion of this journey has been replaced with a cold numbness that finds her drifting away from her own body. Up to this point, she has tried to be a statue of strength for her family, but she now has the desire to climb to the top of one of the peaks and scream directly to God Himself. If it weren't for the comforting arms of her children, perhaps she would.

Time now seems irrelevant, as neither Frederico nor Bartolomeo have reappeared. The only cogent thought that comes into Margherita's mind is that perhaps her husband has somehow bargained his way into the castle for the whole family. He has the skill and determination for such a thing, and maybe he will come back with the news that she will see her son again, and everything will be fine.

Up in the sky, the clouds separate into definable shapes, and the moon can be seen peeking over the top of a mountain beside them. It is waxing half full, and delivers enough light to help make out the surroundings.

Margherita stares out at the silhouettes of the peaks above her, but feels that she might as well be at the bottom of the ocean, with the whole world on top of her and far out of reach. As the moon has made progress skyward, Margherita has moved ever more inward.

"Here they come," says Allesandra.

Frederico and Bartolomeo emerge alone and make their way up to the wagon train. Without discussion, they proceed to inspect the horses and the carts, to make sure that everything is in place. Only sniffles and moans pierce the alpine air, as the family moves out again through the snow, and beneath a bit of moonlight.

"So we need to go about two miles?" asks Bartolomeo.

"It would seem," Frederico replies.

Travelling now at the mercy of his instructions, Frederico has no more desire of adventure, or promise. Leaving his son behind has torn him in two, and he resigns to thoughts of how he has let his family down in the worst way a father could.

In the length of about two miles, precisely as Frederico had been told, the road does narrow, and twists between two large boulders. Frederico stops his wagon and remembers the advice.

"Up to the left, there is a cave."

"I'll go," Bartolomeo offers as he reaches for the lantern and hops down to inspect the mountainside.

Sure enough, up on the hillside, he finds a cave with a wide opening. Inside, the floor is covered in soft brown sand – evidence that this cave has been used many times over the years. A fire pit is visible toward the back, and Bartolomeo moves his lantern all around to make sure no animal has made their home here. He finds no creatures, but finds a substantial pile of logs available to burn, as if this place were created just for them. He leaves the lantern on a large rock as a guide for everyone else, and runs back down to the group.

"It's perfect!"

"Let's carry up all of our food, and bring the hens," Frederico directs in a subdued tone.

Each family member is given something of importance to carry up. Antonio has as many blankets as he can carry, while Isabetta carries two crates of food. Maria brings three of the heavy animal hides for sleeping, and Allesandra takes her mother.

Bartolomeo brings the remaining apples up to the horses, when Frederico notices. "Let's bring their feed up to the cave and untie them. Let them come and go as they please."

Bartolomeo wonders what kind of arrangement that is to let the horses roam free, but at this point, he is too tired to care, and begins to untie every horse. When he finishes, he brings the apples up to the cave.

Within a few trips, the Gallinellis have a great deal of their provisions taken from the wagons, and they find comfortable places to sleep. Bartolomeo starts a roaring fire, and the horses have followed the family, feasting on the plentiful apples and straw.

The cave has proven to be more than suitable for the family's needs. Even the ceiling seems to be made for a fire, as it climbs higher and higher above the pit area. One by one, the children break out their food and share it with each other.

Frederico brings over the three remaining hens, and with them his hatchet.

"We've got an egg," he offers to the family upon noticing the bottom of the crate.

"Give it to me," Allesandra demands, lessening her mother's workload. "I will boil it." Placing the egg into her dress pocket, she pulls out one of the cooking pots to gather snow.

In no time, she has the pot up against the fire, melting the snow on its way to a boil. Frederico holds the three hens in the crate, and has hesitated to take them out.

"What is it, Father?" Antonio asks. "Aren't we going to cook the hens?"

Frederico stares at the birds again, and studies their feathers, their beaks, and their eyes. He sees the alertness in them and understands their single-minded existence. In a new light, he has a feeling of guilt about preparing them for slaughter.

"Can we make do without the hens tonight, Antonio?"

"Oh Father, I have been drooling over those hens for the whole night. I'm tired of bread and cheese and apples."

Frederico looks into his son's eyes and begins to feel for how little his family has had to eat in the last two days.

"Of course. Of course we can have them; you must be starving," he says as he rests his hand gently on Antonio's shoulder.

"I'll slaughter and clean them, Father," Allesandra steps in, and without a word from Frederico, she takes the crate, the hatchet, and one of the lanterns. She proceeds to the side of the cave, and after obtaining some more utensils and another cooking pot, she begins the preparation.

Soon, she is joined by Isabetta and Maria. The girls have followed their sister's lead to prepare the meal for the family so their mother would not have to do a thing. It is the first family meal to be prepared without any participation from Margherita.

As they have been taught, no part of the hens will be wasted. While the meat is cooking, the feathers are stuffed into a pouch for future use.

The roasted chicken meat is a dining treasure for the family. Although intended as a pleasant feast, this meal has turned into nothing more than a practicality of nourishment. It has brought life back into the frozen Gallinellis, and with the fire roaring, they have warmed themselves up with no time to spare.

Frederico settles in next to his silent wife. "You need to eat something, Rita."

She pulls her blanket and rolls onto her side with her back against the fire. Maria has made a bed for them both and lies down beside her mother, who is yet to say a word since her last goodbyes to Ambrogino.

"Maria, you stay here with your mother, and I will keep the fire going," Frederico kisses his daughter on her forehead.

Finding Bartolomeo sawing pieces from the logs, Frederico takes the saw from his hand. "Get some sleep, son. I'll tend to the fire."

"I don't mind, Father."

"You have been through enough tonight. Go and comfort Antonio. I'm not going to sleep much anyway."

Bartolomeo approaches his father, "We had no choice, Father."

Frederico's eyes now glass over, with the dancing fire reflecting in them. He stares at his strong son, who steps into his father and embraces him with all his strength.

"Thank you," Frederico replies, as the two separate.

Watching each family member settling down for the night, Frederico continues to add to the wood pile gathered next to the fire. While a modest fire would do most nights, he builds it up much higher, throwing an overabundance of heat. Nearby, he keeps a few weapons in case of a visit from curious wolves. He thinks to himself that he would relish such an attack, as a bloody battle would be a welcome release for his anger and pain.

After everyone seems to have fallen asleep, Frederico stops to sit. Rousing orange flames climb high, as sparks fly to the top of the cave and bounce sideways against the charred ceiling.

Occasionally, a bright ember will fall back down to the floor like a silent shooting star from the night sky. Frederico watches one of these land at his feet as he sits with his arms around his knees. He fixates on the tiny coal glowing brightly on the sandy ground. Its glow gets smaller and smaller, until it finally goes out.

Chapter 15

Five Years Later

The unmistakable melody of a rock thrush calls outside of Margherita's window as she awakens to a beautiful summer morning. This is the day Isabetta and her new husband are coming to see them. It will mark the first time her middle daughter will be home to Sarnen since her wedding over a month ago.

"Good morning, Mother," says Maria as she walks past the room.

Margherita replies with her warm smile and makes her way out of bed, wrapping herself in her robe.

"Where is Father?" she asks Maria who is now busy cleaning in the fireplace.

"He and Antonio have been out all morning. They said something about picking some flowers."

"That would be nice for today," Margherita responds, and heads outside.

Having finished her morning chores, Maria decides to take one of the horses for a ride before her father returns. Right as she is ready to leave, her mother spots her.

"Where are you going, Maria?"

"I am just giving Rocco some exercise. I'll be right back, I promise."

"Don't go down to the pond by yourself."

"Mother, I'm almost twenty-years-old. I think I can manage." Maria kicks the horse into a run down the road until they both disappear in a cloud of dust.

Margherita knows to the month the age of her youngest daughter. Nonetheless, she can't help but continue offering advice to her children, even when it is not needed. Her concern shifts toward the preparation of the household for Isabetta's arrival, so she goes back inside to get ready herself.

"Fish for sale!" Frederico's familiar voice rings out from outside the window.

While stroking her long brown hair, Margherita walks back to the door to see what the announcement is about.

"Come and see the expert fisherman!" Frederico frolics as he produces Antonio with a string of large fish.

"Well done, Antonio!" Margherita beams. "Did you let your father catch any?"

"No, Mother. He tried, but he has lost his skills over the years."

"Well, let me clean them for you," Margherita offers, and reaches toward her son.

"It's all right, I'll do it... even if they are the biggest ones ever caught!"

"You have all of the skill, Antonio," Frederico laughs. "I'm a useless old man now."

Antonio smiles through the sparseness of his young beard, and turns away from his father, into the house. The two have grown very close over the years, as Antonio has worked very hard to gather his father's knowledge of farming, animal care, and life in general.

"We'll be feasting today, that's for sure, Mother," he says.

"That's wonderful," agrees Margherita, now preparing bread dough at the table. "Without those fish, I thought we were going to have to slaughter Agnola."

Antonio stops what he is doing. "You're not serious, are you, Mother?"

"Well, I never have been attached to that hen. Lord knows, it's a miracle she's lived for five years since coming off that mountain. The day she stopped laying eggs, I was ready to give her the chop."

Antonio is surprised by his mother's confession. It was an unspoken agreement that everyone in the family was seeing to it that Agnola would be kept from slaughter. For as long as she lived, it was a way of remembering that Father had yet to make good on his promise to find Ambrogino.

"What are you saying, then?" he asks.

"I'm not saying anything."

"So you want to serve up Agnola so that Father knows the time has come to go back to the castle?"

"If that's what you think, then that is your opinion," she replies.

Antonio returns his attention to his fish. He makes fast work of the large graylings, and skillfully wraps the meat in paper, setting them aside for his mother. He places the heads and entrails into a small bucket and brings them out to the barn for the hog. Pondering his mother's words, he finds his father over at the anvil, preparing to work on some horseshoes.

"How do those fish look, son?"

"Fabulous, Father. They'll be much better eating than what we used to get out of Lake Como."

"That's because we weren't great fishermen back then. You and your brothers hated it, and thought it was easier to let me go by myself. There were big fish in that lake, but we needed a boat to get them."

"Sometimes I wonder if this farm here is better or worse than the one we left."

Looking up to make eye contact with his son, Frederico responds, "There is nothing here that compares better to the vine-yards we had."

"I know, I know – fifty years it took to cultivate those vines. You've told us many times."

"Then why do you keep asking?"

"I sometimes worry about how Bernardo is doing back on the old farm. Do you think he is still producing wine?"

"If you must know, I expect he was taken by the plague, like everyone else. The vines on that land have grown wild and useless, and all of the animals have either died or run off. I have prayed many times for Bernardo's soul, and the soul of all of my friends we left behind. I am grateful that we have been spared, and my only thoughts are about tomorrow, not yesterday. There, does that satisfy your curiosity about what I think?"

"Not completely," Antonio continues. "I also wonder about a promise that was made to Mother up on the mountain."

Frederico holds his hammer with both hands and stares down at it. He has given many excuses over the years why he hasn't gone back to look for his son.

"So now I have to answer to you directly in this fashion. Is that what it has come down to? Are you the man now, Antonio, who will challenge me on behalf of your mother?"

"No, Father. I don't wish any confrontation at all. I was just determining if you might want to go with me when I make the trip this summer, that's all."

Frederico is caught off guard as his son coolly hangs the bucket on the wall and leaves his father alone.

"You wouldn't have any idea where to look!"

Antonio looks back, "Then I'll get Bartolomeo to go with me."

"Hah! It will take you longer to find him than it will to find that castle!" Frederico laughs.

"Maybe so, but at least I'll try. He is my brother."

Frederico ends the conversation and bangs away at the heated shoe in front of him. Antonio takes a deep breath on his return trip to the house, nervous about having taken on his father. Margherita is waiting at the door, having heard most of the short argument. She gives Antonio a soft embrace of thanks as he enters the house.

"Do you need some more help, Mother?"

"How about picking some fresh flowers to liven things up a bit."

"Oh, that's right. We were going to get some on our trip to the river. I'm very sorry Mother, I'll go right now."

"There's plenty of time, Antonio, why don't you head down to the pond? Your sister took Rocco there a little while ago, maybe she can help you."

"Okay, Mother," Antonio gives his mother a big kiss on the cheek.

Margherita returns to her bread making, feeling confident her son has broken the ice that her husband has kept over the subject for too long. She arranges the burning logs in the oven with the precision of a sculptor, creating the even heat necessary to bake her loaves to perfection. Within a few minutes, Frederico returns to the house.

"Why would your son want to go and intrude on a king?" Frederico asks, without looking in Margherita's direction.

"Maybe because he loves him," she returns with ease.

"So he is willing to risk his life to traipse around for days in the middle of nowhere on the top of some plague-infested mountain, just to find out that everything is as I say it is, and then come home?"

"Yes... " she smiles. "I think that about explains it."

Frederico shakes his head. "Well he'll do it without me. There is too much work to be done around here."

Margherita stops and walks over to the door to see her husband fetch a hoe and begin the least desirable chore of the farm – weeding the garden. She watches him attack the weeds with vigour while stopping to hand pick certain ones so as to not damage the young vegetable sprouts. She sees a very angry and lonely man, and she does not want to leave him to his own thoughts, so she covers her bread loaves and goes out to join him.

Frederico looks up to see his armed wife coming toward him. Without a word, she slips into the garden, and begins the same work as her husband. The two toil in silence for a good length of time, and when Frederico finishes his row first, he goes to get a bucket of water for the both of them. Placing the water bucket on the ground, he hands her one of two cups he has just dunked.

"Thank you," he whispers to her.

"Why, I wouldn't have it any other way," Margherita wipes her brow and lifts up her cup in a toast to both of them.

"Rita, he's a king up there, you know – a king."

"I know, my love," she softy replies, resting her hand on his chest. "I know."

The two enjoy their quiet moment together, and Margherita has decided her husband should not be tortured any more today, so she changes the subject.

"Isabetta will be here soon."

"Yes, I've been anticipating this moment for several days now."

He knows full well that her marriage ceremony could have been much better had Isabetta been able to involve her own parents more, but her fiancé's family was very overbearing and obtrusive. So instead of creating tension, Frederico let his loving daughter be, and allowed the wedding to happen any way the Lippacci family would see fit.

"I'm sure she's looking forward to seeing you as well."

The casual conversation is broken by the sound of hooves coming up the road.

Antonio and Maria appear riding side-by-side up the road to the farm. The brother and sister dismount, with Antonio carrying a large fistful of bright purple bell-flowers, and Maria leading the horse to the water trough.

"Here are your favourites, Mother," says Antonio.

"You are making my day brighter and brighter," she smiles, and places a kiss onto his cheek. "I'll put these in water, and you can see if Father needs any help."

Antonio dusts himself off, and makes his way to the garden where he finds his father relaxing on a bench.

"That was nice of you to get flowers for your mother. I remember that being our job earlier this morning."

"It's quite alright," Antonio shrugs. "I want Mother to have an easy day so she can enjoy herself with Isabetta."

"Why don't you bring some more wood in for her? There is a lot to be cooked today."

Frederico has everything under control, so he does what he prefers in such moments, and retrieves the pruning shears. The apple trees have all been pruned properly in the fall, but now he can see which branches are bearing no leaves or fruit. Even though it has little value to the crop's success, he prunes them anyway – as if somebody was giving an award for the best looking trees.

It's amazing the extent to which Frederico can prune a single tree, and yet leave it looking full and fruitful as if not having been touched. Each snip requires careful consideration of future bud growth and sunlight availability. Hours pass, and the ground beneath a half-dozen trees has become littered with twigs and leaves. This contemplative time alone provides a blissful escape for a troubled man.

"I think you missed a branch, Father."

Without even turning around, Frederico smiles and calls out, "Isabetta!"

She runs up and jumps into his arms as he turns to receive her. Frederico holds on to his slender daughter, keeping her feet off the ground, and spinning her in a circle. Isabetta makes no effort to leave the embrace, and clings to her father like a four-year-old child.

"It's so nice to see you," Frederico exhales as he lowers her down to the ground, pecking her cheeks with kisses.

"Oh Father, I have missed you and Mother very much."

"I regret not being more involved with your new husband and his family, my sweet dear."

"There is nothing to regret, Father. Marco has been very good to me, and he loves me so," she delights, and hangs on to her father's whole arm, leaning against him as they walk along the trees.

"As long as you are being cared for, then that makes me happy."

Isabetta pulls her father closer and reaches up to give him a big kiss on his cheek.

"Thank you Father. Marco is very anxious to speak with you today. He is considering planting a vineyard on his farm."

"Oh, that's a great idea," says Frederico, rolling his eyes.

"You are not impressed."

"I expect he wants me to teach him everything there is to know."

"No, Father," she replies, holding his hand. "He has very modest plans, and only wishes to grow enough for us alone. His horses are always his first interest, and that is how he will make our living."

"Well, I can teach him how to grow twenty high yielding vines."

"Plant forty!"

Frederico smiles in amusement that his quick-witted daughter has not lost her childhood memories.

"You don't need me at all," Frederico warms, and swings Isabetta's hand up and down as they walk.

"It may not seem that way, Father, but I'll always need you more than you know," she looks into his eyes.

Frederico returns a curious look, and the two of them continue on their walk up to the main house. By now, many family members are busy, and Isabetta spies her husband Marco showing Antonio a new trick with his horse. The pleasant scene shows Marco's patience and generosity, and gives great pleasure to Frederico.

Margherita appears from the doorway, eagerly awaiting the return of the two from the orchard.

"Look who I found," Frederico calls out to her.

"It looks more like she found you!" Margherita responds with hands clasped. "Dinner will be ready soon."

"Good, I'm starving," Antonio quips from a short distance away.

"Let me help you, Mother!" says Isabetta, and leaves her father for a straight run to the house.

"You are the guest today, dear. You don't need to help me."

Even so, the two women cheerfully disappear into the house and Frederico decides to make his move over to Marco

"I'll help you finish that in a minute, Antonio," Marco states as he walks toward the oncoming Frederico. "Thank you for having us today, Mr. Gallinelli," he offers in respect.

"My daughter is always welcome in my home," Frederico replies, and reaches out to shake Marco's extended hand.

"Then I look forward to spending those times."

Marco is a fit and strong man, built similarly to Frederico, but a bit taller and has a much lighter complexion. Frederico can see a bit of himself in this man, especially the youthful exuberance and self-confidence.

"You have built a remarkable farm here, Mr. Gallinelli."

"Please don't patronise me, Marco. You know very well that we walked into this place, and have made do as we could. I'm certain your farm is twice as productive."

"More productive, perhaps, but it lacks the touch of efficiency you seem to be able to muster with such ease."

"Well, I am glad to have made an impression here, no matter how small."

"It is your daughter who has taught me all about your clever and indispensable skills."

"She is a bright girl who studies everything. You are a lucky man, Marco."

"Thank you, sir."

Satisfied with the outcome of the first real conversation they have had, the two then head inside to join the activity. Once in the house, they see special place-settings with Antonio's flowers at the center. Wine and cheese are already in place, and the room is brimming with the aroma of baking fish, fresh bread, and stewed vegetables.

"It smells delicious, Rita. We should have Isabetta home more often," Frederico beams.

"That's fine with me," she delights.

"Me, too," Antonio chimes in.

Soon, everyone has settled into their places, and Margherita has led the family in thanking the Lord for not only this meal, but the loved ones around. Each family member enjoys a variety of food including their own personal favourites.

Especially thrilled is Antonio, who relishes the fresh strawberries which have been ripe for picking for about a week now. They are his true weakness, and he could eat three pounds in one sitting.

The conversation is light and merry, as Isabetta boasts to her younger sister about her new home and horse farm. In between, compliments flow towards Margherita for such wonderful food that goes down with great satisfaction for everyone. Regularly commenting is Frederico, pointing out to Marco how important it is to respect the labour of one's wife, even after twenty-five years.

"You flatter me too much. It's only a simple meal. Marco, why don't you tell us about any plans you have for the rest of the summer?"

"Well, there is a fair in Bern toward the fall where we bring our strongest horses for competition."

"Competition? That sounds exciting. Do you often win?"

"No, not very often," he laughs. "But it gives me a chance to speak with other horsemen, and share ideas about successful training techniques."

"He also has stallions that he trains for the royal army, Mother," Isabetta gushes.

"No more than two at a time," Marco downplays his bride's enthusiasm. "They send me the young ones so I can teach them to ride steady for the archers."

"That sounds quite difficult," Margherita continues. "It's amazing you would have any time left at all for a family."

Laughing, Marco gives in, "It would seem that way, but we've got the training down quite well at this point. I expect to be spending a great deal of time with your daughter this summer, if that is what you are getting at."

Margherita smiles, "It's not my place to decide your actions in any way, Marco."

"That's good, because I do have some other plans for this summer... I am going to finally meet my other brother-in-law, Gino."

Chapter 16

Like a tree falling with full force, the conversation stops with a crash. Marco knew what he said, and was prepared for it. No-one else even dared to glance over at Frederico, but the desire to see his expression was almost unbearable. Margherita quickly diffuses the action.

"Well, I don't see any reason why… "

"No, no... that's all right," Frederico interrupts. "He can speak freely here."

Marco remains silent.

"So you have this desire, right Marco?"

"Yes, I do."

"Good, then you want to be sure for your own personal satisfaction that this boy has indeed become a king?"

"So I am told."

"So you are told? So you are told. So what else have you been told?"

Isabetta shrinks in her chair.

"Only bits and pieces, sir, that is why I would prefer to hear the true story from you."

"So it's a story now?"

"It is whatever you wish to call it."

Margherita interjects again, "It's really not necessary that – "

"No, this is very necessary," Frederico interrupts a second time. "Marco here is not satisfied in knowing that his brother-in-law, our son, is living in a castle in the mountains as a king among his people. He is not satisfied to know that he is healthy and strong, and doing God's will with his people. Is that right, Marco?"

Brave, but cautious, Marco measures, "If he has been made king, and not left as a common servant, than we would be received with great honour upon our arrival."

"Or perhaps none of us would be allowed inside, and we would not be received at all," Frederico answers back, prepared for years for these questions.

"I find that very hard to comprehend, sir. I believe he misses you all very much, even to this day."

This conversation stirs up emotions and memories for Margherita, and she pushes away from the table and retreats outside.

"Do you see what you have done now? You have upset your loving mother-in-law with your know-it-all attitude."

"I am so sorry."

"Good, then this conversation is over," Frederico dismisses, and reaches for the wine carafe.

"Then I will apologise to Margherita, and I thank you, sir, for including me on your journey to see Gino this summer."

Slam! The carafe hits the table, causing every dish and plate to rumble in its wake.

"There will be no journey! There will be no calling on Gino with our sad lot! Do you understand?"

Marco remains silent, feeling there is more to come. Frederico stands up out of his chair.

"Why would any man want to seek him out up on that godforsaken mountain? He is the king of his castle, and the rest of us are not welcome! It's that simple! That's all that needs to be said about it."

Marco realises this is his only chance, and doesn't want to let it go. "But he wouldn't even know me," he pleads to Frederico. "I will visit this castle as any man would, and I will seek him out. You don't even need to be in sight, just help me to get there."

Frederico understands the wisdom of Marco's plan, but does not want to give in to anyone's wishes on the subject. With an unwavering stare, he kicks his chair away and leaves to find his wife.

Marco stands, poised to follow him.

"Marco," Isabetta calls for her husband. "Will you keep me company, please?"

"But I'm not sure I got through to him."

"Oh, you did. You most certainly did."

A month has passed since Marco and Isabetta's visit, and Frederico has spent the time cultivating his apple trees and considering his role in this year's summer festival. While he has been gracious in being honoured annually at the celebration, he is growing tired of the attention paid to him for helping the village thwart the great plague. Whether the bonfires were the principle answer or merely coincidence, Frederico has always given credit to the Lord.

Regardless, the festival remains a central event for the village since the savage years, and his new friends all know him as the father of the king. Perhaps there is a way he can skip the main activities and instead present a gift to the townspeople in his place. He looks down at the pruning shears he is holding, and speculates about what gift he could produce. In any event, what he needs to do now is sharpen the noticeably rusty shears.

The sound of an oncoming wagon over the grinding wheel has little effect on Frederico. He has already seen and done everything a man his age could, so a single wagon stopping at his modest farm could only mean somebody looking for something. Must he continue to give and give again?

"Is that you, Father?" a voice calls out from the wagon.

"Who is that?" Frederico emerges from the shadow of the barn and squints through the sun's glare.

"It is your son."

By now, Maria has made her way outside to see what is

going on.

"Bartolomeo!" she shouts and runs into the arms of her older brother.

The two embrace, having not seen each other since Isabetta's wedding. Frederico moves in to get a closer look, and recognises his son, even though he is wearing a full beard.

"Well, look who's here. You look well, my son."

"As do you, Father."

"So what is the special occasion to see you today?" Frederico asks after their quick embrace.

"To see my lovely Mother, of course."

Margherita appears right on cue after being summoned by Maria. She stands out in front of the doorway, looks purse-lipped at Bartolomeo, and places her fists on her hips.

"So you smelled my sweet bread all the way from Lucerne?" she smiles.

Bartolomeo beams with joy, and parades over with his arms wide open. "How have you been, Mother?"

"Oh, a bit lonely from not seeing my oldest son, but I manage to survive."

"Well... if you could get Father to travel a bit... "

"I know, I know," Margherita finishes. "Just come inside and have something to eat."

They retreat into the house, and are quickly followed by Frederico and Maria. Sitting around the sturdy wooden table, they delight in each other's company.

"Where is Antonio?" Bartolomeo asks.

"He has taken Rocco fishing," Maria jumps in to answer.

"Amazing... he's taught Rocco how to fish?"

"You know what I mean, you goose," Maria laughs.

"Of course I do. It's great that he's helping out."

"Seriously, he's done more work since Isabetta's wedding than he'd done in his whole life prior."

Bartolomeo smiles at his sister. "Then that is a good thing for you, right?"

"Sometimes," she smiles.

"So why are you really here, son?" asks Frederico.

"I am here for your help, Father."

"Is that so?" he seems surprised. "Imagine that, Rita. He has come to seeks help from his poor old useless father."

Margherita sneers at her husband's pretense, "I'm sure it must be important then."

"It is, Mother. One of my mares is foaling this week, and she is long overdue. I'm afraid I'm going to lose them both unless I can find someone to help."

"There must be experienced horsemen near you. Plus, you've seen dozens of births yourself."

"Exactly, Father. I have seen many, but this mare is a nervous animal already. Nothing about her pregnancy has been normal, and the only person I trust is you."

"How close is she?"

"She's been leaking milk for days."

"That's normal," Maria interrupts.

"I know, but she hasn't gotten up or eaten in those same three days."

"Oh, that's not normal," she replies.

"So, I want to induce the delivery somehow, the way you did with Forty-seven back in Como, Father."

"I can hardly remember back that far," Frederico shakes his head. "I can't recall doing anything special with that foal's birth.

"Sure you did! You walked that mare around the barn, and talked to her, and she gave birth that night."

"You don't need me, son. You can do all of that yourself. You know more about animals now than I do."

"Nobody knows as much as you do, Father. I thought if you could spare one evening with me, you might have one little bit of wisdom that might make all the difference."

Frederico continues to shake his head, and begins to smile. "You sure do have a way with words," he sighs. "Your mother has taught you well."

"Indeed she has!" Bartolomeo bounds from his chair and kisses his mother on the cheek. "We will have to go now, if we are going to be there tonight."

"Now? We'll never make it in time."

"The roads are excellent, Father, and the weather is divine. With the two stallions out there, we'll arrive in no time at all."

Margherita has already begun preparing a basket of food for her husband and son for the short trip.

"So I am being kidnapped by my own son!"

"Go, Rico, and help out his mare. We can live without you for one night, for goodness sake."

"How will I get back then, Bartolomeo? I suppose you will toss me out with the afterbirth."

Bartolomeo laughs out loud at that one. "I'll take you back home myself," he smiles. "Just get in the cart, would you?"

Frederico throws his hands in the air in jest. He turns to kiss his wife and daughter goodbye, and follows his oldest son outside.

"Please tell Antonio that I am sorry to have missed him," Bartolomeo calls out to his mother as he climbs aboard the wagon.

"I will, dear. I'll be sure to keep him around tomorrow, when you come back."

Margherita then guides the horses out to the road, hands up the food basket, and sends them on their way. "I'll see you tomorrow!"

"Goodbye!" the Gallinelli men yell back and wave in near unison.

Within a few yards, Frederico catches his son's eye and shakes his head as though he were disgusted by being taken away so abruptly. The truth is that he is happy to be needed, for the first time in a while.

"Do you know what this reminds me of?" asks Bartolomeo.

"The time you ran off with that girl who cooked at the church?" Frederico muses.

"No!" Bartolomeo barks, but chuckles at his father's remembrance. "This reminds me of the trips we used to take into Milan when I was a boy."

"Except now you are the driver, and I am the dependant one."

"Is it that different, Father? Aren't we both the same people we used to be?"

"I might be, Bartolomeo, but you are not. You needed me for everything – food, shelter, clothing, and protection. You were in fascination of the whole world, with more questions than I had answers."

Bartolomeo ponders his father's point, "I search for answers every day."

Frederico looks toward his son as the cart bumps along the dry road. "That's good then. That's when you know you've become a man… when you know that you'll never have all the answers."

"So we all simply take what God gives to us, and hope for the best?"

"Yes, but rather than hope, you actually do your best."

"Is that all there is, Father?"

"All there is?" Frederico scoffs at his son's belittling of his wisdom. "That's everything!"

A mile or so passes before either man starts the conversation again. Frederico reaches for the basket of food, and uncovers a mound of strawberries Maria had picked the day before.

"Antonio is going to be angry that his mother gave us the last of the strawberries."

"I'm surprised you're able to pick this late."

"Further up in the mountains you can pick longer. We have some friends up there that we trade with."

"It must feel strange, Father, all these years now without the benefit of your great wine to trade."

Frederico nods, "But now that there is flour back in the marketplace, your mother's bread is as good as gold around here."

"I can't argue with that!"

"So tell me," Frederico changes the subject. "Why did you not request your sister's husband, Marco, to come to the aid of this mare instead of me? He is the great horseman of the family now."

"To tell the truth... he is already there. It was he who told me to get you. He has a high opinion of your knowledge, Father."

"I think your sister talks too much," replies Frederico as he munches on the berries.

Bartolomeo chuckles at the quip, and reaches into the basket for berries of his own. The horses keep up a smooth trot along the ever widening and busy road. On another day, the two might seek out friends or trading partners, but the pace is quick today and they are covering the distance in good time. Sociable hands wave here and there as Bartolomeo shows off his cargo to other farmers along the way.

To their left, the sun sneaks behind the ever-present Mt. Pilatus, and the warm summer heat begins to fade.

"I should prepare a lantern for you," Frederico offers as he looks around behind him.

"It won't be necessary, Father. We are almost there, and these smart stallions would bring us home even if you and I fell asleep."

As if they were listening, Bartolomeo's horses deliver the cart with little direction, and right down the road to their home. At the end of a long meadow, Frederico gets his first glimpse of Bartolomeo's home. It is a small cottage with a large barn sitting naked against fields all around. Although he can't make out any cultivated crops, Frederico does not want to judge his son in the dim light.

Bartolomeo whistles as his cart pulls near the two buildings. Two men appear from the barn. One of them is Marco, and the other is a very short older man that Frederico does not recognise.

"Hooray!" shouts Marco with a big grin. "You did it."

"He did it alright," Frederico responds. "Whether it will have any value remains to be seen."

"How is she doing?" Bartolomeo asks as he steps down and hands the reins over to Marco.

"Tonight, tonight," the older man attempts in what is not his native language.

"Father, this is Max. He is a neighbour who has come by to lend a hand."

"It is my pleasure to meet you, Max."

"Oh, yes, yes," Max delivers in the few words he knows.

Frederico shakes his hand with both of his and notices the extreme coarseness of his skin, almost rock-like. It is rare to find a man with hands tougher than his own.

"Well, let's go and have a look," says Frederico.

All four men enter the barn which is adorned with several well-positioned lanterns. Frederico would ordinarily examine the barn for its construction, but instead is focused solely on the animal lying in the largest stall.

"How long has she been like this?"

"This whole day, and almost all of the last two," Marco replies.

"You've got to get her on her feet, boys."

"She won't move, Father. That's what we've tried to do, she won't budge.

"She won't budge because she's in pain. That foal is all twisted up inside of her. We have to get her on her feet right now."

"She won't do it, no matter how hard we try," Marco adds.

"That's the problem – you are only trying. You have to do it whether she likes it or not! Hitch up those two stallions again and tie this mare to a line at the back of the cart."

"You're not going to just drag her out, Father, are you?"

"A horse doesn't want to be dragged, son. She'll get up on her feet for sure, more mad than she's ever been, but she'll get up."

Marco and Bartolomeo stare at each other for a moment.

"Are you two going to stand there, or are we going to do this?"

The young men jump at the orders, and within no time, the mare is tied to the cart which is out in the yard behind the stallions.

"Bartolomeo, you guide those stallions forward slow and steady. And don't stop until I tell you."

"Yes, Father. Just give me the word to go."

"Okay. Now, Marco, you lead her head in the right direction to follow the cart, and Max and I will make loud noises behind her to get her as mad as possible."

"Do you understand, Max?" Frederico asks, and waits for a response.

Max stares back and makes a motion to the front of the barn. Frederico is unconvinced that he has caught on, so he goes to the wall to retrieve a hammer and a metal bucket. He then offers the two objects to Max, and points to himself first and then back to Max.

"You and me, bang, bang, bang."

"Ah, much noise," Max nods his head in agreement.

"Excellent. Are you ready, Bartolomeo?"

"Ready!"

"Then we go on the count of three," Frederico calls out to everyone. "One… two… three!"

Max and Frederico slam on the buckets and yell as loudly as they can at the startled mare. She is pulled forward toward the stall door, groaning and twisting on the straw. Amidst the noise, she thrashes her legs, and whinnies as though she were being stuck with a pitchfork.

Max and Frederico keep threatening her by banging and yelling like wolves nipping at her heels. Her head is pulled more and more toward the doorway until she has almost no more room to lie, and right at the limit of Frederico's plan, she rolls to her feet in obvious pain.

"Keep going!" Frederico yells up to Bartolomeo. "Keep going!"

Marco has the mare's bridle and keeps focused on the barn door ahead. She waddles and limps on her left side for a few steps, bucking her head up and down, but she is up and moving.

"Don't stop!" Frederico again yells out. "Don't let her lie back down again."

The train keeps moving with Bartolomeo and the stallions up front, followed by the empty cart, and Marco and the mare behind. Within a few more steps, the mare smoothes out her gait and seems much more relaxed. Frederico moves up in front of Marco and gives the commands.

"Keep her going forward after I cut the rope."

"Yes, sir."

Frederico pulls a knife from his belt and slashes the rope a few feet in front of Marco's hands. Marco walks away from the cart and turns back toward the field with the mare in tow, carrying on as instructed.

"Okay, Bartolomeo, you can stop now."

"How is she?" he asks, not having seen what was happening.

"Marco has her out in the field, and he's keeping her on the move. Take the lantern and go find him."

Bartolomeo hands the reins to his father and runs to the barn for a lantern. Dashing into the field to find his horse and brother-in-law, he stumbles and falls. Lifting his head, he sees the mare appear through the darkness coming right back at him with Marco beside her.

"Watch out for that rock," Marco jokes.

"Very funny. How is she?"

"She's very tired, but she seems a bit more comfortable and in control... maybe even calm, if it's possible for her."

"Should we keep her moving, Marco?"

"I think she has the foal into position, and she's ready now."

The two men lead the mare back into the barn, where they find Frederico and Max laying fresh hay on the floor.

"Marco feels she's ready, Father."

"I agree, son. She just needed to get that foal in the right spot, or it wasn't coming out. You can bring her in now."

Bartolomeo guides her back into the same stall where she has been lying for days. She circles the stall a couple of times, and finds a comfortable spot. Upon lying down, her water sack ruptures and pours out onto the floor.

"Hooray!" yells Max as he recognises the progress.

"It shouldn't be long now," Marco adds to the anticipation.

Frederico steps in and ties the mare's tail into a bunch. Within a few moments, two hooves appear from beneath the tail.

"The hooves are up, Father. It's a breech!" Bartolomeo exclaims. We'll need ropes to pull it out."

"Easy does it, son. Give her a moment."

"But he's right, sir. The breeched foal could get stuck."

"Just give her a little bit of time, boys. I see the hooves, too, but she's all mad and ready. Give her a chance to do what she has to."

Max has his hat wrenched in his hands, waiting for any instructions that might come his way.

"Bartolomeo. If it will make you feel better, you can go and get some rags to hold onto the foal's hooves. If it comes to that, you'll want to pull by hand, not with a rope."

Bartolomeo grabs a lantern and races back toward the cottage. When he gets inside, he looks all around for the right type of rags. They can't be too rough, or they will harm the foal, and they can't be too delicate or they will not do the job. He finds just the right ones, and continues to look around to make sure there is nothing else they might need. Within minutes, he heads back to the barn.

Upon his arrival, he sees the three men standing together amidst calm. One of the lanterns has been lowered into the stall, and there in the soft light lies a delicate healthy foal being licked clean by it's mother.

"How did this happen so fast?"

"She was ready, and she had the will," Frederico explains.

"He – beautiful, Bartolomeo!"

"Thank you, Max. He sure is. But I don't deserve much of any credit."

"Sure you do," Marco adds. "You summoned the expert."

"But how did you know what to do, Father?"

"You simply take what God gives you, and do your best. Now, just give me a nice bed to sleep in, will you?"

Bartolomeo smiles and nods his head in satisfaction. "You will have my bed tonight, Father. I'll find some sleep out here."

"Then I bid you all a good night. It was nice to meet you, Max. My best wishes to your family."

"Yes, yes. Goodnight." Max smiles and shakes Frederico's hand with vigour before heading back to his own farm.

Frederico and Bartolomeo gather their things from the wagon and return to the cottage together, where the son shows his father around, and leads him to his own bedroom.

"This must be the only nice bed in here."

"It is, and tonight it is yours."

"Thank you, son. It's been a long day for me, so I'll have a cup of wine, and I'll be asleep before you bury the afterbirth."

"Thank you so much for coming tonight, Father. I hope it has not been a burden."

"Not at all, Bartolomeo. It was like old times out there."

"Like old times, Father. Goodnight."

"Goodnight, son."

Chapter 17

Frederico awakens to the sweet smell of roasting pork, and for a moment expects to be greeted by his wife. Gathering his wits, he realises he is at Bartolomeo's farm. As he makes his way outside, he is impressed with the scene of his son doing the cooking.

"Where were you hiding this pork?"

"Oh, it's from Max, Father. He brought it over to us this morning as a gift while you were asleep."

"He's a strange little man, that Max. But I sure do enjoy his idea of gifts! Where is Marco?"

"He is out in the field with the foal."

"And how is that newborn doing this morning?"

"Bucking like a champion. He's full of the devil, not unlike his mother."

Frederico smiles at the good news, and warms his hands against the fire. "Have you named him yet?"

Bartolomeo pauses, "I hadn't even thought about it, not even for a moment."

Frederico remains quiet, as this is his son's time now.

"I feel so plainly grateful, Father, that he was born at all. There has been so much death these past few years... with Isabetta's marriage and this foal, it's so tremendous to me that anything good is happening. It's strange how I can feel so thankful for even the smallest things."

Frederico looks into his son's eyes and nods, as if twenty years of teaching and knowledge had just been transferred in a single moment.

After a short walk around his son's farm in the morning light, Frederico returns to the cottage and finds the table set for a fine feast with three place settings. Soon, Marco appears and sits down at the table. Bartolomeo presents some apricots, roasted nuts, boiled eggs, and the cooked pork.

"I'd swear that you want me to visit more often, with a meal like this," Frederico offers.

"This meal is humble compared to all you have done for me, Father. I only wish that I had more to give."

"You don't owe me a thing, son. You have much to be proud of."

"Thank you, Father. Let's begin the blessing: Heavenly Father, it is through Your grace that a new foal has been delivered to this simple farm. We thank You for looking over its mother, and I thank You also for delivering my father. Our faith in Your divine guidance never wavers, as we partake in this meal before us, which You have so generously provided. Amen."

"Amen," Frederico and Marco echo.

The hearty breakfast feast is devoured by the hungry men, and the comfort of a brief time together with no immediate work in front of them is savoured. Nearly finished, Bartolomeo decides that the time is right to make an announcement.

"Father, I have something to tell you that is of utmost importance."

"Go on, son."

"Marco and I are going back to find Gino this summer."

Expected silence falls upon the table, and it is Frederico's to break. He takes the last sip of water in his cup, and wears an unmoved appearance from the comment. He places the cup on the table, wipes his lips with his fingers, and stares at Marco with complete contempt.

"You won't quit will you, Marco?"

"No, sir," Marco whispers.

"So this whole trip bringing me here for this unfortunate mare was all a ruse?"

"No, Father, not at all. I could never have created such a story. The mare's needs were real as you saw."

"But your accomplice, Marco, could have solved the problem himself."

"Actually, sir, I had never seen that technique used before. I did have a feeling the foal was out of position, but I only tried to massage it back into place, and it wasn't working."

"Then why make this announcement, Bartolomeo? Why would you want to join Marco in this foolish search to upset and embarrass the king?"

"Perhaps it will be an embarrassment, Father, but we have made up our mind to do it. I will try to guide Marco as best I can. The only question remaining is whether you wish to join us."

Frederico can see the determination in his son's brown eyes. He knows there is no stopping him this time.

"Allow me to tell you two a story, then."

"Please do, Father," Bartolomeo leans in.

"This story begins the day we arrived in Sarnen. There was a widow crying at the altar of a local church over the husband she buried the day before. He did not die of old age, but due to an accident, and this poor woman's life was thrown over in an instant. Then along comes this frozen family from over the mountains. They have no place to go, so they walk into this same church. Was it not a gift from God Himself, that this family arrived when it did? The priest listened to the family's story and granted their salvation by allowing them to live on that farm and to care for that woman. There was no coincidence in the circumstances of that day, only God's will."

"Isabetta has told me many times about that day."

"But did she tell you every bit of God's plan leading up to that point?"

"I don't think so."

"Then allow me to educate you, Marco. I was lucky enough to be in the right place at the right moment in Milan, as God gave me gift number one. Sweet Ambrogino and I heard about the deadly plague right before it ravaged the land and took so many lives. We were told by God to leave our home, and to travel across those horrific mountains to this land here. That was gift number two. Along the way, we found a particular woman who was able to nurse our sick Gino before we travelled into the most impossible pass. That was gift number three. We had conquered our steepest ascent when snow closed the road behind us for the winter. One single day later, and none of us would be sitting here right now. That was gift number four. All of these things happened at precisely the right moment, and in a very particular order. Do you presume all of those things happened by chance?"

"Not as you tell it to me this way," says Marco.

"Then, at our bleakest, Marco, we stumble upon a safe haven, a castle, for little Ambrogino to live in peace and comfort. From there, we received instructions to a safe cave stocked with firewood where the rest of us, including your exquisite wife, are saved from the storm. That was gift number five. We complete our escape into the valley below, and it is we who find our own comfort from the widow's predicament. That was gift number six. Do you think that happened all by chance again?"

"That is the work of God, sir."

"There is no doubt, young man – no doubt at all. So now you want to challenge His word by prying into the past and questioning whether Gino was made to be king or not. You want to see the castle for your own proud self, to satisfy the selfish desires of your feeble mind. Is that what you want?" Frederico stands and opens his arms wide.

"I do believe it is the right thing to do sir," Marco tries. "You tell us all of those things, and you are right about every one. But you can also say that God has continued to show you the way by bringing me into your life."

"Oh, so now you are gift number seven are you?" Frederico

laughs and turns toward the window.

Not at all embarrassed by Frederico's tone, Marco delivers his point. "I am not the gift, Frederico, but I believe it is my presence in your life that will allow you to fulfill the promise you made to your wife that awful night."

"What do you know of promises?" Frederico spins and thumps his fist on the table. "You would think you are Francis of Assisi standing in front of me!"

"Father," Bartolomeo leaps between them, and places both hands on his father's chest. "You don't have to go. You don't have to fulfill any promise. Please, I will go for all of us, and that is all that is needed." He moves his hands up to Frederico's shoulders, much the same way a father would comfort a son, and steadies his shaking father.

Frederico stares through the table, and digests both the logic of Marco's plea, and the love that Bartolomeo has shown him. He never thought it would be possible under any circumstances, but he now finds himself in an unfamiliar agreement with a plan to return to the mountains. "I will go," he says, after a long pause.

"You don't need to, Father."

"Yes, I do. You two fools would be hopeless without me."

Marco smiles at his brother-in-law at the insult, for Frederico's agreement to travel with them is more than they had hoped for.

Frederico turns to exit the cottage with his face down. It is not a moment of happiness for Frederico, but a moment of humility that he has put off for too long.

"We are going to find a king, you know," he mutters back toward the cottage and walks away into the open field. This was supposed to be his journey, under his own terms. Now that Marco and Bartolomeo have forced their will, Frederico finds his anger softening. Perhaps being a passenger will be a blessing to the aging man, and remove the burden of finding the place at all. Perhaps his son's loving determination will ultimately bring peace.

Within a short time, Bartolomeo prepares his wagon to bring

his father home. He asks nothing of Frederico until it is time to go.

"Thank you for staying, Marco," Bartolomeo says as he puts his arm on Marco's shoulder. "I will return this evening, or perhaps tomorrow if my mother has her way."

"Indeed, Bartolomeo. I will keep caring for the animals until you return. Then preparations can begin."

A stoic Frederico sits in the wagon waiting to be returned to his house. No words are spoken during the entire half-day journey back to Sarnen.

Chapter 18

For the last couple of weeks, Margherita has had her husband's things packed for a multi-day journey. She has stockpiled plenty of clothing, lamps and oil, and comfortable bedding for all three men and their upcoming journey.

Frederico is in the orchard pruning apple trees almost without stopping since his return from Bartolomeo's cottage. Today feels like another hot day, so he anticipates that Bartolomeo and Marco have already set out before to make Sarnen before noon.

In the distance, coming toward him, Frederico sees Maria in a bright blue dress, carrying something. He stops his pruning and walks out to meet her.

"Yes, my sweet Maria."

"I have this letter that I wrote to Gino, and I want you to give it to him."

She presents the letter and hands it to her father. It is folded neatly and wrapped in red ribbons, with a red flower tucked into the bow.

"It's lovely, Maria. You have prepared it beautifully."

"You can read it if you want."

"No, I'll let it be for his eyes only," Frederico pulls his daughter in for a hug.

"It sure is hot again today, Father."

As Frederico nods at the thought, he looks up to see Bartolomeo and Marco arrive in the courtyard with a stocked wagon pulled by four horses.

"Your brother is here, Maria."

She turns to look, then races out toward the wagon. Frederico holds the letter out in front of himself to admire its beauty once more before retiring it in his shoulder pouch for safekeeping.

Bartolomeo, Marco, and Maria make the horses comfortable with water and snacks while chatting away with Margherita. The heat of the day and the dirt from the road can be very irritating for the horses, so Maria wipes them down with a cool sponge. Confidence has overtaken nervousness as the preparations are made.

"I knew today would be the day. Another hot one for sure," says Frederico as he arrives on the scene.

"Well, Father, it's best to be hot down here and cool up there. It will be a welcome change for the horses."

Frederico proceeds to inspect the wagon and its provisions. "You've done a nice job, son. We could be gone for a month with what you've got here."

"I wonder where I learned that."

"It's better to have too much, than not enough," Marco adds.

"There is one thing we will have in abundance, that we did not have before."

"What's that, Father?"

"Time."

"Enough time to stay safe, and not take any chances," Margherita adds. "Keep the animals fresh and don't push them, alright?"

"Don't worry about us, Rita, this is nothing more than a pleasure trip. We could do it on single horseback if we needed to."

"I don't want you to get too adventurous. Just stick to your business. And here, give these to Gino," she reveals a pair of wool socks from her apron. These should be the right size, and it's so cold up there in the winter."

Frederico nods and places them into the same pouch with Maria's letter. He then looks for Antonio to see if there is anything that he requires before the journey begins.

"Where is Antonio?" Frederico asks Margherita.

"He is in the house."

Frederico removes his hat and enters the house. He approaches Antonio's room where he sees his son sitting in a chair and staring out the window.

"We'll be leaving soon, son."

"I know."

"Is there anything that you want to say?"

"It's very hot out, so you should make sure you have plenty of water."

"That's good advice, son. Thank you. You'll be sure to keep an eye on things around here while I'm gone, won't you?"

"Of course, Father."

"Then I will see you in a week or two," Frederico smiles, and pats him on the shoulder. "I don't suppose you have a hug for your father, do you?"

Antonio stands up without further prodding, and leans into his father for an embrace.

"Goodbye, Father."

"Goodbye, son. Take care of the women."

"I will."

Frederico turns to leave the room and make one last sweep of the house for anything else he might need.

"Father!" Antonio calls out.

Frederico quickly returns to his son.

"Will you be bringing Gino back with you?"

The simple question stops Frederico cold, and he searches for the right words.

"You know, Antonio, that we are not allowed to."

"Yes, Father, but that was so many years ago! Tell them we need him now more than they do! Tell them, Father!"

Frederico steps forward and pulls his son fully into his chest, and the two share their pain together.

"Okay, Antonio. Okay, my blessed son. I will tell them, just as you wish."

The two separate as Frederico places his hand on his son's head, and gives him a hair stroke of assurance. They look into each other's eyes, and nod through welling tears.

"You are the best brother anyone could ever want, Antonio."

A returned smile is all that is needed from his son to accept his father's praise. Frederico cups his hand against his son's cheek to reaffirm his undying affection for him, and nods. He returns the comforting smile, and departs.

"Whenever you are ready, Father," Bartolomeo calls out from the yard.

"As soon as your horses have had their fill, we'll go."

The heat of the day slows everything down, as over-exertion would lead to exhaustion, or even fainting. They wisely let the stallions indulge on as much feed and water as they need. When that point has been reached, they prepare for departure. The three men ride abreast of each other with Bartolomeo in the middle with the reins.

"Goodbye," Margherita calls out and waves. "Be careful."

Blown kisses are waved towards the strong woman, who now realises it may not be necessary to make this journey after all. Ambrogino is already safe, and the thought now of something happening to any of these men would be catastrophic.

"Goodbye, Mother," Bartolomeo calls back.

"Goodbye," Frederico and Marco add as they all wave and roll out down the road.

Margherita shows them all a happy face as she waves them out of sight, and turns away to say a prayer.

It is past midday, and the sun bakes the road, but the horses are fresh, the wagon is full, and each man is resolute in his own way. This road ahead is very familiar to Frederico for about ten miles or so. From that point on, after the village of Altdorf, Frederico has not travelled since the descent of five years ago.

"So tell me, Frederico," begins Marco. "How well do you remember the roads?"

"My memories are as clear as my daughter's wedding day."

"Even though it was snowing, and you were going the opposite direction?"

"What is your point, Marco? Do you want to drive the team? Bartolomeo, give Marco the reins."

"No, it's not that, sir. I have this map here, you see," Marco pulls a scroll from his carry bag.

"Let me see that." Frederico unrolls and studies the map. Marco is yearning to point out every detail of the map, and their position right now, but he knows the trip will be long, and there is plenty of time. He figures that his observations will be better received if Frederico is the one who asks for his help.

For about a mile, Frederico is fixated on the map and its details. More than once, he has turned the map upside down in order to view it from the opposite direction.

"I didn't realise so many mountains had their own name," Frederico breaks the silence.

"And every river, lake, and pond," Marco adds.

"This is a good map," Frederico concedes and hands it back over to Marco.

"Do you recognise any of the roads, sir?"

"Sure I do. Just keep following this road until I feel we need to make a turn."

Bartolomeo looks over at Marco with an 'I told you so' look in his eyes. Marco nods back in agreement. They both realised days ago that Frederico would want to search his way around the area, and perhaps intentionally keep the group off track.

"That's fine," Marco replies. "I have written down the route that you most likely took, so we can compare my notes when the time comes."

Frederico looks over at Marco to see if he is being smug. Marco earnestly rolls up the map and tucks it away. He notices Frederico and tries to reassure his place with a warm smile.

"You know, you're as stubborn as a mule, Marco."

"I know I am, sir," Marco smiles. "I guess it is how I was

raised. If you feel something is yours, then you must go get it regardless of the price you must pay."

"How about the price others must pay?" Frederico snaps back.

"That's why we offered to make this journey alone, sir. I would not want to see another man burdened at my expense."

"I have only come along because the two of you would have no idea where to look, and you'd be lost up here for months. Bartolomeo's mother would be worried sick, and she'd find some way to blame me."

Bartolomeo laughs at his father's spot on assessment of his mother.

"Especially... " Frederico continues, "since the road we are looking for is not on your map at all."

Bartolomeo loses his smile and looks over at Marco, who has raised his eyebrows in an expression of light bewilderment. Having made his point, Frederico drops his hat over his eyes, and sits back for greater comfort, and perhaps a nap.

"Then I'm glad we have you along with us," says Marco.

Up above, the lack of cloud cover allows the sun to beat down on the men and their team. As they plod along at a leisurely pace, farms along the way bristle with activity from herding, gardening, and the harvest of early fruits and grains. Along the right side of the road, a magnificent vineyard appears, overstuffed with small green berries waiting to ripen in the summer sun.

Bartolomeo wants to wake his father to point out this terrific farm so they can comment on it together, but he knows he has probably seen it before, and would not want to be disturbed.

"That's quite a vineyard, isn't it?" Marco says to Bartolomeo. "Is it similar to what your family had back in Como?"

"We had an equal amount of acreage dedicated to vines. But in addition, we had other fruit trees and a spectacular vegetable garden, each of which were the envy of the town. Those vines you see there are not cultivated to reach their maximum. I can see flaws from here that will distract from the flavour. Also, you will notice that the entirety of this vineyard is in the same area – the same soil, the same sun, and the same air. We had a rolling vine-yard of diversity, so that our yield was always strong, regardless of the season; I always believed that a diverse crop produced our distinct flavour."

Marco is captivated by Bartolomeo's descriptions, and the way he remembers his home with such detail and fondness.

"Why don't we continue right through the pass, and go all the way back to your farm?"

"What?"

"We could easily keep on going, since we have plenty of supplies. Plus, at this time of year, with this team, it will be no trouble at all."

"I don't know, Marco," Bartolomeo whispers, peeking to see if his father is awake.

"It will be difficult enough for my father just to find Gino again. From that point on, I don't know what he's going to want to do. Even if you and I desire to press on, he may not."

"We would all have something to gain from such a journey, Bartolomeo. I couldn't dream of a better opportunity."

"There is no need to discuss any of that now. Please keep those thoughts to yourself, and let's just see how things go," Bartolomeo begs, and looks again over to his sleeping father.

After almost seven hours of riding, the three men find themselves entering the village of Altdorf, twenty-five miles from their start in Sarnen. Most activities are breaking down into dinner mealtime, and the smell of roasting meats fills the air on both sides of the roads.

"Something sure smells good," Frederico straightens up.

"It is dinnertime in Altdorf," says Marco.

"What about us?" Bartolomeo asks. "Should we pay for dinner tonight, or do we cook ourselves?"

"We should buy our dinner while we are in a civilised area," Frederico considers. "We can save our own stores for the remote areas."

"I agree."

"Let's see what we can find then," says Bartolomeo.

Altdorf is the last suitable area of population before the steep grades of the mountains. It is wedged into a small plain at the foot of the mighty Alps thrusting up all around them. Behind the town, Lake Lucerne comes to an end, as do any final thoughts of returning home. Soon, the men come upon two inns that are located opposite each other on the main road.

"Ah, it appears we have a choice."

"Then let us visit the one most rundown, and least appealing," says Frederico.

"I don't understand, sir."

"That will be the place that will be the friendliest, and most apt to serve what we want."

For the sake of timeliness, Bartolomeo agrees with his father and pulls the team into the yard of the large chalet on the right. There they are greeted by a young boy of about twelve years, who ties the team up and fills the water trough for them.

"Thank you very much, young man," offers Frederico as he reaches into his pocket for a coin. "This is for your help with the horses."

The boy nods, and smiles wide, perhaps not speaking the same language.

"Merci," he replies as he fetches more buckets of water for the trough.

Marco then unhitches the two stallions from the rear, and leads them to the trough as well. When all horses are drinking and relaxing, the men step inside.

"Bonjour," offers a smiling young woman.

"Bonjour," replies Marco, who understands a working knowledge of the French language.

Bartolomeo and Frederico remove their hats in respect to the woman and her modest hotel.

Marco and the woman engage in a conversation, while Bartolomeo tries to pick up words that he might understand. Meanwhile, Frederico inspects the room and the structure of the building.

"She says she is expecting us for the night," Marco explains.

"How much?" Frederico replies, while discreetly examining the walls.

"Very little, as long as we stay in one room."

"That's fine," Frederico continues to walk around.

"The food must not be very good then," Bartolomeo whispers to Marco.

"My food is very good," the woman offers, showing off her bilingual ability.

"Oh, I'm sure that it is," Bartolomeo recovers, while Frederico bursts out laughing at his son's innocent misfortune.

"We will be content in any room young lady, and we will be happy to partake of whatever you serve," Frederico smoothes over.

"Very well. Thank you," she replies and goes about her business of preparation.

Frederico wonders to himself if the boy's father is present, or if this woman is able to maintain this building by herself. He continues to explore the inn until he makes his way out back to the courtyard. There, he finds two other working women – one grinding grain into flour, and the other gathering firewood.

Another child, a girl of about ten years, is churning butter with ease, as if she has done it a hundred times before. She looks up to notice Frederico peering at her, and waves to him with a smile. Frederico returns the wave, and heads back inside.

The young woman is busy collecting things for dinner, and firing the wood stove as Frederico approaches her.

"We will be happy to help you with some of your chores this evening, miss."

"Oh, that won't be necessary, sir. We are able to manage quite well."

"My name is Frederico Gallinelli."

"I am Marie."

"I can see that you manage rather well, Marie, and I make no judgment as to your ability. It is just that there are three of us, and a bit of daylight remaining, so it would be a shame to waste it."

"Frederico, you and your sons are welcome to share in whatever activity pleases you as our guests."

"Then what would be the most difficult work that you have not been able to get done?"

"Truthfully, Frederico, we are keeping up quite well."

"I understand," he nods. "We will work on your woodpile then. I have noticed you have many logs outside, and if you will show me to your saw, then we will cut and split them for you."

"You can find a saw that works well hanging on the back of the outhouse."

"Thank you," Frederico smiles and pops his hat back on.

"I thank you, sir."

Frederico gets to work with Bartolomeo and Marco who accept their responsibilities with delight. The painful heat of the day has passed, and the men enjoy the warm evening that is now upon them. Within the time it took for the sun to have set, the men have cut and split two of the logs, and built a handsome wood stack. All the while, the women of the inn have continued their chores and have prepared the table for dinner.

Marco and the Gallinellis have taken advantage of the ample water supply from the cold creek running behind the inn, and have soaked and cleaned themselves from the dirt and sweat of their work. Upon re-entering the building, the fantastic aroma of a seasoned baking fish take the men by surprise.

"Dinner smells terrific, Marie. What is it?" Frederico asks.

"It is trout with a mushroom cream sauce prepared in a flaky pastry."

Marco and Bartolomeo stare at each other in awe of this woman's cooking talent, and can't wait to sample for themselves. They each get seated at the large table that is generously adorned with a variety of colourful flowers and a handful of thick red candles.

An older couple come down from a flight of stairs and joins the dinner party. Frederico immediately stands back up to receive the new guests, and Bartolomeo and Marco follow. This couple speaks the same language as them, so polite greetings and introductions are shared by all.

Marie presents the marvelously prepared plates to her guests, and the compliments flow.

"It would please me if one of my gentlemen guests would begin our dinner with prayer."

Marco and Bartolomeo defer to Frederico out of respect, who in turn, defers to the oldest man at the table.

"No you go ahead, Frederico, please," the old man asks.

Frederico accepts, and asks the diners to bow their heads. "Almighty God and Saviour, we ask that You bless these gifts for which we humble few are about to receive. May You watch over Marie and her family, and allow them to harvest the most bountiful crop this summer, and enjoy prosperity in their home. We ask that You also protect our new friends for the rest of their journey so they may see their loved ones very soon. Amen."

"Amen," the table echoes in unison.

"Thank you, Frederico," Marie says.

Frederico passes around the bowls of bread and cheese to be sure that everyone has been helped before himself, while Bartolomeo takes it upon himself to serve the wine.

"A toast!" Marco breaks out as he raises his cup.

The others raise their cups in anticipation, and Marco continues by pointing his cup in the direction of the boy and girl seated off to the side at a smaller table.

"A toast to the children."

"Les enfants," Marie says out loud so her children will understand.

The girl smiles and raises her wooden cup, while the boy spills his water in an attempt to hit his sister's cup. The adults laugh at the effort, and cheer for them.

"May they always occupy the largest part in our hearts," Marco concludes.

The adults nod in perfect agreement, and sip their wine.

"Do you have any children of your own?" the older woman asks of Marco.

"Perhaps soon, my lady, as I am recently married."

"Then cheers to you, Marco, and to your bride."

The guests raise their drinks again in celebration, and then turn to sampling the lovely fish creation.

"This is the best I have ever had, Marie," Marco prompts.

"Divine, simply divine," the older woman follows next, with her husband too busy stuffing in a second mouthful.

"This pastry, Marie… it is like a piece of Heaven on Earth," Bartolomeo mumbles.

"Yes, you are spoiling us with this dinner," Frederico heaps on the compliments.

"Thank you all very much. I can't do very much else, but I have had much training with pies and pastry in my homeland."

"What you do is more than enough," Frederico encourages her.

"You have pies as well?" Marco asks to the amusement of the table.

"Yes, two of them."

"It will be good to be full when we embark on our trip tomorrow," Bartolomeo says.

"Where are you young men going?"

"We are all going to visit my brother."

"And where is he?"

"He is living in a monastery high up in the mountains," Marco presents on behalf of Frederico. "He is a king there."

"Really," the woman beams at the news. "Do you know where that monastery is, dear?" she asks her husband.

"There is no monastery on this road here until you get to Bellinzona, and even then, there aren't many residents left from the plague of '48."

"Well, it may not be a monastery as one would expect," Marco corrects. "But it is a castle, and he was left… rather, he was accepted to live there in the late autumn of the previous year."

"The only thing you'll find up there is a few deserted farms, and a lot of goats," the man continues.

"Maybe you have the wrong road," the woman questions.

"This is the right road, my lady. I am certain of that," Frederico responds. "We are going off the main road, so it may not be noticed by most folks who travel the road."

The older man shakes his head and points his fork at Frederico. "If you stay on this road, and take it all the way down the other side, there isn't a side road that goes anywhere, but up the face of a cliff."

"We'll take this road all the way to the Riviera if we have to, then we will know if it is the right road. If it isn't, then I guess we'll have to turn around and come back here for another meal with Marie."

The old man smiles at the calmness of Frederico's tone.

"Perhaps getting lost would be a blessing," Marco adds to the point. "That could mean more pie!"

With great satisfaction, the meal has come to a close, as Marie and her two children clear the table with ease. Frederico, Marco, and Bartolomeo withdraw to the patio with a full glass of wine each, and relax in the solitude of the evening.

"I have prepared your room with an extra bed," offers the ever-appearing Marie as she lights the lanterns on the patio.

"Thank you, Marie," Frederico replies.

"We would like to settle with you now, since we will be leaving very early in the morning. Are you sure this is enough for the three of us?" Bartolomeo asks as he counts out his coins.

"We have agreed already, and your work with the wood is most appreciated."

Marie then retires for the evening, and leaves the men alone. They continue to enjoy the quiet of their mountain surroundings, each having his own thoughts about the reunion awaiting them.

Soon after, the stars have come out in full force, and Frederico decides to head to bed. In his absence, Marco and Bartolomeo discuss their trip in more detail, contemplating road conditions, and the availability of game. After discerning the proper travelling route, Marco makes an observation.

"Why do you suppose your father has wavered all these years on his promise to go back to find your brother?"

"I would not call it wavering, Marco. My father was content in his knowledge that what he had done was right."

"Yes, but do you suppose he would be embarrassed to find out that Ambrogino is not a king at all, but a common young man, forced into common daily labour?"

"I can't comment on what my father thinks or feels," Bartolomeo stares out into the hills.

"Then what are your feelings, Bartolomeo?"

"My feelings? I have kept my feelings to myself since that snowy night. It was my father's decision, and I faithfully obeyed him. I respected his decision, and it is impossible for me now to choose between my love for my brother and my love for my father."

"I do not mean to cause you any pain, Bartolomeo. Please accept my apology."

"You have no need for an apology. Our journey tomorrow means as much to you as it does to my father."

"I'm going to turn in for the evening," Marco says as he walks off the patio toward the outhouse. "I'll see you back inside."

"Goodnight, Marco."

Feeling finished with his wine, Bartolomeo empties his cup over the rail and onto the ground. It creates a tiny pool that reflects the glow from the lantern. Bartolomeo is captivated by its momentary presence all alone in the dirt. It slowly seeps into the earth, sinking smaller and smaller within itself, until finally, it is gone.

Chapter 19

The morning sky is brightening in the east, and an excited fox crouches beneath a small spruce tree, her eyes fixated on the subtle movements of some tall grass nearby. Sniffing and nibbling his way around inside the grass is a brown field mouse, oblivious to the vixen waiting for him. Poking for grains, the mouse inches his way toward an open area beyond the grass, while the fox tightens her crouch in giddy anticipation. Just as the little mouse is about to appear, a loud crunching sound startles him, and he darts deeper into the tall grass and disappears from sight. Four huge stallions stomp their hooves into the open road up this mountainous terrain. The startled fox retreats herself as Marco's horses begin their arduous ascent.

"How far do you estimate we can get in one day?" Marco asks his companions.

"As far as we can," Bartolomeo replies.

"Should we try to find a village to spend the night again?"

"I'm sure we'll find a village, or a farm or two for this night, but after that we'll be on our own."

"Do you think they will all be friendly toward us?"

"Marco, we should stay focused on this road, since it will do funny things. Mistakes and stumbles will cost us dearly if we don't pay attention, especially if we want to make our ten miles per day. We should also keep our eyes open for berry bushes, and small animals to make a meal from."

"If there is anything substantial moving in the bushes, then I'll take a shot at it," Marco says as he moves to the back of the wagon to pick up his bow.

"Good idea," Frederico cracks to him. "Just yell out for us to stop if you've got dinner in sight."

Bartolomeo is relieved at his father's playfulness, as he knows the odds of Marco hitting anything from the wagon are about a thousand to one.

Travelling is slow, but steady, and the strong stallions are having little problem with the grade. Frederico is pleased with the preparedness of his party, and feels comfortable they will find few problems along their route.

"So, Father," Bartolomeo begins. "How has Mother been holding up now that Isabetta has left home?"

Happy to have a new topic, he responds with enthusiasm, "It is more a question about your sister, Maria. You know the work your sisters have done does not go away, and with each year, one more child leaves home and the chores get more difficult."

"That is why I ask."

"Your mother is a hard worker, son, you know that. Maria works very hard, and Antonio is coming into his own very well now."

"Yes, but aside from the daily chores, I wonder how she feels every day with so many of us gone."

"While it is certainly a burden for you to have left, I know she agrees with me that each one of you were smart to have taken advantage of the open lands after the great mortality. You know your mother – she is happiest when she knows that you are safe and well fed."

"I suppose I should visit more often. I don't live that far away."

"She would like that."

"Then I will definitely be around come harvest time, so you and Mother should not become burdened with too much work at your age."

"At our age?"

"You know what I mean, Father."

"I don't think we need any such help this year... but it would be nice to have you around just the same."

Bartolomeo smiles at his clever father, who is looking straight ahead now to avoid eye contact.

Soon, one mile becomes two, and two becomes three, as the bright sun breaks in through the tall pines. The morning haze has lifted, and once again, the heat of the day begins to make itself known.

"Stop!" bellows Marco from the back of the wagon.

Bartolomeo immediately brings the team to a halt.

Tew! goes Marco's bow, as he lofts an arrow into the hillside.

"I got it! I got it!" Marco yells out as he leaps from the wagon. "Follow me!"

Bartolomeo looks at his father in disbelief, and shrugs his shoulders. He hands his father the reins, and hops down to go with Marco, and the two young men disappear into the forest on the side of the road. Frederico listens to his son and son-in-law thrashing through trees and shrubs until they fade into the distance.

Frederico gets down from the wagon and blocks the wheels with two sticks of wood. After waiting for too long, he yells into the woods.

"What are you two doing in there?"

Some branch-snapping sounds comes back, but he can't decipher them. It does not sound like panic, or a cry for help, so he relaxes and feeds a carrot to each of the horses while he waits. Eventually, the sounds of men thrashing through trees again get louder, as Frederico can now make out that the two men are dragging something.

"Good gracious Marco," Frederico cries out. "What have you got?"

"Take a look!" Marco brags as he shows off a full-grown ibex.

"This isn't real! How were you able to hit that beast with one shot from the road?"

"I don't know, I saw it standing there up on a rock, so I shot."

"You could have shot a dozen arrows from that distance, and not even scared the thing. I can't believe you hit it with a lethal shot."

"Maybe I got lucky, but what does that matter? He is ours now."

Frederico walks closer to inspect the animal. "This one is far too big."

"Too big?"

"It's too big for us. "We can't eat all this meat. There is too much. It will spoil on us."

"So what if some of it spoils. We'll get all we need, keep the hide, and sell off any other parts."

"But at least half of this creature will go to waste, Marco," Frederico presses. "Why couldn't you have shot at a marmot?"

"I don't understand why this is a problem, Frederico."

"Because it is needless, and wasteful, that's why. If anything, we should bring it back to Marie, and let her have it."

"Bring it back? We're not going that way. We would end up wasting the whole day."

"And what is the price of one day, Marco? What was this day compared to any other that we could have left? What is so special about tomorrow or the next day that we should waste this food?"

Marco throws his hands in the air and turns away from Frederico. He doesn't understand the uselessness of this whole conversation and shakes his head in disgust.

"Maybe we will see some travellers coming the other way, and we can give what remains to them," Bartolomeo searches for common ground.

"No!" Marco mocks in argument. "We're going to waste the day and this good weather returning to Marie, all for the sake of one half an ibex."

"Listen to yourself, Marco! So young, so strong, and so smart, but not an ounce of wisdom in you."

"I am a generous man, Frederico. I give more than I take from this world. A hundred ibexes die every winter here and nobody cares. You tell me where the wisdom lies in caring so much for this one. Perhaps you are delaying this trip any way you can."

Frederico ignores the last comment, "You have now shown us your ignorance in your own statement, Marco, "It is the wolves and the crows and other creatures who scavenge on those hundred carcasses every year who care a great deal, and whom you have forgotten."

"So it seems that you know everything, Frederico. You are the all knowing and the all wise. Perhaps someday I, too, will have the wisdom you have, and know it all."

"Your argument is the source of your lack of wisdom, Marco. You see, wisdom is not gained by knowing everything, wisdom is gathered by asking."

Being put in his place, Marco goes back over to the ibex and studies it more closely. Bartolomeo doesn't want to take sides, but wants to make peace if he can. Whether they go forward or backward, he does not care at this point.

"You are right, Frederico," Marco accepts. "Let's take it back down before it spoils in the heat. We can help Marie butcher it, and just take a few cuts with us. It will be late in the day, so we should spend the night again and start out tomorrow morning, the same as we did today."

"Now you are thinking, Marco."

"Then it is settled," Bartolomeo says.

"Yes," Frederico announces. "We take what we need right here, and leave the rest in the woods for the wolves and the crows."

Marco and Bartolomeo look at each other, shake their heads, and break out smiling.

"Lessons abound everywhere when you are with my father," Bartolomeo says to Marco.

The three men then begin to work as a team to gut and strip the ibex, keeping the fabulous skin and the best cuts of meat, while the horns will make for good trading. They clean up in a nearby stream, and before long, they are off again.

This part of the road is long and uninhabited, chiefly due to the ravaging pestilence of the last few years. Many of the cultivated lands have overgrown, and it would seem rare to find an inhabited cottage. If this road didn't lead somewhere, there would appear to be no use for it.

Passing the middle part of the day, the sun now pokes in and out of puffy clouds. The men nibble on snacks while they travel, and save their biggest meal for nightfall so they don't waste the daylight.

"How are the horses, Bartolomeo?" Marco asks from the back.

"As strong as ever."

"Good, let's get them into this stream again soon."

"You and I are thinking the same thing, Marco, and I believe there is a spot up ahead to do so."

Shortly thereafter, the three men and four horses find themselves enjoying another refreshing break down in the streambed. They have no need to rush, since the timing is perfect considering the distance they have travelled up to this point.

Bartolomeo climbs to the top of a boulder to look back down on where they have come from to see if it looks familiar from that perspective. "It's hard to imagine how these mountains can be so dangerous, when they are so magnificent right now."

"Even when the weather is mild, there are plenty of hazards on the road itself, so let's not lose our focus," Frederico adds.

The remainder of the day is uneventful, and the men make good travelling time. They set up camp in a wooded area not far from the road. Much of the meat is roasted over a fire, and the men are able to stuff themselves before turning in to sleep. With the first day having passed, there will be at least one more to follow before they can get to their target area. Night falls upon the modest camp of Frederico, Bartolomeo, and Marco, who take comfort in the warm air. Their fire flashes brightly in the darkness and tosses wobbly shadows against the tall pines.

Chapter 20

Day two is much more challenging than the first, as the road is now presenting steep inclines and unpredictable conditions. Not surprisingly, few engineers remain who can maintain such a route. At last there is comfort in the cooler temperatures. At the top of a wide turn, the journeymen reach a small village. Bartolomeo recognises one of the buildings without question, as it has a waterwheel with the water running over the top.

"Father, I recognise that wheel."

"You do?"

"Yes, this is the only place I have ever seen such a wheel."

"I don't remember it myself, but I trust your observations, son. Marco, where are we on your map?"

Marco is thrilled that his map has been called for, and quickly fumbles to retrieve it.

"There is no name for any village here, but by judging the direction of the stream, I would say that we have covered about eight miles so far today."

He looks up and around at the surrounding mountains, then back at his map. He glances at the three cottages and the waterwheel, then up to the mountains.

"It appears we are right at the spot below our feet."

Frederico laughs, "You're an accomplished navigator."

"At least we're going in the right direction, Marco," assures Bartolomeo.

This collection of homes and barns combined with the alpine

scenery gives Frederico a feeling that this piece of land is not at all like the place he descended from years ago. Perhaps it is because of the season, or the fact that so few people remain. Once, there was serious activity going on here, and now there is only the sound of water trickling over the squeaky wheel.

The men stop the wagon, and seek out anyone they can find. Between two of the cottages, they find two older men carrying freshly cut hay towards the barn.

"Greetings," Frederico calls out.

Neither man pays much attention as they continue their work.

"What do you make of these two, Father?"

"I tired of trying to figure everything out, son. Let's just water and feed the horses, and keep moving."

Just then, one of the men approaches the group. He looks very tired, and is older than Frederico.

"Hello, folks."

"We would like to rest a moment and water our horses," Frederico endears himself to the man.

"Please feel free to do so. Do you have anything to trade?"

Presenting the ibex remains, Marco steps in. While maintaining the secrecy of their journey, the men enjoy getting to know one another, and before long have completed several trades. As usual, Frederico allows himself to come up the loser, gaining only a small sack of wool and a pot of honey for the ibex, and a great pair of boots. While this is not much of a return, Frederico accepts it with great enthusiasm for the dignity of the poor man. Marco and the Gallinellis are asked to spend the night, but they decline, wanting to get as many miles behind them as possible each day. They offer sincere thanks, but move onward and upward with their team.

As night falls on the second day, there begins to develop a sense of excitement, as it is possible they can reach their destination at some point tomorrow. Making camp for the evening, Frederico takes special care to make sure both Bartolomeo and Marco are fed well, and are as comfortable as possible. Clouds have begun to circle above, contrasting the night sky and the mountain tops. A half moon appears for brief moments in between.

On the morning of the third day, the men find themselves awakening to a damp campsite. Light rain showers have passed through during the night, and left a soggy ground.

"Well, at least the horses are happy," Frederico says to himself as he shakes off the puddles of water from atop the wagon covering.

"It's somewhat refreshing," Marco adds, climbing out of the wagon to his feet. "I rather enjoy sleeping to the sound of rain against a canopy." He wanders over to his stallions, who are each tied to nearby trees. "Good morning to you, boys." Taking two of them and walking over to a glen nearby for grazing, he lets them indulge on some fresh green grass. Even though they are well fed from last night, he endears to keep his horses happy, and let them know he is always looking out for them. After a modest snack, he takes the two horses back and does the same for the other two.

Meanwhile, Bartolomeo has risen and taken it upon himself to tend the fire back to flame, where he begins boiling water for tea. Soon, all three men have collected themselves around the morning fire, and are enjoying Bartolomeo's tea.

"This is delicious, son. It has an orangey taste."

"That's right, Father. I mix in bits of orange peel with the tea leaves. Isn't it grand?"

"It's terrific! You could trade this."

"I don't know, It seems easy enough to do. Oh, I almost forgot… we've got that honey."

"You are spoiling us, Bartolomeo," Marco smiles, as his brother-in-law caters to them by drizzling a small amount into their cups.

"Thank you, son," Frederico enjoys. "So, Marco, how do your stallions look this morning?"

"Excellent, they look very bored," he smiles.

Frederico laughs, "Their boredom will dispense today."

"Mmm… " Marco sips as he looks up the road. Around them,

there is nothing but jagged peaks, and sheer cliffs taking the place of trees.

"I'm glad you like my tea," Bartolomeo says. "I'm looking forward to some smooth travelling today."

After their pleasant breakfast of tea and biscuits, the men have the stallions hitched and ready for action. Frederico has left all of the wagon inspecting to Bartolomeo, figuring that if his son needs his help, he will ask. They are back on the road with great efficiency, and underway.

Within the first mile, they come to a fork in the road. It is an open area, so they can see the road continuing in both directions. Making their choice is more difficult because they must recall how it would have looked from the opposite direction. It's possible they might get many miles up before they notice they have taken the wrong fork.

"Any ideas, gentlemen?" Marco poses.

"We are going to have to go up, and look back down each road," says Frederico.

"Why don't you both take a horse and go up each road separately for about a half mile or so, then come back, switch roads, and do it again. Whatever you both agree on is where we go."

"Excellent idea, Marco," agrees Bartolomeo.

With the plan in place, Marco blocks the wagon, and releases the two lead horses. He fashions them with saddles for the Gallinellis, and the two men ride up in opposite directions and disappear into mountainsides.

A short time later, they come back down, almost in unison. They pause momentarily to look around for landmarks, then cross paths to do the same thing again on each other's fork. A longer time passes this time, and Bartolomeo is the first to come back to the wagon. Frederico returns moments later, and doesn't want to give away his thoughts just yet.

"Okay," Marco begins. "When I count to three, I want both of you to point up the road you think we should take. One... two... three."

Bartolomeo thrusts his hand toward the road on the right, while Frederico watches his son, and raises his, in the same direction.

"Are you sure?" Marco asks both of them.

"Definitely," Frederico states, and dismounts his horse.

"To the right it is," Bartolomeo agrees.

With no second guessing, they remove the saddles, tie both horses back to the wagon, and continue up the narrow road, climbing higher and higher on the steady grade. They have now covered a distance of about twenty-five miles from their start in Altdorf, and figure to have less than ten to go. But whether it is ten, or nine, or even fifteen, they do not know for sure.

"Do you smell that?" Frederico asks his two companions.

"I do smell something," Marco replies.

"There must be a house nearby, doing some cooking," Bartolomeo adds.

It is difficult to see very far ahead due to the curvature of the road and the increase in elevation, but there is a plateau that is beginning to appear on the horizon. Soon, several rooftops pop up, and their wagon rolls into a small village on a fertile green plain.

"I remember this village, Father," Bartolomeo offers with glee. "Do you?"

"Maybe... is this where we traded the last of our wine here?"

"Yes, yes it was, Father, to that man with the very long beard."

"No, the long-bearded man we saw was on the way up, not on the way down."

"I thought he was on the way down, Father."

"Couldn't there be more than one man with a long beard?" asks Marco.

Both Gallinellis shrug their shoulders and accept the positive fact that at least the village is familiar to them.

"Either way, this village is not too far from the cave."

"The cave... that's right," Marco acknowledges.

"The cave... the cave..." Frederico changes the subject. "Let's just see if anyone is here and get a break."

Bartolomeo drives the wagon into the middle of the village, and an older woman is the first to greet them. She is wearing a bright dress with wooden buttons and is carrying two buckets of milk from one house to another.

"Good day, gentlemen," she offers and keeps going on her way past them.

Marco looks at Bartolomeo and smiles at the woman's unapologetic brush off.

Frederico laughs, "At her age, she doesn't have any time to waste with the likes of us."

Soon, two teenage girls come out from the house the old woman entered. They too are brightly dressed in colourful attire, and appear to be about twelve and sixteen years old.

"We can care for your horses," the blond haired, younger girl states.

"What is your price?" Bartolomeo asks.

"How much do you have?"

"Anna!" the older girl scolds, and slaps her sister on the arm. "I'm sorry, sir, she is not very polite."

"That's quite alright," Frederico replies as he climbs down to greet them. "If you water and feed them for us, we will pay the both of you a fair wage."

The two girls smile at each other and get to work untying the stallions to bring them to the nearby stream.

"They are very big and strong," the younger one states as she draws up against them.

"Are you sure you don't need any help?" Marco offers.

"No, we can take them," the older one replies with complete confidence, not wanting to give up their wage to any others who might appear.

"Then we thank you," Frederico replies. "Are there any adults around?"

"My grandfather is in that house, along with my aunts," the older one points up one more house away. "There's my Aunt Anna now."

"Is every girl here named Anna?" Bartolomeo asks.

"No, just me and Aunt Anna."

Frederico reaches into the wagon for whatever gift he can find, and the three men stroll up to their directed destination.

"Greetings," Marco offers.

"Hello," Aunt Anna replies. "What can I do for you men?"

"We only wish to rest our horses for a short while, if that is okay with you," Frederico explains.

"It seems my nieces have already attended to that."

"Would you mind if we came inside to get out of the sun ourselves?"

"Please be our guests. I am Anna, and this is my sister Helen," Anna opens her hand toward another woman standing inside the doorway.

"I am Frederico, this is my son Bartolomeo, and my son-in-law, Marco."

"It is nice to meet you."

Frederico then presses a bit, "Let me ask you... have you always been here, or did you take possession?"

Understanding his question, since the taking of land was such a common occurrence a few years back, Anna answers. "My father, Philip was the only survivor here. He lost eleven of his family, mostly children."

"I'm so sorry."

"It's okay, Frederico... I'm sure you lost plenty also... like all of us."

"Actually, my family was spared if you can believe it."

"Your whole family?"

"From the pestilence, anyway," Frederico continues in a rare moment of candour. "I lost my oldest daughter during childbirth two years ago, but I must say that God has been most gracious to me, Anna."

"What was her name?"

"Excuse me?" Frederico is surprised by the question.

"What was your daughter's name?"

"It was Allesandra, and she was the most beautiful and brilliant woman you would have ever known."

"I am certain she was," she comforts.

Bartolomeo nods to himself at the description of his sister. "Let's go inside, Father, and get out of the sun."

Frederico looks over at him, agrees, and leads the group inside. There, they find a much older man carving a bowl out of a small oak stump.

"This is my father, Philip," Anna presents.

Philip waves to the men, but does not rise to greet them. Frederico is not offended due to the man's advanced age, and also because of the sight of a walking cane that is resting near him. Everyone finds a seat in different parts of the room, and Helen has brought out a pitcher of water and some cups.

"We don't have much to eat, so I hope you have what you need with you," Philip calls up from his carving.

"We are fed well, my good man, and have plenty with us. Save your food for the girls, please."

"You look like you are from Tuscany. Are you on your way home?"

"Lombardy, in fact, and we are visiting my son, if you should need to know, sir."

"Does he live in Tuscany?"

"He lives very close to here," Marco can't help but to join in.

Philip stops his carving and looks up through one good eye and a wrinkled face, "Is that right? And where is that?"

"Marco," Frederico interjects. "Let's not bother this man with our trials."

"It's no bother at all," Philip replies. "Kind of keeps things interesting around here... seeing what folks are up to and getting news from the valley."

"Perhaps you know some of the roads around here, Philip," Marco pries.

"I don't know much, young man, but I do know where the roads go."

Bartolomeo tries to reassure Marco, "We know where we are going, Marco. This is all very familiar to me, including the cottage we are in right now."

"Have you stayed with us before?" Philip asks.

"I think it's time to go and check on the horses," Frederico says as he raises from his chair.

Marco rises as well, and the three men thank their hosts and leave a small wheel of cheese behind. They exit the modest house for the small but rich pasture where the stallions are grazing.

"Do you suppose that man remembers you?" Marco asks.

"I don't think that man remembers what he ate for dinner last night."

"At his age, he probably has a hard time finding the outhouse before bedtime!"

Bartolomeo looks up to gauge the sun's progress. The men agree without speaking that it is time to get moving again. They thank and pay the girls, then position the well-trained stallions back in place. They wave in cheerful fashion as the wagon rolls away from the village and up into the heart of mountains.

Their pace is more deliberate now than ever. Anticipating each obstacle and turn, Marco maintains complete control at the reins. "I can't imagine making this trip in a snowstorm," he wonders out loud.

"Neither can I," Frederico answers.

Chapter 21

"Father, can we can make the last leg before dark?"

"If we do or do not, what would it matter, son? We should camp as soon as we can find a safe spot. We'll get there eventually."

"But aren't you anxious, sir? I am." Marco says.

"We've waited this long. There's no sense going over a cliff now."

"I must agree with Father, Marco. Let's stop at the next long straightaway.

"We're not planning this very well, are we?"

"You have something against making camp along the road, Marco?" Frederico replies.

"It doesn't bother me in the least, sir. It just seems smarter to sleep in the villages rather than between them."

Bartolomeo does not want their weariness to turn to argument, so he again finds himself mediating, "We're going to need plenty of daylight to find the place, so it's best to stop here. I'm getting hungry anyway."

"Of course, I'm sorry."

"No, you're right. We could have planned the camps better."

"Goodness, the two of you getting along is confusing me. I preferred it when you were fighting."

They both chuckle at Bartolomeo's comment, and Marco pulls his horses to a stop. They climb out and maneuver the wagon to a safe position. In no time, they are seated on rocks and logs, and are passing around another wheel of hard cheese. Also appearing for the first time, is a sweet uncut salami they have been saving. Frederico opens his jug of whiskey and passes it around.

This campsite is much more relaxing than the others, and the men take time to move about some additional rocks and logs to give themselves greater comfort. Another fire is prepared with ease, as there are many fallen branches and trees with in reach.

After about an hour of eating and relaxation, Marco begins to ponder out loud.

"Look at that peak up there with the moon rising beside it."

The Gallinellis indulge him.

"I wonder how many men have sat in this same exact spot over the years on this same day to see the moon do the same exact thing."

"I wonder how many men have had as much to drink as you have tonight, Marco," Frederico pokes.

"No, I'm serious, Frederico. Try to envision all the different people who have come this way for so many different reasons."

"I think of the Roman soldiers all the time," Bartolomeo adds.

"That's what I mean. They would have marched right in front of us hundreds of years ago, and stepped on these same stones, and looked up to the same moon."

"So what's your point?" Frederico asks.

"I don't have a point, sir. It strikes me as awesome to consider how other people have come before me, and how many more will come here after me."

"There was a short time ago that we didn't believe anyone would come after us," Frederico contemplates.

Changing the subject, Bartolomeo asks, "How long before you guess another army comes through here on campaign?"

"Less than five years."

"That's scary to project, but I agree with you, Marco," says Bartolomeo. "It seems like we can't have peace for any amount of time at all."

"How about this, boys… " Frederico takes a turn. "How long will it be until there are no more wars at all?"

"Never," Marco scoffs.

"A thousand years," Bartolomeo guesses.

"I figure about five hundred years," says Frederico.

"So in the year 1853, there will be no more soldiers on the earth?" Marco poses.

"There will be soldiers, but they will be armed with food."

"They will be beating each other with loaves of bread?" Marco chuckles.

Frederico shakes his head, and smiles a bit himself. "No, follow me on this, Marco... every time there is a war, it is because somebody is hungry. Whenever there is hunger, there are desperate men. It is only desperate men who go to war, when they have nothing to lose. Imagine a world where everybody has enough food for his family and his neighbours. We won't have any need to fight amongst ourselves, and there will be no more wars."

"That's interesting, Frederico. I will give you that. But what about the jealousy and greed of men? You can be as fat as you want, but if one man desires the woman of another, then you will have a fight. Then somebody gets killed, and the family wants revenge. Pretty soon you've got soldiers again."

"I don't know, Marco. Five hundred years is a long time for us to get over jealousy."

"It will never happen, Bartolomeo. As long as there are men, there will always be greed and jealousy. I hate to say it but it's true."

"I don't agree," Frederico retorts. "We have to grow up some day, and realise there is more to be gained by saving ourselves instead of killing ourselves."

With that last point, Frederico rises and retires to the wagon. Marco and Bartolomeo stay up a bit longer.

"You're not convinced mankind will ever live like Christ, and put his fellow man before himself, Marco?"

Finishing the last of his whiskey, Marco stares back out at the moon, "We would sooner step foot on the moon, my brother, than we will eradicate our greed."

"So it's impossible then."

"In my opinion. But as my father always told me in my youth, Heaven will be a very quiet place because there won't be many people there."

"Sure there are, Marco. There are a lot of people there. For every one thief, there are ten who were stolen from. There are many more innocents there than you think."

"Okay, Bartolomeo. I'm too tired myself for this discussion. I was just letting my mind wonder, that's all. We'll have an exciting day tomorrow. Let's turn in."

For a change, both men prepare beds for themselves under the stars tonight, and settle under the soft light of the moon.

In the morning, the three men take their time packing up. They know they have given themselves plenty of daylight for this last leg, and they don't want to rush the animals, even though they have performed well to this point. With casual effort, the wagon departs on this monumental day.

Well before noon, the travellers have put several miles behind them, and since the pace has slowed from the grade, Marco decides to get out and walk. He wants to lighten the load a little, and encourage the stallions by being out in front of them.

Following their master's lead, the horses press on over the dry stony road. Marco finds a staff to keep his balance and energy, while he walks on ahead. Perhaps three days of riding has made him restless, or perhaps he simply wants to be out in front should he see something.

"We might go a little bit faster if we tie you into the team!" Frederico says to Marco.

Bartolomeo laughs out loud, and Marco himself can't help but to laugh.

"I often see myself as a stallion," he replies back, and begins to walk backward with his arms open to the men.

Frederico laughs at the reply.

"You know, it's rather easy walking backward," Marco muses. "It gives my legs a chance to catch their breath."

Marco continues his backward march, and watches as Bartolomeo slows the horse team to a stop.

"What, do you need another rest already?"

But Frederico and Bartolomeo sit in silence, fixated on something off to the side. Marco spins to see what it is, and sees nothing.

"What is it?"

"Come and get in the wagon, Marco," Frederico calls out to him in a fatherly tone.

"What do you see?" Marco begs as climbs back aboard.

"Up there on the right," Bartolomeo points.

"I only see piles of rocks."

"Look further away, up on that crest."

"Just tell me what it is, please!"

"Those rocks are a small pass, Marco. Our horses will go right in between them in a double curve. I would know that rock formation anywhere."

"That's great then, are we getting close?"

"Very close, brother-in-law."

The stallions behave like champions as they cover the ground up to the narrow road in the rock pass. As expected, they are now turning side to side as they maneuver in the difficult turns that cut through the immense boulders. Once they emerge from the other side, Bartolomeo stops the wagon in a level spot and gets down.

Marco spins with excitement, as he surveys the entire area for any clues at all. He stops with his hands out, and is looking in the same direction as both Bartolomeo and Frederico.

"Is that the cave?"

Silence befalls both Gallinelli men as their eyes focus on that spot – Frederico rekindling old emotions in his eyes. Bartolomeo glances around the area to soak in the concept that this is indeed that one singular place on earth. Marco does not ask anymore, and runs up the hillside to see for himself.

All of Marco's words, the noise from the grunting horses, and any other sounds have disappeared from Frederico's ears as he gazes at the cave that is up to his right. Bartolomeo tries to move his feet, but his heart is pounding so fast, he can't move at all.

Frederico climbs down and leads the horses up to the entrance of the cave. He puts back on a face of resilience, and forges up the hill. Stopping to make sure his son is behind him, he holds his hand out, palm down, to collect his hand. The two men join together and walk up into the entrance.

This is the spot where the family spent their first night without their beloved son, and this is the cave that sheltered and protected them from the snow storm while Margherita wept through the night.

In their own respectful way, all three men proceed to inspect the area. Each rock, log, and footprint take on an almost Biblical meaning. The horses are not tied up, but stand and wait for their master. Frederico makes his way into the fire pit area, and kneels down to look into the ashes. He scoops some up with his hand and lets it spill back down in a gray dusty cloud.

"This is the cave, Marco," Bartolomeo reminisces. "It may not seem like much right now, but with the snow knee deep, and blowing sideways, it made for a first rate sanctuary. Nobody would take us in that night, except for this cave."

"Allesandra sat right there," Frederico points to a spot near the fire ring. "She cooked for us, I remember. I remember her working very hard, but I don't know what I was doing." He turns his head side to side to look for more images of that night. "We were scattered all over, and had a great fire going."

"It was a huge fire, Father," Bartolomeo adds. "We burnt everything long and hot to shake off the cold. I can't believe how much distance we covered in that weather in the middle of the night."

"But your brother, Antonio… he stayed away from the rest of us. He hated me that night."

"That's not true, Father."

"It wasn't? He hated me that night, and for a month later he wouldn't talk to me."

"What he hated was that night itself, Father, not you."

Frederico wants to accept his son's words, but will not let himself. It is much easier if he alone takes the blame for the decisions made that snowy night five years ago.

"So we are close to the castle now," Marco brings the conversation back to the present.

Bartolomeo turns his attention toward the sound of the voice. "Right… right, Marco, we are close, indeed."

"We should get going then," he pleads.

Frederico and Bartolomeo are slow to move to Marco's demands. There is so much history at the cave, and with all of the memories flooding back, it is difficult for the two men to continue with any speed.

"Give us a moment, Marco, would you?" Bartolomeo asks of his brother-in-law.

Marco nods and decides that a slower and more thoughtful pace would be best considering how close they are now, and what a big moment awaits them when they will all soon be reunited with Ambrogino.

When Frederico is satisfied, he scoops up some sand and puts it in his pocket. He makes his way back down to the wagon and climbs in. Waiting on his father for every action, Bartolomeo climbs up as well, and drives the team onward.

The mood is very somber, and even though Marco is filled with excitement, he finds himself sympathising for Frederico and what he must have endured for his family that night.

Nestled in the vast solitude, mountain peaks rip into the sky all around, offering what would appear to be impossible walls to escape from. If one were going to build a monastery to remain hidden from the world, this would be the place.

"About how far is it from here?" Marco asks of Bartolomeo.

"There weren't any landmarks that I remember. We'll just keep going, and I'll let you know when something looks familiar."

Travelling at a deliberate pace, Bartolomeo searches left and right, and up and down. Frederico has his eyes fixated on the rugged cliffs on the left, and he sits upright, glued to his spot on the seat.

There is occasional movement and calls from crows in the scrub trees, but no other sounds of men or beasts in the area. The sturdy wagon wheels keep turning, and more distance is put between the searchers and the cave.

Bartolomeo looks down at the side of the road, and a creek has shown itself out in the open right beside the road. It is swampy on both sides of itself, with tall green grass cushioning its edges. He remembers stepping into wetlands like this through the fresh snow that night.

He studies the ground, and imagines the scene blanketed with snow. Just ahead, he sees a faint trail wiggling to the left up to the base of the cliffs. He slows the horses and stops at the junction of the trail.

"I think this is it."

Marco sees the path as well, and bounds into it, surveying its dimensions in every direction. He begins walking upward in its direction toward the base of a very rocky cliff. About one hundred feet above his head, the cliff plateaus, creating a perfect ledge to build on above the road and out of sight.

Frederico and Bartolomeo have now left the wagon, and they look around to see if anyone else is anywhere near them. They reach Marco's side and the three of them head straight up the path and towards the cliff. Marco is breathless walking out ahead of Gallinellis, encouraging them to move faster.

"It's perfectly hidden," Marco adds with great excitement. "What do we do now? Get some ropes? This is the place, right?"

"We'll find out in a moment," Bartolomeo replies, and begins walking ahead.

Walking closer, the men see the rocky cliff becoming more complex, as what looked like a shear wall has turned into several layers of broken rock, cracks, and fallen boulders.

Frederico bends his head from side to side to study the area, and often looks back to measure their distance from their wagon. Bartolomeo, too, is inspecting the rocks with careful concentration.

"There must be a pathway up somewhere," Marco anticipates. "It must be here somewhere, right?"

"We're here."

Frederico, about fifty feet away, hears his son and stands at attention to his words.

"Where?" Marco asks as he makes his way to Bartolomeo's side. "Where are we?"

"Right here," Bartolomeo repeats, and points to a small cave opening in the cliff.

"This little cave is the entrance to a castle?" Marco asks with a puzzled look.

"No, Marco," Bartolomeo whispers. "This is where we buried Gino that night, five years ago.

Marco's face falls as he stands stunned at the sight before him. As Marco puts together the pieces of the Gallinelli's journey that evening, he is ashamed of his enthusiasm for this trip.

"Oh, Dear God, Bartolomeo. Please forgive me."

"There is nothing at all to forgive, Marco," Bartolomeo replies, as he puts his arm around his brother-in-law, with tears welling in his eyes.

The two embrace, and when they look up, they see Frederico, who has moved closer, but is twenty feet or so from the cave opening. He is steadying himself on the boulders with his left hand, and covering his mouth with his right. He gauges each step, not only to keep from stumbling, but also to not disturb a single stone, no matter how small, from its position.

Marco steps away from the cave, to give Frederico all the room he needs, and Bartolomeo backs away with him. Frederico's eyes are swollen red, and his face is trembling with emotions that there are no words for. He glances into the cave opening, and creeps toward it.

Using both hands now, Frederico bends over a bit and holds

onto the large rocks for balance as he inches his way into the dark opening. Gaining a look inside, he sees the bottom of a pile of rocks that sit neatly in place, precisely as he and Bartolomeo had laid them.

His fight to stay composed is over, as Frederico can't contain his crying for his son. He crawls down to his knees and falls forward onto the carefully arranged rocks and embraces them. Five years has become five minutes.

"I'm so sorry, Gino," Frederico sobs uncontrollably. "I'm so sorry, son."

Bartolomeo now feels his father's pain flowing into him, and has to turn away. He sits on a nearby rock and buries his face into his hands.

"I should have saved you," Frederico struggles through his tears. "I should have found a way, my sweet beautiful boy!"

Marco steps into the cave to be with Frederico and share his misery if it is somehow possible.

"Why couldn't I save you?" sobs Frederico, as he caresses the rocks, and straightens them out. "I can build any stupid house, and grow a thousand miles of vines… and it was all worth nothing."

Marco holds his hands over the stones, and for Frederico's comfort, recites the prayer for the dead that's been too common in recent years, "God our Father, You raise us from dust through Your power alone, and we return to it by Your command. Let our deceased join Christ in Your Heavenly kingdom, where tears are shed no more, and the songs of Your praise are heard forever and ever."

"Amen," Bartolomeo finishes, as he joins the tiny service.

"Amen," Frederico wipes the tears and dirt from his face, and resumes the straightening of the gravesite.

"Thank you, Marco," Frederico says and puts his hand on Marco's shoulder.

"I am so, so sorry, sir."

They embrace, and Frederico begins to cry a little more.

Brushing off his tears this time, Frederico stands up, mindful of the headroom in this small space. "It is time we marked this site properly."

"I agree," says a proud Marco of his fallen brother-in-law.

They all leave the cave and hike back toward the waiting wagon. Frederico retrieves the items he brought from home, and also begins to remove two planks from the side of the wagon. Marco assists with vigour.

Bartolomeo understands their meaning, and rummages around to produce two strong straps of leather. Within a short time, all three men are headed back up to the site with items in hand. When they arrive at the cave, Frederico begins to whittle and shape one the planks on the edge of one of the rough boulders.

"Do you have the cross piece or the stake piece, Father?"

"The cross."

Bartolomeo then works the bottom of his piece into a point, and fashions a small hole into the upper part with his knife. When he is finished, he takes his father's piece.

"Should you carve it, Father, or should I?"

"You do it, please," he replies. "Gino, beloved son."

Bartolomeo carves those exact words with skillful precision, and makes another small hole in the center of the piece. He then uses a piece of twine to weave the two pieces together in the shape of a cross, and then finishes the job by strapping the leather pieces over the joint for strength.

Marco has already prepared a hole in the ground at the head of the grave, and has a stone ready to pound in the cross. Bartolomeo delivers it, and drives it into place with the stone. They reinforce the base of it with more heavy stones, and Marco adorns the moment with another short prayer from his own heart, "Most merciful Jesus, Shepherd of Souls, we mark this grave in Your presence."

Frederico now brings forth the letter from Maria, it's bright red ribbon contrasting the earthen brown of the cave. He places it halfway under one of the stones with the little red flower poking out above.

"This is from Maria, Gino. She loves you very much and wants to tell you so. She misses you terribly… " he pauses to collect himself. "… and hopes that everything is all right up here in the mountains. Maybe she will come up here to see you herself someday."

Frederico then pulls out the pair of stockings that Margherita has knitted, in the size his feet would have been five years ago.

"These are from Mother. They are extra warm, so your feet will not be so cold during the winter months. You have feet like hers, you know. She wanted me to give you a kiss for her. She loves you so much, my sweet."

He leans over and kisses a stone near the head of the grave. Further down, he tucks the socks next to Maria's letter and delicately rearranges the stones to keep them all in place. Bartolomeo kneels down to be with his father and puts his arm around him. The two take comfort in each other's presence as Marco re-enters the cave with a handful of blue and gold wild flowers.

He kneels down and arranges the dainty alpine flowers. "You are much stronger than I ever knew, little man, and you are a treasure to God's kingdom."

"He gave his life for all of us, Father," says Bartolomeo.

"Do you really think so, son?"

"Of course. He saved seven of us that night, and we all lived through that horrible pestilence as proof. He saved Isabetta for Marco, and all of the children they will have. And he saved Maria and Antonio, and their future children. And the people of Sarnen who would have perished without your advice, he will have saved a hundred lives."

Frederico nods and climbs back to his feet. He nods again more to himself and puts his hand on his son's shoulder. "He did save all of us, didn't he?"

"He's a king, Father. He always was."

Marco adds with great feeling, "I believe it with all my heart, sir. He is the king of salvation – like no other."

Frederico smiles at Marco's realisation, and turns back toward the wagon to leave. Drained from the emotion, he looks up into the sky with an odd feeling of renewal. Marco and Bartolomeo follow behind arm in arm.

A light breeze rattles some low bushes, and Frederico hears a hawk's piercing cry high in the sky.

A few low clouds roll over the craggy peaks around the men, and the horses snort with restlessness. One-by-one, the composed men climb back into their wagon and sit together for a moment.

"You know," Frederico says to his two sons as he observes the mountains around them. "I never realised how beautiful it is up here."

Ken A. Gauthier was born in New Hampshire, USA. Married to Susan for 22years, they have two sons, Cuyler 17, and Traynor 14. Ken is an avid golfer and general sports enthusiast. He has owned and operated a golf shop in Concord, New Hampshire for five years.

www.legendpress.co.uk

www.twitter.com/legend_press

Lightning Source UK Ltd.
Milton Keynes UK
172696UK00002B/2/P